CRITICAL PRAISE F

• Finalist for the 2021 ~~~~ ~~~~~~~~ Prize
for Children's Literature
• Winner of the *Guardian* Children's Fiction Prize 2016
• Nominated for the CILIP Carnegie Medal 2017

For *Cane Warriors*

• Short-listed for the 2020 Caribbean Readers' Awards
(Best Young Adult Novel)
• Short-listed for the YA Book Prize 2021

"Wheatle brings the struggle of slavery in the Jamaican sugar cane fields to life . . . A refreshing and heartbreaking story that depicts both a real-life uprising against oppression and the innate desire to be free. Highly recommended."
—*School Library Journal*, starred review

"Alex Wheatle departs from his award-winning contemporary novels for a superb foray into historical fiction . . . Wheatle's characteristic kennings and coinages . . . heighten this intense, affecting story of courage, bloodshed, and commitment to freedom at all costs."
—*Guardian* (UK)

"*Cane Warriors* centers the voice of the enslaved rather than white abolitionists. In this way, readers face the reality of enslaved people who fought for their own freedom."
—*Worlds of Words*,
Book of the Month recommendation

"I read it in one sitting. I simply could not put it down. *Cane Warriors* is such a powerful narrative of trauma and triumph . . . Wheatle celebrates the heroism that Tacky inspires. He tells the riveting story of fourteen-year-old Moa who bravely joins Tacky's army."
—*Gleaner* (Jamaica)

"Set in 1760, *Cane Warriors*, the latest young adult novel by Alex Wheatle, is a fictional account of a key but often overlooked event in Jamaican history: Tacky's Rebellion, a major revolt by enslaved Africans, planned via an island-wide conspiracy. In Wheatle's narrative, a fourteen-year-old named Moa is caught up in the growing revolt, driven by a fierce desire for freedom and self-determination."

—*Saturday Express* (Trinidad & Tobago)

For *Home Girl*

"With a tough exterior and brash attitude, Naomi is an authentic character in an unfortunate yet accurate picture of modern-day foster care in the UK . . . The ending is neither predictable nor sugarcoated, leaving readers rooting for this determined heroine."

—*School Library Journal*

"Wheatle returns to the world of his award-winning Crongton books with his most powerful and personal novel yet. Naomi Brisset is a teenage girl growing up too fast in the UK care system. Her journey through a series of foster homes exposes the unsettling, often heart-wrenching truth of this life. Yet despite the grit, Wheatle's writing is as rich and warm as ever, bringing courage and hope to an unforgettable heroine's story."

—*Bookseller* (UK), Editor's Choice

"Teenager Naomi, old before her time and as vulnerable as she is fierce, is growing up in the care system. Foster homes and pupil referral units revealing the unsettling, often bewildering reality of this existence. Wheatle's empathy, authentic characters, and rich dialogue illuminate the dark."　　　—*Observer Magazine* (UK)

"Another powerful and poignant novel deftly created by one of the most prolific master novelists on either side of the pond. *Home Girl* is a page-turner, with not a dull moment. Loved it from the rooter to the tooter."　　　—Eric Jerome Dickey, *New York Times* best-selling author of *Before We Were Wicked*

"Alex Wheatle's latest novel offers no unrealistic fairy tale happy ending. But the award-winning writer, who draws on his own experiences of a childhood in care, does offer some hope for Naomi, a sometimes difficult but very likable heroine."

—*Irish News*, Children's Book of the Week

Kemosha
of the
Caribbean

Kemosha of the Caribbean

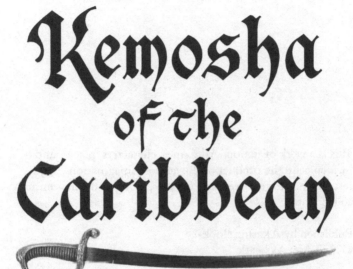

A young adult novel by
ALEX WHEATLE

Published by Akashic Books
©2022 Alex Wheatle

Paperback ISBN: 978-1-61775-982-6
Hardcover ISBN: 978-1-63614-000-1

Library of Congress Control Number: 2021935240
First printing

Black Sheep
c/o Akashic Books
Brooklyn, New York
Twitter: @AkashicBooks
Instagram: @AkashicBooks
Facebook: AkashicBooks
E-mail: info@akashicbooks.com
Website: www.akashicbooks.com

CHAPTER 1

A New Master

Captain Tate Plantation, St. Catherine, Jamaica, 1668

I was scrubbing the pots in the cookhouse with the split ends of a thick sugarcane when I heard the bell ringing from the front of Captain's big house. The afternoon sun would soon sink behind the northern hills. The high clouds were still today but I awaited a hint of the rising full moon. The small creatures in the fields had come out to quarrel again.

My cookhouse sister, Marta, paused her drying of plates, knives, and forks. She was twenty years older than me. It might have been twenty-two—she wasn't sure. The bell rang out again. Marta squeezed her eyes shut. She reopened them and dread crept over her face.

"Asase Ya!" she bawled. "Mama of de world! Dem about to lash another one. Why cyan't they behave demselves?"

I dried my hands on my frock. I looked at my palms and they were hard, red, and blistered. "It might not be dat, Marta," I said. "Sun soon fall. It could be someting else."

Marta shook her head. Strands of gray collected around her temples. She hadn't secured her black tie-head tightly today and it almost slipped off her forehead. She didn't seem to notice. "Kemosha! Kemosha!" she repeated. "Foolish chile. What else could it be? Captain don't bother shake him bell for anyting else. Him love to whip somebody in front of everybody before him tek him rest."

"You never know," I said. "Captain might give we our freedom. Mama used to say to never stop believing. He might be going off to de broad blue waters once more to war wid de Spanish. Captain nuh love de Spanish."

Marta laughed hard. "Foolish, foolish chile! Don't your fifteen years teach you anyting? You dream too plenty. Just like your dead mama. Me used to dream too. But now me don't waste me time."

"They will never tek me dream from me," I said.

Marta shook her head. "Captain sword get tired. Him want to mek plenty money and sit down on him veranda counting sugarcane and cocoa and drinking firewater."

"De top of de top English soldier might come for him," I said. "And mek him fight ah next war."

"Come, Kemosha," Marta beckoned. "Don't make we be late. Let we see what madness somebody do."

"De only madness me sight on this land is Captain lashing anybody who vex him," I said.

"Me wonder if it Hakan getting up to him runaway ways," Marta replied. "Him long foot too itchy."

"Me nuh want to see another beating," I said. "Me seen plenty blood running already."

Marta side-eyed me and placed her hands on her hips. "And you will see and *feel* your very own lashing if you don't move your skinny toe quick like hungry chicken."

"Nuh worry, Marta," I said. "If it is another whipping, me will turn me face to de moon. When it all over me could get to talk wid Gregory."

"You better teach Gregory not to pick up any runabout ways," Marta warned. "Captain will mash up him back just like him leave him mark 'pon Hakan."

I didn't reply.

We made our way along the dried footpath that ran behind the back of Captain Tate's big house, past the smokehouse, and up by the side of the mansion. I sniffed hog meat, cocoa, and the breath of boiled sugar. The hills in the north were wrapped in shadow and there was no breeze to disturb the treetops.

Marta and I were the last to arrive. In total there were twenty-five of us assembled on the front lawn of Captain's big house. Hakan was there, tall and strong from cutting the sugarcane. So was Iyana, a sister from another mother. The skin on her left cheek still hadn't grown back.

Four overseers watched us from each corner, including Misser Lyle Billings. His flesh-scraper was longer than anybody else's and he had customed his whip with small jagged stones.

Three women carried their pickney strapped to their chests. Men leaned on their billhooks and other long tools.

Nobody was tied to the post in the middle of the lawn ready for Captain's lash. Marta and I let out a long breath. Asase Ya smiled on us.

What is this all about?

Gregory was present, his mud-stained pants rolled up just below the knees. There were new mosquito bites on his calves. I hoped I could find time to treat his legs with a bush remedy. He tried to stand tall, but his shoulders slouched forward and his mouth sucked in big air. He was eleven years old. I tried to catch his eye, but he stared ahead at Captain's big house.

"Kemosha!" Marta pulled my arm. "Kemosha! Look forward and pay attention. Don't get weself inna trouble."

I gazed ahead.

Two white men stood on the veranda. One of them was Captain Tate. As usual when the afternoon grew old, he was dressed in his uniform: clean white shirt, baggy white slops where I couldn't see the shape of his legs, a dark blue cravat tied around his neck, shoes with shiny silver buckles, and a three-peaked hat. His cheeks were almost as red as my palms. His lips had as many cracks as Hakan's back. He held his flesh-scraper in his left hand.

The other man was a strange sight under the falling sun. I'd never seen anyone like him before. He only had one eye. There was a hole where the other should've been. His skin was reddish light brown, as if he had spoken with the sun every morn. His mustache was thick like a scrubbing brush and as long as Captain's boot laces. And his pink cravat was the longest I had ever seen. It was wrapped around his throat two or three times. I could've mistaken his orange shirt for fire, and the buttons on his jacket caught the gaze of the lanterns on the veranda. His boots were black and longer than Captain's.

This burned white man only had his one eye for me. His glare wouldn't let me go. I glanced to my right and shuffled my feet. Still he stared at me. Heat rose in my cheeks and I felt my heartbeat deep within my throat and behind my ears.

"Nyame save we, Marta," I whispered. "You ever see such ah wicked-looking mon? Angry John Crow must ah peck out him eye."

"Hush, Kemosha! Nyame won't come down from Him sky and save we if we nuh quiet!"

"This is Quartermaster Mr. Antock Powell," announced Captain Tate.

"What's ah quartermaster?" I whispered to Marta.

"Me nuh know," she replied. "Stop asking question and pay attention."

"Mr. Powell is a brave man who has given his good service to the English Navy," Captain Tate went on. "Indeed, he helped push the Pope-loving Spanish back to the filthy hole where they come from. And he's helped protect our waters around this island. You should give him your allegiance."

"What is allegiance?" I said.

"Quiet your mout', Kemosha!" hissed Marta.

Someone else muttered in Spanish behind us. I dared not look over my shoulder, but I guessed it was Hakan. *Hasn't he suffered enough of Captain's whip?* We were forbidden to speak Spanish. I had always warned Gregory not to do so.

"What Hakan say?" I whispered again to Marta. "Me never ketch all of it."

Marta leaned toward me and spoke out of the corner of her mouth. "Him say why cyan't de English go back to de dirty hole where *they* come from?"

I bit my bottom lip to stop a grin escaping.

Mr. Powell ran his one eye over my fellow slaves. He fixed his gaze on Iyana, who stared at the ground. I side-eyed Hakan and I could read the fury in his eyes.

I didn't think Mr. Powell liked what he saw. I glanced at Gregory. He looked exhausted. I wanted to put him to bed but he was too old for that.

"Mr. Powell is here to buy an obedient Negro to work in his tavern at Port Royal," Captain Tate went on.

"What is ah tavern?" I asked Marta. "Where is Port Royal?"

She shrugged and screwed up her nose. "Me nuh sure. It could be ah place where de white mon drink their firewater. Stop ask me question!"

"If this slave works hard and don't offer no quarrel"—Captain Tate paused, and looked hard at Hakan—"it could be a very fine life."

Mr. Powell walked down the three steps from the veranda and inspected the male slaves.

"The tall and broad ones will cost you ten pieces of eight each," said Captain Tate.

My heartbeat cannoned when he approached Gregory. He stopped in front of him and studied his frame. Gregory could hardly keep his eyes open. He passed him and my chest returned to normal. I dropped my head and stared at my feet, hoping Mr. Powell wouldn't select me.

I sensed his boots approaching. He had a short stride. Hot sweat dampened my eyebrows. I could feel it on my back, between my breasts and my belly. I closed my eyes and shifted my feet. I felt the ground ripple as he stood in front of me. His one-eyed gaze bored into me. His breath wasn't fresh. I opened my eyes but didn't dare lift them. I only stared at his dirty boots.

"What's your name?" Mr. Powell asked.

I tried to pretend he wasn't talking to me. *Maybe he'll ignore me and move on. Maybe he won't. Marta always tells me I'm too pretty wid me brown eyes, heart-shaped face, walk-good legs, and a behind dat mek any mon look twice. Me glad me hair look wild today. Me never had de time to plait it.*

He slapped me hard on my left cheek. The silver ring he wore on his right hand scored my face. I soothed the stinging pain with my right palm. Pure hatred burned inside of me.

"They call me Kemosha," I said.

"Kemosha Tate," added Captain Tate. "Every slave here has my surname."

Mr. Powell grinned. His teeth were brown like the cocoa field. "Take off your frock," he ordered.

I stood very still. It felt like my blood had stopped flowing. I hoped he wouldn't do to me what Captain Tate did to Marta.

I did what I was told. I let my garment slip off my shoulders and it fell about my feet. I wasn't wearing any underclothes. I shut my eyes once again. I sensed all attention on me. My skin breathed but perspiration ran down the inside of my arms and over my buttocks. The breeze returned and it cooled the corners of my naked flesh.

Mr. Powell walked around me. I was glad there wasn't no flesh-scraper in his hand. He paused. I felt his dirty breath upon my neck.

He said to Captain, "They will enjoy a dark creature. To add a spice of variety."

"She can cook too," said Captain. "She's fifteen and yet to be with child."

"Good, good," nodded Mr. Powell. "How much for her?"

"Five pieces of eight," replied Captain Tate.

"Five pieces of eight," repeated Mr. Powell. "You barter a hard price."

"But your pockets are deep and full," said Captain Tate. "I know your booty was a generous one following your last voyage to the Spanish Main. You have done well under Captain Morgan. And Kemosha has yet to be spoiled."

I wondered who Captain Morgan was, and what "spoiled" meant.

I picked up my frock and squeezed into it. I caught Gregory's anxious stare. He took a step closer to me but then he remembered himself. I felt his rage. *Nyame, me beg you. Don't let dem tek me.* I *had* to speak. "Me nuh want to leave," I said. "Me want to stay here so wid me liccle brudder. Him nuh have no mama or papa to mind him. Not even ah big brudder or sister."

I glanced at Gregory once more. He was perfectly still but tears dripped from one eye.

"He's of age," Captain said. "If he keeps growing at this rate of knots, he'll be worth ten pieces of eight. Maybe more. But until he grows to his size, he has Marta."

Marta stared at the ground. Then she glanced at me with sorrow in her eyes. "Me will mind him," she said. "Nuh worry about Gregory."

I offered Marta a vicious look. She turned her gaze away from me.

Mr. Powell addressed Captain Tate: "Can you give her a clean frock to travel in? I don't want to present her in rags. I want the good drinking and seafaring men of Port Royal to gaze upon her like the shiny coins in a Spanish conquistador's chest."

"Of course." Captain Tate nodded, and went inside.

Mr. Powell placed his right forefinger under my chin and lifted my head. My nerves stood to attention. It felt like a worm crawling through my spine. He looked at me hard. I tried to look away from the empty hole where his missing eye should've been. His one eye dropped to my figure. I wished I didn't have the backside where men looked twice, nor the curves that they enjoyed. "You have defiance in you," he said. "The buckos and mateys who I sail with will like that."

Moments later, Captain Tate returned with a scarlet-colored frock. I guessed it had belonged to his dead wife. Toilet sickness claimed her like it did to my mama. Before she passed, Captain's wife looked whiter than the high midday clouds. I helped soothe her passing with bush tea and warm palms to her cheeks, though she had always run to Captain Tate complaining about me. I couldn't imagine hating anyone as much as Captain's dead wife. When I was beaten because of Madam Tate's cruelty, I used to close my eyes and wish I was somewhere else.

My mama's last words to me were: "Vuela a casa, Kemosha, vuela a casa"—*fly away home, Kemosha, fly away home.*

Captain tossed the dress over to Mr. Powell. Mr. Powell grinned and stared at me as if I was still naked. "You will look *desirable* in this," he said.

I didn't know what that meant, but Mr. Powell's gaze told me what he wanted. I pulled off my old frock and wriggled into my new one. It was too tight, and I could barely move in it. Captain Tate nodded his appreciation.

"My horse and cart are by the side of the house," Mr. Powell said to me. "Your legs, your buttocks, your breasts, and the rest of your black Negro self better be in there before the sun drops anchor beyond the horizon."

"Yes, Misser Powell."

He aimed his one eye on me once more. He spoke slowly. "I own you now."

What fresh cruelty will lash me life now? I glanced to the western skies. *Asase Ya, why you nuh come down from your high place and save me?*

Mr. Powell turned to Captain Tate. "In the meantime, I will barter with Captain Tate for a fairer price over a generous shot of rum. It's worth a try."

The two white men strolled back inside the house, their steps echoing off the wooden boards. They closed the door behind them. Fireflies buzzed around the lanterns. The slaves returned to their huts, except Hakan, Marta, Iyana, and Gregory. Lyle Billings watched for any signs of disobedience before he walked away.

"No te vayas!" Hakan shouted as he marched over to me.

"Keep your tongue quiet before you lose it," warned Marta. "She *has* to go. Otherwise there will be big trouble for we."

"One good day," Iyana whispered, "*we'll* be de ones carrying de flesh-scraper and de long blade. We should fight dem now!"

"Not now, Iyana," said Hakan. "Our time will come."

"And when dat time come," said Marta, "your foolishness and your itchy toe will bring tribulation to all of we."

I didn't want to hear Marta, Iyana, and Hakan's cuss-cuss. My thoughts were on Gregory. He stood very still under the afternoon sky. His eyes found new energy and fresh anger. His glare was fixed on Captain Tate's double front doors. I went over to him and hugged him. "Gregory, Marta will mind you and look out for you."

He didn't respond. His eyes remained locked on Captain Tate's big house as if he was planning a bloody revenge.

"Listen to me, Gregory," I said. "Me swear, as long as me draw good breath and me two foot cyan carry me, me will do everyting to come back to you."

Gregory finally turned to face me. "Mama dead liccle after she give birth to me," he said. "They send Papa away before me even born. When you gone, nobody lef' for me."

His words carved deep notches into my heart. I had to take a moment to steady myself.

"But me here for you, Gregory," Marta said. "Me will mek sure your belly never empty and do everyting to keep Captain flesh-scraper from your back."

I cradled Gregory's jaws but eye-water drowned his cheeks.

"Don't mek promise if you cyan't keep dem," Gregory said.

I struggled for a response. "Me will try me best," I said after a short while.

Hakan shook his head. "Si peleamo', nadie tiene que irse," he said. *If we fight them, no one would have to leave.*

"Hush your runaway mout'!" Marta warned. "Talk like dat will get we all killed. Me nuh want to tek me long rest inna de pit just yet. Go back to your hut, Hakan, before me get mad wid you and fling chicken bone after you. Rest your runabout ways."

"Him cyan't rest him runabout ways," said Iyana. "Dat day will come. So Asase Ya tell me so! Mighty she is."

Hakan stood his ground for a moment. He offered Marta a fierce glare before he shook his head and made his way to his cabin.

Gregory dropped his head. I met his eyes and gripped his shoulders. "Me will *never* forget you, Gregory. As Asase Ya and Nyame see me now, and mek dem hear me words. Me will do me very best and come back for you. Dat me cyan promise."

Wrapping his arms around my neck, Gregory held me tight. "Every morning when de bird sing inna de treetop, me will look for you," he said. "And when me finish me work inna de field, me will see if you ah come."

"And me will t'ink of you when me first open me eye inna de morning and before me close dem at night."

"Sun soon fall," Marta said. She glanced at the heavens. "And moon will soon wake. You better climb up in Misser Powell's cart."

Gregory didn't want to let go of me. "You promise you will try to come?"

"Yes, me will try and try ah liccle more," I said.

I didn't know how I would return. I didn't know when. But I had to keep it as a whisper in the corner of my head to keep me living.

Gregory offered me a smile. I returned it.

I gazed into Marta's eyes. I sensed the many years of hurt and agonies in them. The despair. The loss.

"Me cyan give you some corn and ham for your journey," she said. Tears washed over her fleshy cheeks.

She ran to fetch the food, leaving Gregory and me gazing at each other. "Me better go back to me hut," he said. "Captain nuh like we lingering outside when sun about to fall."

I nodded. "Yes, you better. Keep living. Don't do anyting to ketch Captain's flesh-scraper."

He wiped his face and turned around. He slowly made his way to the side of the big house and he disappeared behind it. He didn't glance over his shoulder once. Despite my promise, I didn't think I'd bless my eyes on him ever again. But I had to offer him hope.

"Nuh worry, Kemosha," Iyana said. "One good day, we will chase de white mon from this land. So Asase Ya tell me so." She gripped my shoulders and looked at me hard. "Stay strong like your mama before you and your mighty ancestor." Then she turned and made her way to her own cabin.

I was alone.

The fireflies kept busy around the lanterns. Other tiny flying things hovered above the pit toilet. *Me swear to all de African gods dat me will come back for me liccle brudder.*

CHAPTER 2

Port Royal, the Wickedest Place on Earth

I climbed into Mr. Powell's cart. The horse reared up slightly, but it soon settled itself. The wheels were bruised and bent and had collected plenty mud. I laid myself down on the straw in the cart, my feet resting beside a large barrel. I thought of my Spanish-speaking mama. Almarita, they called her. She had a Spanish surname too, but that was changed to Tate. Her cheeks shone under the fat moon, no line dared to touch her forehead, but there was always a deep sadness behind her brown eyes. At night, the last words she would say to me before I caught sleep was, "Pueden acabar con tu cuerpo, pero no deje' que destruyan tu mente"—*they might break your body, but don't let them break your mind.*

Marta returned with three pieces of corn and a generous portion of ham. I took a bite from the meat then quickly covered it with straw. "May Nyame keep you until me return," I said.

Marta didn't say anything in response. Instead she shook her head. Tears fell over her jaws. She reached out and grabbed my hands. Her lips moved. She searched for words, but they never came. I had plenty quarrels and disagreements with her, but parting from her tormented my good heart.

"Me *will* come back," I said. "For Gregory and you. Maybe me will return wid ah hundred pieces of eight and buy Captain's big house and set we all free."

"Foolish chile," Marta wept. "Always dreaming. Just like your mama."

I tried to raise a smile. Marta cried some more. I felt my own tears, but they wouldn't show themselves. Then I heard Mr. Powell's boots stepping along the veranda. For a short moment, the fireflies took fright. Marta gave my hands one last squeeze before she turned, hitched up her frock, and jogged her way back to her hut. *Me will never feel her waking me up again to lead me to the cookhouse. She always rose to greet the morning before me.*

Mr. Powell checked his stride and looked at me before he climbed into the driving seat. He picked up the reins, gave them two mighty shakes, and the horse began to trot. I watched the lanterns circling Captain's big house becoming smaller and smaller until they were like fireflies. It was only then that eye-water drenched my lips.

* * *

Guided by the late amber sun, the horse picked its way through the trees and bushes. I sat up because my head bounced off the cart whenever we rode over a divot or the wheels fell through a crack in the hard earth. I stared at Mr. Powell's back, his shoulders moving whenever we made a turn. I thought of Gregory. *Maybe me shoulda said someting to Captain. Me shoulda drop down to me knee and beg to stay. Who else going to help Marta wid big cooking? Gregory need me. Me nuh want to come back and find him dead. Me will never forgive meself if dat happen. If sickness ketch him, me want to help him. If him back get lash by Captain flesh-scraper, me want to be there wid ah blood-cloth.*

Without further thought, I stood on my feet, watched the ground disappearing beneath me—and leaped. My knees wobbled on impact but I just about managed to rescue my footing. Then I pulled up my frock and ran for my good life. Mr. Powell restrained his horse and jumped down from the driver's seat.

He came after me. His stride was long. Curses flew from his mouth and petrified whatever flapped over my head. My heart raced quicker than my feet.

I couldn't see where I was going. I pushed my hands in front of me, trying to feel my way through the trees, but the tightness of my frock restricted my stride. Pure fear compelled me to keep going. *Kemosha! Kemosha! Foolish chile. You shoulda tek off de frock before you jump.*

Before I knew it, I was struck on the back of my

neck. I fell facedown onto the ground. I tasted dried mud. Intense pain shot through my right shoulder. A rough hand turned me over. Mr. Powell's one eye was only an inch away from my forehead. It was like an ugly, scarred moon. He bared his rotten teeth and I watched the hairs of his nostrils dance as he snorted. He gripped a curved dagger in his left hand. I closed my eyes, expecting my flesh to be split and ripped open. *Foolish chile, Kemosha. Now Gregory have nobody. Asase Ya, will you save me foolish self? Me must have vexed Her.*

Instead of carving me, Mr. Powell backhanded my face and stamped on my right leg. His heel left a red mark on my ankle. *Aaaaarrrrggghhh.* He held the tip of his blade before my left eyeball. There, he threatened me for a long moment. I could hardly breathe. He spoke slowly and his breath stank. "If you ever decide to flee from me again, I will cut out your eyeballs and sew them onto my slops."

"Sorry me sorry," I stuttered. "It's me first time me ever been outside Captain's place and me get mighty scared."

"Get up to your feet!"

I slowly stood up. I rubbed my right shoulder and thought I might have broken it. He then hit me on the back of my head with the black handle of his dagger. "If you want to breathe again, *do* what I command. Never forget, *I* own every last piece of flesh on you."

I nodded.

"Get aboard the cart!"

I climbed back onto the wagon and lay down as

comfortably as I could. I closed my eyes, wanting death to take me.

"They will appreciate you in Port Royal," Mr. Powell said. "Oh yes, by the shine of Spanish coins, they will like you."

I wondered who *they* were.

We rolled on, the horse not in a hurry despite Mr. Powell shaking the reins and cursing bad words.

Sometime later, I sniffed salt. I sat up and could just about make out the dark waters in the distance. Mama once told me "vengo de una tierra al fin del mar"—*me come from ah land at the end of the sea.*

I couldn't imagine where that place could be. We neared the coast and the dark waters met a black sky.

"Ahoy!" Mr. Powell called out. "The lights of Port Royal are over yonder. Look beyond Kingston Harbour where the land kicks out into the ocean."

He pulled up the horse and pointed with his dagger. At first, I thought he was gesturing to the curved lights before the sea, but there was this thin strip of land that jutted out into the ocean. If four men walked abreast, one of them would suffer wet boots. It reached out to what looked like an island. Lights like tiny moons filled it. I could make out the dark shadows of ships and boats around it.

"Aye," Mr. Powell said. "Port Royal. My heart wants to ride the waves again. Too long have I allowed the weeds to grow around my feet."

He shook the reins again and the horse trotted on.

We neared the coast. For the first time in my life, I heard the breath of the sea. Salt was on my lips. I chanced a bite or two of my corn and ham. It tasted good. I wanted water to wash it down, but I dared not ask.

We reached the narrow strip of land where I watched the waters on both sides. At times the weak waves lapped over the path and filled the wheel ruts. The dark sky seemed so broad here and the breezes made themselves known. The lanterns of Port Royal twinkled in the near distance.

There was a gate guarding the entrance of the town. It was manned by two men. "Who goes there?" one of them called.

"Insolence!" Mr. Powell shouted back. He showed the length of his sword and gave it a swish for extra effect. "Insolence! You don't know me? Be careful, guardsman, or you might deny Captain Morgan's very own quartermaster."

Again, I wondered who Captain Morgan was. *He must be even wickeder than Captain Tate.*

One of the sentries stepped up to take a closer look. He held a lantern. "Oh, my apologies, Mr. Powell. We offer you safe passage and fare you well."

Mr. Powell offered an evil look and snorted like the last hog Marta and I had killed. The men opened the gate.

I looked around and there were many buildings, some of them even bigger than Captain Tate's big house. One of them had a big cross on top of it but there were no lights inside or outside. No one seemed to live there.

I heard the laughter and shouts from loud men. As we climbed uphill, I watched men dressed like Captain Tate and others like Mr. Powell. They wore bright feathers in their hats. The gusts fanned their baggy slops and they sang strange songs. Shiny buckles were on their shoes. Only a few of them walked straight. Many reeled and staggered sideways, their swords and daggers dancing by their sides. They reminded me of Lyle Billings and Captain Tate when they had drunk firewater.

I lay flat on the straw, not wanting any of these rum-loving brutes to spot me.

"This town will be your new home," Mr. Powell said. "If you do what I command, your cheeks and back will be left untouched."

The dried mud path had changed to cobbled stones. I peered out to the sea: many ships were anchored there. Some tall with broad mainsails, others short and narrow. I couldn't count them all. *Maybe Epo, Mama's sea god, cyan save me. Yes! Mama said Epo is kind.*

We passed a strange wooden structure by the road. It was a tall post with a shorter length of timber fixed to the top of it. It looked like a misshapen cross. It was stained with something dark and had cruel hooks and long nails protruding from it. Thick flies and other winged creatures buzzed around it.

Mr. Powell caught me staring at it. "You're looking at a gibbet," he said. His mouth curled into a grin. "Where we hang thieves and traitors and Spanish men, if we can find them."

The ham I had ate made a reappearance in my throat. I just about managed to keep it down.

We trotted on for another half mile or so before Mr. Powell pulled up his horse outside a two-tiered building. I heard roars of laughter, cheers, and singing. I sniffed rum once more. There was a man lying face-down near the door in his own vomit. There was another on the opposite side of the path. With his one hand, he clutched an empty wooden mug. For a moment, I thought of taking the reins and trotting back to Captain Tate's plantation.

"Stay here," Mr. Powell ordered.

I did what I was told.

He came back moments later with a bucket of water for the horse and some vegetables for it to eat. He patted it on its head. When the horse had finished with the water, Mr. Powell brought the bucket over to me.

"Drink," he ordered.

There wasn't much left, but I drained it to the last drop.

He secured the horse to a post outside the building and then narrowed his eyes. "Time for you to meet my fellow owner of this enterprise, Indika Brown. She looks after my affairs when I'm away at sea and runs a fair ship of our tavern. She's worth her weight in Spanish coins but I will not marry her yet. Climb aboard, my dark one."

CHAPTER 3

Indika Brown

I hesitated, not wanting to enter the tavern. Instead, I stared at my feet.

Mr. Powell backhanded me again. "Move your land-hugging feet!"

He grabbed my wrist and pulled me down onto the ground. I lost my footing and fell onto my damaged shoulder. I wanted to scream but didn't want to give Mr. Powell the pleasure of my pain.

"Get up, you black strumpet!" he raged again. "My temper is still blowing after you tried to flee. *Insolence!* You will do well to remember the gibbet. The hooks will easily hold a slender figure like yours. Death comes slowly hung up there, my dear dark one."

I knew I would never forget the gibbet or the winged things that circled around it.

I stood up, shook my arm free, and followed him to the door. I sucked in a deep breath before Mr. Powell pushed his way into his tavern.

Noise bruised my ears. Alcohol fumes rose from the floor. Rough-chinned men puffed smoke from thumb-long pipes. It stung and watered my eyes. The chanting, if you could call it that, fouled the air. Insults were swapped. Chairs were scraped, thighs slapped, and mugs slammed on bare tables. Men with long ears weighed down by shiny things drank from wooden tankards. Their hair was long, and their scars were deep. Their skinny scarves, slops, breeches, and shirts were colorful like the pretty birds who sometimes visited the plantation. *Me wish me could fly.* I thought of Mama. *Vuela a casa—fly away home. Nyame, god of de sky. Me calling on you.*

Many had missing fingers and dented cheeks. Those who still had their full hands wore bright rings. A few stood on one or one and a half legs. Long curved swords and short daggers dangled from their belts. In a corner, men played some sort of game where untold pieces of eight decorated a table.

One of these gamblers called Mr. Powell over. "Have you been avoiding us?" he said. "I cheated the sea last week, so Lady Luck is gracing me once more. Will you not chance your fortune tonight?"

"If your pockets are heavy, then yes," replied Mr. Powell. "But before I grace you with my presence, I have to finish my errand with my new slave girl."

For a moment I stood still, looking around at my fresh hell. I wondered what I could do with all those shiny Spanish coins. *Maybe me could buy Gregory's free-*

ness wid dem? Foolish chile, how you ever going to get even one Spanish coin?

By now the men had stopped singing, and gazed at me like I was a generous serving of pork.

Mr. Powell pulled my arm again. "This one will not be spoiled tonight," he said. "She'll be apprenticed this evening in the ways of my tavern."

The chanting started up again. Mugs and tankards were raised. The voices were rough like the inside of a corn dumpling pot.

> *"Isabella was taken from the Spanish Main*
> *She wore a red frock and couldn't be tamed*
> *Her temper was wild*
> *She was little more than a child*
> *But her fiery tongue caused her to be caned*
> *The man who tried to spoil her*
> *Suffered the dagger under her garter*
> *Never did he molest a maiden again*
> *The governor tried her for murder*
> *But no gibbet claimed her*
> *And the rope grew impatient to choke her*
> *She escaped into Kingston Harbour*
> *No one knew if she was an able swimmer*
> *Maybe the crocodiles had feasted on her*
> *Some claimed she fled to the hills in Jamaica*
> *Sea-riders speak fondly of her quick brain*
> *And her pretty looks still carry her fame*
> *Seven moons later*

The governor changed his opinion of her
He cried, injustice was to blame
Send word that she is not to be slain
But she was never to be seen on these warm shores
again
That pretty Isabella from the Spanish Main."

"MORE! MORE!" the men hollered as they raised their tankards.

Mr. Powell had to barge his way ahead to clear a path. He led me to the counter where behind it stood a sun-scorched white woman with feathers in her ears, shiny rings on her fingers, and a silk green headscarf. Brown freckles dotted her nose. Her green frock wrapped her generous breasts like a tight manacle.

She offered Mr. Powell a foul look. "Two days!" she shouted. "Two days you have been gone! Can't your one eye find its way back to Port Royal? Left me to barter with the scum of Jamaica. None who find pleasure in paying for their rum and whiskey." She glared harder. "I hope you haven't been gambling away your fortune."

She spoke the same language as Mr. Powell but there was a different flavor to her words. None like I had heard before.

"But, my sweet Indika, I *have* returned," Mr. Powell said. "And I can assure you I have not visited any dark gambling house. I have brought help for you."

Indika turned and gazed at me. Her stare was long. It felt like she was undressing me, just like the men.

"Who do we have here?" she asked. She leaned in closer and grabbed my chin as if she were studying a piece of eight.

"Me name is Kemosha," I managed. "Kemosha Tate."

"Kemosha Tate," she repeated. "Do you know what you have to do?"

"Yes . . . yes," I replied. "To cook and serve."

She grinned a dangerous grin. I hoped she wasn't as evil as Captain Tate's wife. "You'll soon get to know what is expected of you," she said. "In the meantime, wash those tankards in the end barrel. I'll show you to your place of rest when you finish your night's labor."

"Yes, Miss . . ."

I had forgotten her name.

"Indika Brown." She raised her voice. "I'm the poor woman who looks after Mr. Powell's affairs when he sails the seven seas, winning his fortune."

"Are . . . are you soon to be married to Misser Powell?" I asked.

Indika laughed hard like I had never heard before. She held her belly and her breasts nearly spilled out of her frock. "Married!" she said. "Married! Only Mistress Sea will ever claim Antock Powell's salty hand in marriage. This sea-rider wants me to take care of his business on land."

"Oh," I managed.

Mr. Powell gave me a brutal stare.

"Let me start on those mugs," I said, to escape his one-eyed gaze.

"And this tavern needs scrubbing," Mr. Powell added.

I climbed onto the counter, swiveled, and dropped down beside Indika. There were five barrels against the stone wall and they all reeked of something that churned my stomach. I had to swallow my rising vomit. Through a doorway, I spotted a wooden staircase. I longed to escape to rest my bruised body and my half-broken mind.

Indika looked me over once more. "I hope you last longer than the one before," she said.

"What . . . what happened to she?" I asked.

"Diseases. The most dangerous diseases. Wasted away, she did. A small barrel of bones. What was left of her was buried at sea."

This time a cold snake curled around my spine. I hoped that Mama's sea god, Epo, had saved her spirit.

Indika pointed her finger. "The washing barrel is over there. Dry those tankards well with the rags. Buckos and mateys don't like to taste water in their spirits."

I did what I was told as the singing and chanting started up again.

Once I washed the mugs, Indika showed me the ale, beer, spiced red wine, whiskey, and rum barrels and how much I had to pour into a tankard.

"If you give the sea-riders even a spit extra, I'll take it off your food," she said.

Before I finished my lesson, there were three men carried out after drinking too plenty, two fistfights and one slashed neck as men in the corner gambled and fought over their pieces of eight. They hollered and quarreled and drank and spat.

"Clear up the blood," Indika ordered. "It brings in the ants and the cockroaches. And I *hate* them both."

I rinsed out a rag and nervously went over to a fallen chair that had been spotted with blood. As I wiped it down, someone smacked my behind. It was a fat brute with eight and a half fingers. Before I could protest, Mr. Powell warned, "She will *not* be spoiled tonight. You know my price for touching any of my strumpets! Be gone with your squiddly tentacles or otherwise lose 'em!"

The ruffian who had molested me backed away as Mr. Powell showed him the curve and sharpness of his sword—it glinted under the lantern lights. "It's only a friendly greeting I was showing your dark strumpet," the man said. "My appreciation, if you like."

"Appreciation costs pieces of eight," Mr. Powell replied. "She's a fine looker and she will not be cheap."

I felt safer when I returned behind the counter. My whole body shook when I thought what tomorrow may bring. *They will surely tek me like how Captain Tate tek Marta when me was liccle. Me could sniff de drink from him before he entered our cabin. He kicked me off the bed me shared with her. Marta covered her mouth with her palms as if making any sound was a sin.* Marta never spoke of it, but she knew I had seen it all.

Later, Indika showed me my place of rest out back. It was beside a hog pen, a chicken coop, and a small cookhouse. The wooden fences were shoulder high and a pit toilet lay behind these open outhouses. In a corner, there was part of a soiled white sail that was secured to three skinny posts. It could just about cover the length of me. Old clothes, rags, and animal hides were beneath it. Indika pointed. "That's where you sleep, my black one," she said. "There are cabbages, potatoes, and carrots in the cookhouse, and Mr. Powell will be killing another hog when the sun rises tomorrow."

I glanced into the pen: there were three hogs chomping chicken bones.

"Tomorrow you can scrub the tavern," she went on. "And aye, I want it as clean as the calm waters of the sea on a Sunday morn. You cook in the afternoon—your blackness can take the heat at that hour, I can't."

"Yes, Miss Indika."

"I don't want you addressing me with all this fancy *Miss* talk," she said. "I'm no English lady and nor do I want to be. I crawled out from a hut in Cardiff and I had to kick two older sisters out of my way to find my fortune. Some fortune! Just call me Indika, and do your work without fuss or complaint. You will be watered and fed well."

"Yes, Indika."

"But on *no* account will you venture upstairs to my cabin," she told me. "Do you understand?"

I nodded.

"If you do, I will dig out your eyes like I'm scratching for buried treasure. I don't want any foul breathing near my place of rest. My end will not be a barrel of bones tossed in the sea."

"I understand," I said.

"Sleep well. There's plenty work for you to do in the morn."

I made myself as comfortable as I could under the filthy white sail. The stars above looked so far away. The chickens clucked and the hogs rolled in their dirt.

My rest was disturbed by men using the pit toilet. One of them took a long look at me before he relieved himself. His three-quarter-length jacket had shiny buttons. He wore a blue cravat. His thumb was missing on his right hand and he wore three feathers in his hat. I kept as still as I could, but he still wandered over to me. His feet weren't steady. His eyes looked hungry, yet I didn't think he craved food.

"Sit up," he ordered.

I thought again of Captain Tate and Marta, and pretended I didn't hear.

"*Sit up!* I command you."

I did what I was told.

The man grinned and bared his crooked teeth. He undressed me with his eyes. "Mr. Powell doesn't want you to be spoiled on this warm night," he said. "But tomorrow I shall request your company."

I didn't reply.

He tipped his hat, its three feathers dancing in the breeze. "Sleep well, pretty black one. You will need your strength when the moon sails high again."

I slept little on that night. I even wished that Mr. Powell had killed me with his dagger when I tried to flee. I wondered why Asase Ya had kept me alive.

Mama, me ready to join you.

CHAPTER 4

A Hairful of Dagger

I woke up to the sounds of a hog's final squeal as Mr. Powell used an ax to chop off its head. Blood squirted everywhere, staining my face and my frock. He tossed it into a gully behind the pit toilet and fixed his one eye on me. Under the same sun, Marta would be preparing chickens. Gregory would be carrying his tools into the fields. I'd wave to him as he passed the cookhouse.

I tried to avoid Mr. Powell's gaze and glanced toward the sea. It looked so calm. There was no white or gray in the sky. The ships and boats were perfectly still in the harbor. I concentrated my eyes but couldn't find Mama's land at the end of the ocean. I wondered if this fair place was only in Mama's dreams.

"Make yourself something to eat and then scrub the floors and stools of my tavern," Mr. Powell said. "Be thorough with your work—you don't want to displease Indika this morning."

"Yes, Misser Powell."

"She will take her breakfast later."

I ripped an old frock that I had slept on and fashioned a headscarf out of it. Not bothering to plait my hair, I wrapped my head and made my way to the small cookhouse. I found Mr. Powell already there, chopping the carcass of the hog. There was corn, sweet potatoes, carrots, cabbages, and a small sack of ground wheat on a wonky wooden shelf. Two large pots rested on a wooden fireplace. They were not clean.

"There is a stream half a league away up the hill," Mr. Powell said. "Go and fill the pots after you have eaten. Do you know how to start a fire?"

I nodded.

"Good," said Mr. Powell. "I will salt the meat."

I decided to fetch the water before I made breakfast. I found other women near the top of the rise filling their buckets and pots. Three of them washed clothes.

At the top of the hill was a stone fort. Men in uniform patrolled the battlements. The location offered me a magnificent view of Kingston Harbour and the soaring green hills behind it. I wondered which direction lay Captain Tate's plantation. I hoped Marta would manage without me and Gregory would not suffer Mr. Billings's lash.

None of the women looked older than twenty. A few seemed even younger than me. They were of all shades—some Black, mixed race, and others with sunkissed skins. I counted nine white women. No smile touched their lips and they all shared sad eyes. None of us greeted each other but we all knew we owned a common misery, swapping quick glances. I made three trips and no one offered me a single word.

I was eating my second corn dumpling when I spotted Indika coming out of the back door of the tavern. Her eyes were red, and her stride was short. She seemed to be in pain. "What's troubling your eyes, my black one?" she said. "Haven't you had the pleasure of seeing a white woman suffering monthly cramps in the morning?"

"No, Indika," I replied. "Captain's wife dead and gone some moons ago and she was de only white woman me know."

"Don't waste your time when you finish," she said. "I want that tavern scrubbed like Captain Morgan's upper deck."

Again, I wondered who this mysterious Captain Morgan was.

I set about my work with a bucket and plenty of rags. I had to make a further four trips to the stream to fetch more water. There was no bush or tree to escape the sun in Port Royal.

I longed to be with Gregory, Marta, Iyana, and Hakan.

The sun trotted toward the west when the man with the missing thumb and the three-quarter jacket stepped into the tavern. I wiped a stool as he approached the counter. Indika stood beside me, drying mugs and tankards.

"I'll have half a whiskey, my sweet Indika," the man said.

Indika poured the drink without comment. The man stared at me. The serpent returned to slither through my rib cage. Its skin was prickly and its fangs sharp like Mr. Powell's sword.

"No need to fear me," said the man. "Back in Portsmouth they say I'm a gentle soul. My wife cares not if I ever return but my mother still pines for me."

I didn't reply but wondered where in this bad world was Portsmouth.

"My name is Oliver Marsh," he said. "A trusted privateer."

"She wouldn't know what a privateer is," said Indika. "She's just a slave girl."

"What . . . what is ah privateer?" I asked her.

"Privateers offer their services to help the English Navy defend this island," Indika explained. "And they're not shy to assist them to rob from the Spanish."

"And kill them too," added Mr. Marsh.

"Port Royal is flooded with Spanish gold," said Indika. "It's a shame that most men don't know what to do with their fortune. They could find a wife, build a home, but no. They drink till they can't drink anymore, buy women of the night, and gamble what they have left."

"Where is Mr. Powell on this good day?" Mr. Marsh asked. "I want to barter with him about the company of this dark one this very evening."

"He's running errands for me," said Indika. "I need

salt, spices, and sweet potatoes from the harborside. The men of my tavern are not like the Spanish. They like their wine to spit fire."

Mr. Marsh laughed hard. "Yes, you can always tell a Spaniard by the way they drink their plain red wine."

"They believe they're drinking Jesus's blood," chuckled Indika.

"It won't save them from the cut of my sword," said Mr. Marsh.

"And the way Mr. Powell gambles," Indika said to him, "Jesus will not save him either."

As they laughed, I watched them and wondered who Jesus was.

I remembered the work I had to do, so I swiveled over the counter to wipe tables and chairs.

Mr. Marsh locked his gaze on me again. He walked over. I couldn't take my eyes away from his four-fingered hand. "Take a rest, my dark one," he said.

I glanced at Indika. She nodded.

I paused my work. Mr. Marsh placed his hand on my throat. His fingers were hairy and thick. I nearly choked. His nails were black, long, and twisted. I raised my head. He then gripped my chin and looked at one cheek and then the other. "Shall I pay for her now?" he asked Indika. His eyes never left me.

"Not now," Indika replied. "Pay Mr. Powell on his return. We have an agreement, although it is not written. I collect the price of drinks, and he barters for anything else."

"I hope he returns soon," Oliver said.

"Even if he does return now, my slave's place is in the cookhouse. Seafaring men crave meat when the sun falls. And I don't want to disappoint them."

On Mr. Powell's return, he carved the hog meat with his sword, gave me six pieces to cook, and salted the rest. I made a broth, adding corn, carrots, and cabbage. I boiled sweet potatoes with the meal and served nine plates of dinner. My customers licked what fingers they had clean. Meanwhile, Mr. Marsh sat on a stool beside the counter, tipping whiskey into his mouth. Every time he placed his tankard down, his hungry eyes flicked about me. I may as well have been naked.

I had scrubbed two cooking pots when I spotted Mr. Marsh speaking quietly with Mr. Powell. A piece of eight was handed over. Mr. Marsh grinned at me, and it wasn't just the sea breezes that blew through me.

"Black strumpet!" Mr. Powell called to me.

Green and yellow lizards sometimes scrambled along the floor of my cabin back at the plantation. Marta hated them. When she caught one, she battered it with a broom. Now, it felt like one of them scurried along my spine. *No broom.*

I took my time approaching the two men. The moon was high, and the tavern still had three men draining tankards of rum, whiskey, and spiced red wine. A fourth man snored in a corner. When I reached Mr. Marsh and Mr. Powell, I adjusted my head-wrap and stared at the floor.

"Mr. Marsh has paid a good price for your company tonight," Mr. Powell said. "He will do what he will with you but not before you clean the tables. And I have two other men who are more than eager. You can give your body to them tomorrow but *not* while you're working."

The lizard inside me turned cold. It fed on my bones.

As I started cleaning, I felt Mr. Marsh's eyes burn into my flesh. My heart punched my ribs like the drop of a hammer driving a post into the ground. I couldn't stop my hands shaking. I didn't swab any stools near where he was seated. I prayed to Asase Ya for him not to hurt me. I remembered Marta's silence whenever Captain Tate had his wicked way with her.

"Be swift, my black one!" Mr. Marsh shouted. "The night is sailing on and I have paid a just price. The last time I had a woman, the stars above looked different and the winds were in a foul temper."

I imagined his four-fingered hand molesting my private parts. I could almost sense his whiskey breath blowing into my mouth. I saw his craven eyes devouring me. Rage grew slowly within me and resistance pulsed in my good heart. *Why should me allow him to tek me? Asase Ya, me nuh want to go through wid this. No, mon. This cyan't go so. Me cyan't let it be so.*

I rinsed out the cloth. Mr. Marsh watched my every move. He took a generous glug of his whiskey. He licked his lips. I wiped the counter. The man sleeping in a corner suddenly stood up and went about his business.

Someone shouted from outside, "Close to the midnight hour and all is well!"

"Go to your place of rest and do the deed there," said Indika. "Don't frighten the chickens and don't get your belly fat. I need you to work, not suckle babies."

I had to think fast. Keeping my eyes to the floor, I quickly made my way to the cookhouse. When I got there, I checked if Mr. Marsh had followed me. *Not yet.* I picked up a dagger that I had used to peel carrots and sweet potatoes. I quickly placed it under my head-wrap and secured it tightly. I stepped to my sleeping place. It still reeked of hog blood and urine. Next door, the chickens clucked. Flies buzzed over the pit toilet out back. The sea breezes were a little stronger. I laid myself down.

I heard Mr. Marsh's boots before I saw him. His eyes were keen. Impatient. His cheeks swelled with a grin. It was hard to make out his filthy teeth in the dark. I closed my eyes. *Asase Ya, mek me hand strong and mighty.*

My entire body tensed like a thick, stiff cane.

He kissed me first. His beard scratched my cheeks, and the stench of whiskey was all about me. His teeth grazed my lips. I pulled away but he laughed a horrible laugh and lunged for me. His hand reached for my garment. He pulled it up. His mouth searched for my neck. He bit my ear and I felt his tongue licking my temple.

"Never had a black strumpet before," he said.

His hand moved toward my woman parts. He squeezed roughly above my knee and forced my legs apart. His breath was heavy and wet. *Me cyan't tek this.*

I grabbed the dagger beneath my head-wrap and gored him just above the elbow. I drove the blade as far as my strength allowed. He didn't scream. His mouth opened wide, as broad as I had ever seen. His eyes were in perfect shock. I could see the whites around his eyeballs as clearly as a full moon in a cloudless sky.

I let go of the dagger and he fell backward. A long groan came from his mouth. I thought of the gibbet and the tale of Isabella who was taken from the Spanish Main.

I glanced behind me. The fence was shoulder high. Without further thought, I climbed the barrier and dropped down into the gully. It was steep, dark. I couldn't keep my footing and I tumbled down. I almost crashed into the hog's head that was being eaten away by small flies and other tiny things that wriggled and crawled. Mosquitoes buzzed around my head.

Everything hurt. Pure dread pulled me to my feet. I ripped off the bottom part of my garment and ran like I never ran before.

Something cut my foot, but I kept on going. I dared not look behind. The gully bent to my left. Toward the sea. There was a sheer drop ahead of me, a crag face inviting quick death. The ships looked mighty in the harbor and I was higher than the tallest mast. I came to the cliff edge. Again, I thought of pretty Isabella from the Spanish Main. *Me cannot swim and if me could, where would me swim to? And if me drop, me would mash up meself 'pon de rocks below. What step do me tek now?*

I glanced over my shoulder. No one hunted me. Not yet. *Nyame, did me kill Misser Marsh?* The gibbet grew large in my mind.

There was a row of buildings on the gully ridge above me, some two-tiered, others one level. I guessed most of them were taverns. I peered into their backyards. I spotted several white men relieving themselves. I pushed on.

I headed for the smallest building before the sea. *Maybe it could be a storehouse?* I had to climb up the face of the ridge. My foot leaked blood and I couldn't feel my shoulder, but I had to pull myself up. I wished I had broader fingers and longer nails.

Asase Ya must have blessed me with Her strength because somehow, I managed to drag myself up to the top of the ridge. Before me was a head-high log fence. I couldn't squeeze through the gaps, so I clambered over and fell down on the other side. I hit the ground with a mighty thud. I think I passed out for a few seconds but I'm not sure. All I remember was being surrounded by barrels.

CHAPTER 5

The Barrel Maker

black face looked down on me. His eyes were hard and brown. Grayness flecked his beard. An orange scarf wrapped his head and a gold ring dangled from his ear. His lips were fat. *Maybe Nyame and Asase Ya listened to me cry. Maybe not. This mon might kill me.*

I sat up, feeling a sharp pain in my foot. I tried to climb the fence.

"Flee if you will," the Black man said. "But I'm probably the only man in Port Royal who can help you."

The words from his tongue sounded strange to my ears. No Black man I knew spoke like that.

I had no strength to climb the timber wall. I groped for my dagger beneath my head-wrap but it wasn't there. All I had left was a fierce glare.

"You have the eyes of someone who has been molested," he said. "Such is the way Port Royal treats its women. You don't have to fear that from me."

I didn't reply.

"And you don't even carry a blade," he said. "Even long-toothed sea-riders refuse to be abroad at night without a sword."

"Me . . . me nuh have no sword," I managed. I was in no condition to fight and I searched for mercy in his eyes.

"We can continue to swap looks," he said. "Or I can see to your foot."

I lifted my left foot and it poured with blood. Suddenly I felt dizzy. He caught me before I dropped.

"Fire has to seal it," he said.

I nodded weakly.

"They call me Ravenhide," he said. "Master barrel maker and carpenter. But sometimes they ask me to seal their wounds as I have patient and skilled hands."

I didn't say anything. Instead, I looked around Ravenhide's backyard. Strange tools were on the ground surrounded by barrels, lengths of wood, and piles of sawdust and chippings. In a corner was a small cookhouse and next to that was a chicken coop.

I watched Ravenhide kindle a fire. He gave me a stick that he had wrapped in rags to bite on. I lay on my stomach and raised my left foot. He didn't hesitate.

The agony was unbearable. I did my best not to scream but I spat out the stick. The stench of burning flesh attacked my nostrils.

"It won't bleed anymore," Ravenhide said. "But you will carry the mark for the rest of your life."

He went to fetch a rag and tightly secured my wound. "You will live," he added.

It felt like I was dying.

"Now," he said, "who are you fleeing from?"

The intense pain from my foot made me stutter. "Mr. . . . Aaaahhh. Mr. . . . Mr. . . . Pow . . . Powell."

If I had guessed Ravenhide's face couldn't get any darker, I'd been wrong. My news troubled his eyes and cut a gully in his forehead. He raised his eyebrows. "Mr. Powell," he repeated. "He's Captain Morgan's quartermaster. An important man."

I didn't say anything.

"He will hunt you down to the lowest cabin and the highest crow's nest. He's not a man who suffers any loss of property well."

"There . . . there is more," I said.

Ravenhide offered me a long look. "What more have you done to offend him?"

At this moment, pain and fear overwhelmed me. I couldn't stop my tears. I thought of Marta, Gregory, and Mama. I so much wanted to return to the plantation. I remembered Mama's soft words to me at night: "Seca tus lagrimas, hija mía. El mundo puede que sea má' amable en la mañana." *Dry your tears, my daughter. The world might be kinder in the morning.*

Before I could reply, there was a fierce knocking on a far door.

"Inside the end barrel," Ravenhide urged. "The shortest one. Now!"

I thought he was jesting. "I will not be able to squeeze myself—"

"Do not parlay with me!" Ravenhide cut me off. His eyes blazed. "Inside!"

There were barrels of three different sizes. One was shorter and skinnier than the rest. I hopped over to it.

I'm not sure how, but I managed to climb into it. I twisted my shoulders and hips and wriggled myself in. My knees kissed my chin and I sat on my heels. Ravenhide secured the lid and rolled me onto my side. He then went to answer his front door. I felt like I was a piece of corn being ground by stones on all sides. It was almost impossible to breathe.

My panicking heart recognized Mr. Powell's voice before my ears did.

"My insolent black strumpet harpooned the good privateer Mr. Marsh," he said. "Almost cut off his arm, she did. Indika's sealing his wound. I had to pay back his piece of eight! Have you seen her fleeing by your backyard?"

Footsteps approached. Mr. Powell's voice was plenty closer now. There was a pause. I held my breath. My throat tickled but I managed to kill a cough.

"No, Mr. Powell," Ravenhide said. "I've been taking my rest. Been sawing, shaping, and smoothing in this burning sun all day."

"Five pieces of eight I paid for that black strumpet! *Five!* When I catch her, I'll have her fingers hanging from my ears and sew her eyes onto my slops."

"If you kill her, she will never be able to repay you," Ravenhide said.

Silence.

"Where do you take your rest?" Mr. Powell asked.

"In a corner of my shack."

"So you will not protest if I check your barrels?"

A long pause.

Something strange happened inside my belly. It almost made me sick. Fear had shaken my shoulders. I tried to keep as still as I could, but my hands trembled. My throat suddenly dried. *This will be my end.* I recalled the efficient way Mr. Powell chopped off the hog's head. Its blood stained my lips and the taste was evil. *At least me will see Mama again. But not if Mr. Powell sews my eyes onto him slops.*

"Why should I have cause to protest?" Ravenhide casually replied.

Is he mad?

I had to let out a breath.

I heard hard footsteps very close by. *Mr. Powell must be wearing him long boots.*

Then a tapping sound. I guessed Mr. Powell went about checking the barrels with his sword. My heart drummed against my rib cage. My tongue felt as dry as a small dead lizard left to rot in the midday sun. Captain Tate's wife used to order me to remove them from her veranda. I pressed my hands together to stop them shaking.

Tap tap, tap tap, tap tap.

"Maybe she went down to the sea," Ravenhide said. "She'll be long gone, drowned like Isabella from the Spanish Main. Or she might be over on the Port Royal Road. If you jump on your horse, you might find her yet."

Mr. Powell didn't reply.

Tap tap, tap tap, tap tap.

I felt the ground tremor. My shoulders cracked. Or it could've been my feet. I placed my mouth around my kneecap and breathed into it.

This time the taps were louder. *Pung, pung, pung, pung.*

I stopped breathing.

Pung, pung, pung, pung.

"Maybe you're right, Ravenhide," Mr. Powell said. "I'll check the Port Royal Road, the harbor road, and the shore. Her dark neck will join the hogs' heads in the gully, I promise you. The rest of her will be nailed to the gibbet. The crows will have her."

Footsteps. Then the opening and closing of a door.

Desperate to breathe, I struck the lid of my barrel with my head. It didn't move. *"Aaaaarrrrrgggghhh!"*

Ravenhide twisted off the lid. I puffed out a long breath and was mighty glad to see the stars.

"You want to wake up the dead at the bottom of the sea?" Ravenhide said.

"Me could nuh breathe in there," I replied, feeling the bump on my head.

He helped me out of the barrel, but I was so weak

he had to carry me inside his hut. He laid me to rest in a corner upon rags and hides. Bright-colored scarfs, tops, and slops hung from a rope suspended from the ceiling. There was a small table in the middle and a wooden chest in a corner. He brought me water to drink and food to eat, watching me closely as I greedily swallowed my cold chicken and corn.

"You're . . . you're not ah slave?" I asked. "Nobody own you? You never come from ah plantation? You have plenty-plenty garment."

"No," Ravenhide replied. "I was never a slave."

"Why? Every Black mon me see is ah slave."

Ravenhide laughed. "You haven't seen much of the world."

"Isn't *this* de world?" I asked.

"Jamaica is just a small island in the big ocean," he said. "And to survive here, you have to learn something that makes money."

"How do you mek money?"

"In my guess, I am the top barrel maker in the island," Ravenhide said. "They'd have to sail far and wide to find a pair of hands skilled as my own. So, they pay me a fair price and don't insult me too much."

"You? They pay *you* ah fair price? Ah Black mon?"

Ravenhide laughed again.

I was confused.

"Barrels are very important," Ravenhide said. "On ships it keeps food fresh and seals in good water and spirits. And tobacco too."

"Tobacco? Is it dat someting dat white mon put in dem pipe and smoke?"

"Yes," he replied. "The brown weed that they love to smoke. Some of them believe it can cure you from the plague."

"What is this plague?"

Ravenhide shook his head. "You ask many questions . . . all I see is that tobacco makes men cough and spit."

"Then me won't try it," I said.

"My barrels are very important. Nobody would last long if they sail the great blue and all their barrels are leaking. They would perish from thirst."

"Perish?"

"Die!" Ravenhide raised his voice. "It's not pretty seeing a dead man's eyes and tongue who has died from thirst."

"Where did you learn to mek barrel?" I asked.

"A long tale is that. And I haven't shared it with any living soul to the coming moon. You have to excuse my leave."

"Your leave?" I repeated.

"Yes, I have to fetch some seawater for your foot."

"And dat will mek it heal up?"

Ravenhide didn't answer. Instead, he collected a pot from his outdoor kitchen and left by the front door. I closed my eyes. *Thank you, Asase Ya. Me will never question you again. But if Ravenhide want to molest me, me will jook him up too.*

I hobbled out near to the back fence in case Mr.

Powell returned. *If me sore foot allows me, me will jump over if me hear anyting.*

I peered out to the still seas and wondered what world Ravenhide had talked about. *Maybe Mama was not dreaming.*

Ravenhide returned shortly, and applied the seawater to my foot.

"*Aaaaarrrggghhh!* You want to kill me?" I cried.

He offered me the stick again to bite on, but I spat it out and swung a wild punch at him. Ravenhide easily parried my blow and laughed hard. "You have fire," he said. "I like that. It will keep you alive. Trust me, the seawater will heal your foot."

"It's *killing* me foot!"

"Now, fiery one," he said as I settled, "what name do I call you?"

My foot stung like I had danced barefoot over angry rocks. "Kem . . . Kemosha. Kemosha Tate."

"Kemosha Tate. And you were a slave girl?"

I nodded.

"And you have taken your master's last name?"

"Yes. From Captain Tate at de plantation."

Ravenhide shook his head. "I'm going to rename you Kemosha Black."

"Kemosha Black," I said. I liked it.

"You will take your rest here tonight. And when the sun rises, I will teach you how to lengthen your days."

"Me cyan't stay here so," I said. "As soon as me foot

heal up me want to go back to de plantation. Me have ah liccle brudder and—"

Ravenhide shook his head. "If Mr. Powell finds you hiding on the Port Royal Road or near the shores, he will kill you and nail your body onto a gibbet. Do you want that?"

In my head I could see the hooks and stains on that misshapen cross by the roadside.

"What are you going to teach me?"

"How to keep yourself alive," he replied. "A woman who hates being molested in Port Royal has to be apprenticed in the arts of the sword. And there are robbers, killers, and bad-minded people everywhere you look."

"But me never even pick up ah sword in all me life."

Ravenhide chuckled. "You will tomorrow."

"Tomorrow?"

"Yes, Kemosha Black. For a price."

"What is it?"

"My cooking is not as good as my barrel work," he laughed. "You cook, and I teach you how to live."

I thought about it. At least I didn't have to sleep beside any hogs.

I nodded.

CHAPTER 6

Sword Woman

The rooster in Ravenhide's chicken coop startled me out of my sleep. The barrel maker still lay snoring, so I decided to step outside. Morning light spread in the eastern sky. The clouds were high and skinny. White birds beaked the surface of the clean blue waters. I stood up, closed my eyes, and heard the fresh breath of the sea. My body ached all over and my foot throbbed with pain. *Mama, me cyan't fly away home if me body paining me.*

I hobbled over to the cookhouse, spotted pieces of chicken wrapped in broad leaves and two sticks of corn. I soon started a fire to make breakfast.

When the meat was warmed, Ravenhide rose. He sniffed the air, stretched his arms, and smiled. "How is your foot?" he asked.

"Ah liccle better," I said, offering him food.

For the first time in my life, I didn't have to worry about what size portions I had for breakfast. I ate two chicken thighs. *Two!*

"Do you want some tea?" Ravenhide asked.

"Tea? What is tea?"

Ravenhide chuckled.

By the fence was a tall green plant. Ravenhide pulled off ten broad leaves and brought them to the cookhouse. He boiled water in a pot and placed the leaves inside, then handed me a mug. "This will help your healing. Tea. Drink when it cools down a little."

"Marta call it bush leaf," I said.

"When you finish the bush leaf, as your Marta calls it, it'll be time to start your first lesson."

"Wid de sword?"

"Yes, with the sword," answered Ravenhide. "Best to take your lesson now because everyone else in Port Royal will be at rest—including Mr. Powell and Indika. There is too much firewater in this island."

I drank the tea. It didn't have a strong taste, but it freshened my mouth.

When I finished, Ravenhide pulled a sword from under his bedding. Taken from its cowhide sheath, it was a long, straight weapon that curved near the tip. It reflected the rising sun. It had a wooden handle and a metal knuckle guard. He brought it outside and ran his finger down the length of it, before swishing and swinging it as though he was fighting an enemy. "*Ayaah! Ayaah!*"

When he wielded the sword, he seemed to grow another long finger. His blade danced in his hand. Mighty he looked. *How cyan liccle me swing sword like dat?*

He suddenly stopped and called to me. "Kemosha Black, take my blade. They call it a hanger sword. Never ask about who owned it before I claimed it."

For a moment, I wasn't sure. I hesitated. *Me never seen ah woman wid ah long blade before.*

"Kemosha Black!" Ravenhide raised his voice. "Do not waste my time! Come here and *take* the sword."

I did what I was told. The handle felt cool and was too big for my fingers. Ravenhide watched me with hard eyes.

"I have sailed to the Spanish Main and back again seven times," he said. "Been at war with five Spanish ships, killed at least twenty men, and I haven't lost a finger yet. Nor has any blade notched my head. I am skilled with a sword and my reflexes are swift, but white captains still only see me as a barrel maker."

"They only see me as ah cook," I whispered to myself.

"Get used to the sword," he said. "It will become your sharper third arm. Thrash it here and thrash it there."

I slashed, jabbed, and sliced for the next half hour or so. I couldn't remember having such big fun since I was a little girl flinging sweet potatoes at Marta's head.

"*Ayaah! Ayaah!*" I imagined Mr. Powell and Mr. Marsh being in front of me. "*Ayaah! Tek dat and tek dat! Ayaah!*"

Meanwhile, Ravenhide went to the cookhouse and collected three pieces of corn.

He watched me for a while with a smile spreading from his lips. I cut, thrust, and chopped.

"Stop!" Ravenhide cried.

He came over to me and adjusted my stance: one foot forward, left hand behind my back and facing side-on. "You have to make yourself a skinny target," he said.

"But this uncomfortable. And me foot still sore."

"Would you rather be uncomfortable or have a sword find its way through to your heart?"

I shook my head and quickly positioned myself into the pose.

"I will toss the three pieces of corn into the air," Ravenhide said. "You will slice each one in half before they fall to the ground."

"Jest, you ah jesting," I said. "Impossible! Me cyan't do that."

Ravenhide didn't reply. Instead, he slowly walked up to me and held me in such a fierce glare that I dropped the sword.

"Pick it up!" he shouted. "That is your lifeline. To survive in Port Royal you have to keep a sword close to your hand like your mouth is close to air."

I picked it up quicker than any portion of accidentally dropped ham for Madam Tate.

"If you question me again," he added, "I will cut out your eyes and sew them onto my own breeches! Do as I say!"

I stepped into my stance. Ravenhide tossed the corn high into the air. I slashed and hacked as quickly as I could, but the three pieces dropped to the ground uncut.

Ravenhide bent over and slapped his knees with laughter. I didn't find it funny.

"Again!" he roared. "Maybe a one-armed oarsman would prove to be a better apprentice."

I'm not sure how many times Ravenhide tossed those cursed pieces of corn into the air, but when the sun had passed the midday hour, I managed to scratch only one piece.

"Bravo!" Ravenhide clapped his hands. "Now, take your rest."

He offered me a mug of water from a barrel in the cookhouse. As I drank it, I watched him closely. He had long delicate fingers, thick arms, and broad shoulders.

"So, if you not ah slave," I said, "where you from?"

Ravenhide stared at the ground for a long while as if he was thinking of some cruel memory. He sipped his water. "I come from a place far, far away," he said. "And that place is not Spain, England, or the Spanish Main. I come from a land south of the European sea. A place where people speak many tongues, have many shades, and where they study the skies. A place where we have our own Black history, counted back to the ancient years, tell Black stories. Oh yes, we have our own Black heroes and legends. And let me tell you, we have pretty pieces of art too."

"What do they call your place? Do you have ah mama, papa? Any brudder or sister?"

He stared at the ground again. Just when I thought he had ignored my question, he spoke softly: "My people are Mandinka. My parents walked tall. They named me Souleymane. I had brothers and sisters, I was the oldest. Many in our village wanted us to pray to their one god: Allah. My father refused. So he took us on a long journey north. Across the mighty desert. To the sea."

"Who are they?" I asked. "What is ah desert? Who is Allah?"

Ravenhide glanced at the sky before he fixed his hard, brown eyes on me. "Kemosha Black, you ask too many questions."

"But me want—"

"No more talk! Take your rest. I'm going to Kingston harborside to barter for more corn. Prepare yourself for more sword schooling on my return."

Before I could say anything else, he left.

He returned an hour later but soon departed to fetch a barrel of water. As soon as I refreshed myself, he told me to stand up.

He stood before me with two long sticks in each hand. "Pick up the sword," he ordered.

What Ravenhide doing wid dem long piece of stick? Him going to lick me wid dem?

"You're going to defend yourself against my attack," he said. "Listen to me good. Don't look at my legs nor my arms. Don't even look at my face because those parts of my body will not strike you. Concentrate on the wood in my hands. *This* will be your torment."

I nodded, but before I could ready myself Ravenhide launched a ferocious attack, swinging and clubbing at me. I could barely raise my sword to defend myself. I scrambled backward to the log fence.

He wasn't impressed.

"Concentrate!" he yelled. "Keep your eyes on the two sticks!"

I was struck on my arms, back, legs, and chest.

"Me cyan't do this," I said. "Why don't you just let me go back to de plantation?"

Ravenhide seized me with a glare. He marched up to me and ripped the sword from my grasp. He raised it above his head. "*This* is your life," he said. "Don't you understand? You have wounded a man who serves the English Navy. The only chance you have is to learn how to wield the sword and defend yourself."

"But me nuh want to fight anyone," I replied.

"You have no choice," said Ravenhide. "Don't you understand? This is Port Royal. If you run back to the plantation, Mr. Powell will find you and kill you there. And then he will take your body and nail it onto a gibbet to warn other women in Port Royal. Or he might feed you to his hogs. They care not what they eat. The rum-swiggers of this town will care no more if you die than a fly on their brow."

I thought about it.

"*Concentrate* on the sticks," Ravenhide said.

Until the sun dipped beyond the west, Ravenhide instructed me, adjusted my stance, and raged at my mistakes. I went to my rest that first night not afraid of Mr. Powell capturing me, but dreading Ravenhide's long pieces of wood. Bruises marked my whole body.

When I finished, I could barely raise a hand over my head. I was in no condition to cook. Ravenhide fed me well, serving sweet potatoes with my chicken and corn. "You need to build up your strength," he said. "You're going to need it."

"Need it for what?" I asked.

"I have a plan," he said.

"Ah plan?"

"Don't worry about that for now. Take your rest and think about what I taught you today. It'll save your life."

I closed my eyes and thought of Gregory and Marta. I wondered if they could see the moon as clearly as I did.

The night was still deep when I woke up. Ravenhide slept silently. I peered over the log fence toward the dark waters. I wondered about the fate of Isabella from the Spanish Main. *Was she ah real girl or some mad story dat ah rum-drinker tell?*

My foot still ached but I managed to climb the fence and make my way down to the shore. I had to be careful over the harsh rocks. *One slip could be me end.*

Foolish chile, I heard Marta whisper in my ear.

I thought of Mama's words when I would get up at nighttime as a small girl and go wandering. "Eres demasia'o curioso y no escuchas"—*you're too curious and you don't listen.*

Up close, the ships looked gigantic. Lamps lit the decks. The sails could have covered Ravenhide's hut and his backyard. The masts and poles seemed to touch the stars. I spotted men loading barrels and chests on deck. Some climbed rope ladders and others mopped and scrubbed. *It's ah strange ting watching white mon doing slave work.*

On shore, men sat in circles drinking, smoking, gambling, and cursing. I couldn't help but wonder what it was like to sail the great blue. *Epo, is dat where me journey end?*

I carefully made my way back up the craggy ridge. I just about managed to clamber over Ravenhide's log fence, but when I landed on the other side, he was there with his hands on his hips and wearing a look fiercer than a Jamaican hurricane. He bit his top lip and shook his head. He spoke very slowly.

"If you go away again," he said, "I will hunt you down myself and feed your liver to the hogs!"

"Me sorry," I said. "Me just wanted to see de big ships."

"Do you want to live, or do you want to die?" Ravenhide shook his head again before turning away in disgust.

"Me want to live," I whispered to myself. "Me have to live if me want to go back for Gregory and Marta."

CHAPTER 7

Ravenhide's Challenge

I lost count of the days that I was trained by Ravenhide in the art of swordplay. Two fat moons and a thousand bruises came and went. If Mr. Powell was still hunting me, he never revealed it. I didn't sleep well.

Every day Ravenhide bathed my burned foot with seawater. He gave me a baggy red pair of slops to practice in. During the afternoon he would sometimes walk down to the harborside and barter for food, nails, bolts, and lengths of wood. He often received customers in the evenings and sold his barrels. Before they arrived, I climbed the fence and lay low on the rocks until his guests had departed. I once hid in a barrel as he bartered over prices with a drunken shoe merchant. On a few occasions, he would disappear for hours and refuse to tell me where he had been. Before he would leave, he'd collect a crocus bag of refreshment, a barrel of water, and then be gone without a word.

"You ask too many questions," he'd say to me on his return. "Don't leave my cabin or my backyard."

"Me promise," I said.

I kept my word and never left.

One breezy morning, Ravenhide hurled three corns into the air and I managed to slice two in half and wound the third. I danced and screamed with delight. "Me did it! Me did it! Oh, Asase Ya, Nyame, me did it but me cyan't believe it!"

Ravenhide stood and nodded. "Bravo. But keep your voice down. They will hear you in a ship's hull sailing the horizon."

I danced a little dance, something I learned from Marta. I was in no mood to speak in whispers. "Ayaah! Ayaah! Kemosha Black de sword woman! De sword woman wid de quickest hands inna Port Royal."

He allowed me to have my moment and we celebrated with spiced red wine. I felt a bit dizzy after two glugs and had to sit down.

"Me cyan go back to de plantation now?" I asked after a while. "And fight Captain Tate and find Marta and Gregory?"

Ravenhide shook his head. "No, Kemosha. Best way to help your brother and Marta is to have pieces of eight in your pocket so you can buy their freedom."

"Then why you teach me de ways of de sword?"

Ravenhide drained his wine before answering. He side-eyed me. "You have to face Mr. Powell before we think of any other plan."

"What . . . what you ah say?" I stuttered. "Misser Powell will kill me for true. Me cyan't fight him. You see how long him sword is?"

"He has a weakness," Ravenhide said.

"Me nuh see no weakness when him chop off de hog's head. He will kill me for true. And if Misser Marsh about, he will want to murder me after Misser Powell kill me."

Ravenhide shook his head. A smile crept over his lips.

"Me nuh want to fight him. Me want to go back to de plantation."

"And if you go back you will have to slay Captain Tate, Mr. Billings, and all the overseers. And you can't stay here. I'll be sailing to the Spanish Main soon on the new moon."

I thought about it. "What is his weakness?"

"His weakness is gambling," Ravenhide said.

"How . . . how this will go?"

"I will set the challenge. You will defend yourself against his sword for a count of a hundred."

"Ah hundred? How long is dat?"

"Long enough for you to prove yourself."

"But . . . but if him see me he will kill me before ah John Crow fly from one branch to de next."

"Don't question your ways with the sword. You have improved day by day."

"Me hear what Misser Powell say. Him want to dig out me good eye and sew it onto him breeches. Even if me dead me will never see me mama again."

Ravenhide killed my words with one of his hard glares. "Mr. Powell is not as swift with the sword as he once was. Drink, bad women, age, and the Jamaican sun have slowed him. And you have two eyes to his one. All you must do is parry and block for a count of a hundred. If you concentrate, you can do that."

"But—"

"Quiet! No more talk. No more *can't*. Just think about your sword defending his sword. Remove Mr. Powell from your mind. We go to the tavern in three days."

CHAPTER 8

Duel Beneath an Amber Sun

The three days went quicker than a yellow dawn. An amber glow began to fall beyond the western hills when Ravenhide ordered me to sit down cross-legged in his backyard. I clutched my sword in my right hand, and now it fit like a glove. I wore my red slops. It was a still, early evening. The chickens had stopped clucking. The sea looked so pretty, with a golden streak that stretched to the horizon. I wanted to swim to the end of that light rather than clash blades with Mr. Powell. *Mama, where is your land? Me might be flying to you quicker than me have planned. Maybe Epo cyan ride me over de waters and tek me to you.*

Ravenhide asked me to close my eyes. I did what I was told. He spoke slow and calmly: "People will be cursing, hollering, and screaming. But you only have eyes for his sword. When we enter the tavern and deliver our challenge, they will laugh at you. They will mock you. *But you only have eyes for his sword.* You are not just defending yourself, but Gregory and Marta too. And everybody else at your plantation."

"Me know dat," I said. "Iyana, Hakan, and—"

"Quiet!"

"Me sorry."

A long pause. Then I heard his soft words again: "The secret of a duel is to remain calm. Take a good stance. Feel the ground beneath you with the soles of your feet. Balance is everything. Defend the blade."

I nodded.

"How is your foot?" he asked.

"Me foot heal up," I replied. "Me nuh feel it too much."

"Don't even think about your foot."

"Me won't."

"Get up," he said. "We go."

Half of me wanted to flee back to the plantation and the other half urged me to dive into the deep blue. I wanted to join Isabella from the Spanish Main wherever she could be. *At least me good black skin would not be split this way and dat.*

We left Ravenhide's shack by the front door. The cannon of my heart could have sunk the ships in the harbor and half of the island.

Mr. Powell's tavern was only two hundred strides up the hill. We reached the front door to find a carved-faced ruffian asleep beside it, holding onto an empty tankard. I heard the hollering from inside. Ravenhide gazed at me. This time his brown eyes were soft. "Concentrate on his blade," he said. "Pay no attention to the cursing."

"Me will try me best," I said.

"Grip your sword. Remember what you're defending. Marta, Gregory, your mama, papa, and everybody else who came before you. You're fighting for them and the Mandinka people who I come from."

He pushed through the door ahead of me. I followed him in. Smoke curled around me. I could barely lift my eyes from the floor. Drink fumes attacked my nostrils. The tavern was packed. Groups of men gambled in opposite corners while two men groped a one-legged mulatto girl in the shadows. Others chanted their strange chants. Some only had eyes for their mugs and tankards.

I lifted my head, seeing Indika behind the counter serving a seven-fingered customer. Another girl was beside her, drying a mug. She looked younger than me, her face bruised. Mr. Powell was behind her. A chill colder than night rain spread from my good heart and reached down to my toes. I found myself puffing hard. I closed my mouth and breathed through my nose. The grip on my sword tightened. I heard mocking laughter and cruel comments.

"Hear all!" Ravenhide suddenly shouted. "Hear all!"

All eyes turned on him and then to me.

"I have found your black strumpet," Ravenhide announced.

First, Mr. Powell glanced at me. Then his eyes narrowed and glared. Disbelief marked his forehead. "The night man of the barrels!" he shouted. "A long time since you have bought rum from my tavern or even bartered for a mug of water. And you claim you have *found* my black strumpet. I say you have given her shelter!"

He went for his sword, leaped over the counter, and rushed toward me. The crowd backed away as he waved his blade high in the air. I was too shocked to move.

"Before you take the life of this slave strumpet," Ravenhide said, stepping between me and my onrushing owner, "is she really a fair challenge to you? What sport is there if you kill her so easily?"

"The black witch fled from my ownership after wounding Mr. Marsh," Mr. Powell raged. "Her liver is mine to nail where I choose. I bartered five pieces of eight for her! *Five!* Will you compensate me?"

"No," replied Ravenhide. "But if you kill her now you will never recover those pieces of eight."

The tavern hushed. Men paused their drinking. The mulatto girl managed to free herself from the two men and fled with her crutch. I heard her hopping over the cobbled stones. *Bop poom, bop poom, bop poom.* I concentrated my gaze on a red stain on the floor. I spotted an ant scurrying to a corner.

"May I present a challenge," Ravenhide went on.

"You dare present me with a challenge?" Mr. Powell responded. "Insolence!"

"It could increase your fortune and luck," said Ravenhide. "And if you win, it'll make me the poorer."

Mr. Powell considered his options. He flicked his

one eye at me. *Me cyan't tek this. Asase Ya, save me good self. Me heart going to bounce outta me chest.*

"Name your challenge," Mr. Powell said with his voice raised.

Ravenhide hesitated. Doubt crept into his eyes. His lips moved but no words were spoken. He coughed, placed a hand over his mouth, and steadied himself. *Maybe him finally realize me cyan't do this.*

"Name your challenge!" Mr. Powell repeated.

"If you can part her black skin with your sword and make her blood flow before a count of a hundred," Ravenhide said, "then there will be no price for the barrels I make for you for a year nor any other work you might desire for me to perform."

The sword loosened in my hand. A strange feeling grew from my feet to my stomach. My forehead was suddenly wet with hot sweat. I felt my heartbeat on my forehead. I couldn't look up. Someone laughed; others joined in.

"A count of a hundred," said Mr. Powell. "You jest with me, Ravenhide."

The laughter grew louder.

"What say you?" challenged Ravenhide. "Do you accept my challenge? Brave quartermaster of Captain Morgan himself. One who has conquered the Spanish Main and walked its sands!"

I lifted my gaze. Mr. Powell glared at Ravenhide. He scratched his chin and chuckled with an evil pleasure. Behind the counter, I spotted Indika with hands on her hips, shaking her head. She wasn't impressed. The young girl with the swollen face only had eyes for the floor.

"Give the black strumpet a chance!" called a man from a corner.

"What have you to lose?" shouted another.

"And, if by slim fortune," said Mr. Powell, "that the black strumpet manages to defend herself for a count of a hundred, what do I lose?"

Without hesitation, Ravenhide answered, "You lose the five pieces of eight you paid for her. She wins her freedom."

Indika shook her head. "If she wins, you better find me another who can cook and scrub in this God-cursed sun. Your gambling will be the death of me."

Mr. Powell rubbed his chin once more. He gazed at his sword and smiled. "I accept," he said.

I think what blood I had in my legs had escaped me for I could barely stand. I held onto Ravenhide's arm. He whispered into my ear, "Remember what I taught you. You're not fighting him, you're defending against his sword. His blade is your enemy. Be a skinny target."

I wanted to be a target that was plenty miles away.

"Outside!" someone yelled.

"OUTSIDE!"

Ravenhide led me through the tavern's front door. An arch of an orange sun still shone over the western hills. Not only did this tavern empty, but other places of drink too. There must have been over a hundred and a score men, all eager to see my death. Maybe two hundred. They ranted and cursed. They had taken their mugs and tankards with them. They puffed on their pipes and sniffed their tobacco. A few women were in the crowd too; I saw the one-legged mulatto girl watching from behind a horse and cart. They made a circle on the cobbled road for the duel. Some climbed on shacks and low-level buildings on both sides.

"This will be quick," said one man.

"The strumpet won't last the first plunge of a sword," said another.

"It's better entertainment than seeing a strumpet waste away on a gibbet."

Gripping my shoulder, Ravenhide whispered into my ear, "Think on all we practiced. Only have eyes for his sword. Turn off your ears to the crowd. Unlike me, they haven't seen how swift you wield your blade."

I nodded.

I stood at the edge of the circle. Mr. Powell walked side to side, opposite me. The grin had grown on his cheeks. His one eye seemed to turn into an angry moon. It glared at me in contempt. He performed thrusts and slices for the crowd. They roared, cheered, and supped their drinks.

I stepped into my stance. Left hand behind my back. Side on. Right foot forward. *Kemosha, mek yourself skinny.*

"Who will count to a hundred?" Ravenhide asked.

"I will," said Indika. "Though I doubt if I will reach ten. The sooner this is over with, the sooner you buckos and mateys will be back in my tavern buying my rum."

She gave me an evil eye-pass.

"When you finish," she added, "toss her body far away from my gully. The stench of my pit toilet and my hogs is bad enough."

Asase Ya, Nyame, Epo. Mek me hand strong and mek Mr. Powell arm weak. Give me quick sight so me cyan see which way him sword go.

"One!" yelled Indika suddenly. "Two! Three!"

Mr. Powell sprang toward me. He flailed his sword this way and that. I managed to parry his first blows. He went for my neck and then my knees. I jumped over his wild hack and had to move swiftly to my right to dodge his straight jab.

"Seven! Eight! Nine! Ten!"

I managed to deflect a thrust aimed between my eyes. Mr. Powell bared his teeth and cursed my being. I almost fell over backward, but was able to regain my footing and step away to my left.

"Face me, black witch!"

"Fifteen! Sixteen! Seventeen!"

Me still alive!

Mr. Powell wasn't pleased. His cheeks turned red. He lunged for my neck again and I raised my sword just in time before he split my chin and everything else. He sliced, chopped, and stabbed, but I saw his sword coming. It was longer and broader than mine. The dying amber sun reflected on its blade.

"Twenty-six! Twenty-seven! Twenty-eight!"

I breathed hard but I had no time to stand still. My feet were quicker than his and I used the full circle.

"Stand still, strumpet!"

He came for me again, his sword held high. He slashed at me from right to left and then left to right. Our blades met and sparks were about us. His spit covered my cheeks. Creases circled his empty eye. I sniffed rum from his tongue.

"The hogs will feast on you, strumpet!"

I danced on my toes. I leaned this way and that. I ducked and weaved.

"Forty-seven! Forty-eight! Forty-nine!"

Me legs were getting tired. Sweat poured from my forehead and dripped through my lashes. I felt my burned foot once more. Mr. Powell tried to crack me open from left shoulder to right hip. I parried his blow but the force of it made me fall onto my back. Mr. Powell seized his chance. His one eye grew large. I could see the skinny red veins in it. He gripped his sword in two hands and tried to cut off my head. Seeing my peril, I rolled to my left, leaped to my feet, and his sword met stone. *Thwaaaanggg!* He let out a roar of frustration. "Arrrrrhhhhgghhh! Black witch!"

Asase Ya. T'ank you for giving me foot speed and strength.

The crowd was silenced. I caught a quick glance of the one-legged mulatto. She raised a half smile, but she then covered her eyes.

"Sixty-three! Sixty-four! Sixty-five!"

I blew hard. Mr. Powell took in a deep breath. His neck was as red as his face. His hair stuck to his forehead. His eye boiled with rage. Sweat poured off me like a hard rain falling off a broad leaf.

Me cyan do this! Me cyan do this!

Mr. Powell let out an ugly cry and swish-swashed toward me. He cursed, spat, and attacked me from all angles. His foul temper had got the better of him. I remembered what Ravenhide had said: *The secret to any duel is to remain calm.* He slashed, hacked, and chopped, but each time I met his sword with my own.

I could have driven my blade into his wobbly belly. But I decided not to. If I did, I might have two hundred men to defend against.

Now, his blows were not as powerful.

"Ninety-two! Ninety-three! Ninety-four!"

"Who taught you the art of the sword, strumpet?" he yelled. "Tell me! Who?"

I comfortably deflected his last three blows. Mr. Powell puffed hard enough to launch a ship into the great blue.

"One hundred!"

Roars were all about me. Tankards were flung in the air. Mr. Powell offered me a demon look before turning away in disgust.

I searched for Ravenhide. He smiled and nodded, coming over to me. "Kemosha of the Caribbean," he said, "you're alive! And you've done your people and this Mandinka proud."

Men offered to buy me drinks. Some wanted to buy me for ten pieces of eight and others asked for my hand in marriage. Ravenhide fended them off. He eventually bought a bottle of spiced wine and we started back to his shack.

I spotted the one-legged mulatto again, emerging from behind a cart. She was very pretty. Half of her left leg was bound in rags. "What do they call you?" she asked.

"Kemosha," I replied.

"Kemosha Black of the Caribbean," Ravenhide said.

"Miss Kemosha," the girl said, "in all me days me never seen such ah ting. T'ank you. You mek me good heart sing. Maybe there is ah tomorrow for me."

Then she was gone.

"Who . . . who is she?" I wanted to know. "Where she come from?"

Ravenhide didn't break his stride. "She survives by selling her flesh," he replied. "But this is Port Royal. Many drunken men have no love for paying anything for a girl of the night. Especially one with one and a half legs. But she makes enough to eat and drink and find a place to rest her young head at night."

The gods were with me that night as I crawled over Ravenhide's fence. She wasn't so lucky. "Me will pray to Asase Ya for she before me eyes close."

"Yes, you do that," said Ravenhide. "Tonight we will drink the spiced red wine and chant to our gods. Tomorrow we rise with the sun to start a journey."

"Ah journey?" I said. "Where are you teking me?"

"Sunrise will give you the answer."

CHAPTER 9

Sister from Another Mother

The spiced red wine had made me sleep long. When I finally awoke, the sun had risen above the eastern hills. Ravenhide had already cooked breakfast. The inside of my head felt bruised. He had left me three corn dumplings and a round piece of green fruit I didn't recognize.

"Eat your food," he said. "I'm going to barter for a horse and cart by the harborside. And I need a new sword as you have earned my own."

"You sure you want to give me your blade?" I asked.

"I'm sure," he said. "You can have the sheath and the belt too." He paused, as if remembering some long-ago battle. "If it could speak, it could tell an interesting tale."

For a moment, I couldn't say anything. No man had ever offered me a gift before.

"Why you need ah horse and cart?" I finally asked. "We moving?"

"No, Kemosha," he replied. "We're taking a voyage."

"Ah voyage?"

"A land voyage on wheels, hooves, and feet. You ask too many questions, Kemosha Black. Eat your food and be ready on my return."

I ate my breakfast, but my headache raged at me. I drank plenty water, kept out of the sun, and took my rest again.

I hadn't slept too long before Ravenhide shook me awake. A new sword and sheath dangled from his belt. "Come, Kemosha," he said. "I want to return before the sun dies. Many a traveler has gone missing or been found with a ripped neck on the Port Royal Road."

"Where we going?"

"Stop asking your questions and get to the cart."

I stood up and collected my blade. A brown horse and an unsteady cart were waiting for us outside. Ravenhide untied the animal from a post and offered it water from a bucket. He stroked its flank before climbing on the carriage seat. "I have the horse and cart for a day," he said. "I paid for it with two barrels. Very expensive, but no other horse was available."

He picked up the reins and beckoned me to join him. It felt very strange. *Ah Black mon driving ah horse and cart? Me wish me mama and Marta coulda sight this.*

I recalled my first journey with Mr. Powell into Port Royal. He'd owned me. *Now me is free! How long will dat last? Me better not smile too wide yet. Could it be true? In all me years me never seen ah free Black girl or woman. Maybe me dreaming Mama's dream again.* I kept thinking that at any moment, a white man could send me back to a plantation.

We started up the hill to the stream, where we filled two barrels of water. The women there offered us double glances. I wanted to introduce myself to them but Ravenhide would not wait. We set off again.

The wheels were wonky and didn't run straight. We wobbled and rattled a hundred yards down the road when I spotted the one-legged mulatto girl once again. She was hobbling up the hill with an empty pot. A new bruise darkened her left cheek. I turned to Ravenhide. "Cyan we stop this time?" I asked. "Me want to talk to her."

Ravenhide thought about it, then pulled on his reins. I smiled at the girl and she returned my greeting. "Tell me someting," I said. "What dem call you?"

"Lillet," she replied. "That's what me owner used to call me."

"How old are you, Lillet?"

"Fourteen dem tell me? Me nuh sure."

"You don't have ah owner anymore?"

She shook her head.

Ravenhide jostled the reins. "We have to go, Kemosha. The sun always keeps to its own time. I can't ask it to pause."

As we trotted on, I glanced over my shoulder at Lillet. I wondered what her story was. She was free too, but misery marked her gaze.

We left Port Royal and trotted by the coastline. Sunburned men bartered for food, clothes, gold, and many other things by the Kingston harborside. Then we turned inland where the track narrowed and curved around trees. A short climb uphill later, the dirt road quit. Suddenly, we were surrounded by more green leaves than blue seas. Strange sounds came from the trees. Things talked in the grass. The bushes were wild, thick, and very green. The air was fresher here. Every now and again, Ravenhide would pull on the reins and offer the horse water and carrots. I wondered if Ravenhide was lost, but he seemed to know just where he was heading.

"Where are you teking me?" I asked. "Nobody ah live up here so apart from bird wid long beak and de small someting inna de grass."

Ravenhide didn't answer.

I glanced behind. I enjoyed the view of every single ship and boat in Kingston Harbour. The shore bent in a long arch and at the end of that curve was Port Royal. It was very pretty. I peered into the horizon and wondered about Mama's land. *Maybe de land was only inside her head.*

Ravenhide watched the seas. "Soon, Captain Morgan will be dropping anchor in Kingston Harbour," he said.

"Who is this Captain Morgan?"

"The richest man in Jamaica, and probably the

whole Caribbean. Some say he has gold pouring out of his ears."

Before I could ask more, Ravenhide checked the horse. We came to a halt. He peered into the bush and called out, "Isabella! Isabella!"

No one answered.

"Isabella!"

A rustling sound. I could see where the grass seemed to be trampled down. Two birds flapped above. Then came the steps of light feet. Leaves and twigs parted, and she emerged. I opened my mouth, but my eyes were wider.

Ah song mek flesh. She living for true!

She wore a golden scarf and a brown frock that had been ripped from the knee. She wasn't white but she wasn't Black either. She had a skinny nose; she didn't look like a mulatto. Her hair was long, dark, and curvy like gentle waves. Her eyelashes were thick. Her feet were bare. A red scar ran from her ankle to below her left knee.

She offered me a long glare. I felt threatened and placed my hand on the hilt of my sword. She turned her gaze to Ravenhide and spoke: "No te dije que nunca trajeras otra alma viviente a mi casa?"

Captain Tate may have banned any slaves speaking in Spanish, but I recognized the woman's words: *Didn't I tell you never to bring another living soul to my place?*

Ravenhide climbed down from the cart. He patted the horse. "Her name is Kemosha Black," he said. "She has fought for her life against the English quartermaster Antock Powell. She cheated death. I taught her the ways of the sword. And her way is swift."

"Los ingleses son unos diablos," the girl said. "Y los españoles son demonios."

Englishmen are devils and Spanish men are demons. Mama spoke those words plenty times.

"Isabella," Ravenhide said, "shall we all speak in English?"

Isabella nodded. I couldn't pull my gaze off her. I blinked hard and opened my eyes again. *She real for true!*

"Me try," she said.

"Are you going to help us off-load the barrels?" Ravenhide asked. "I've brought you water. I'll be sailing the Caribbean on the new moon."

"The deep blue kill you one day," she said. "Many times, it brought death close to me. And I don't need water barrel. Find stream up in hills."

"I'm not taking them back to Port Royal," said Ravenhide.

For a long moment, I couldn't move as Ravenhide and Isabella lifted the barrels off the cart. I eventually jumped down to help.

Isabella led us into the bush. The trampled path widened, and we wheeled the barrels through it. We stopped at a clearing where she had built a small wooden shack. I recognized many of Ravenhide's barrels circling the hut, all marked with the letter *R*.

Perched on the roof, strange birds watched us. It was

a burning hot day. No cloud blocked the sun's fierce rays.

Isabella had a small chicken coop and a strip of land where she grew corn and other vegetables. Next to that was a small cookhouse. There were two trees behind it with odd curved green fruit. The broad leaves of it seemed to be slashed by a sword.

"I don't know how long this voyage will take," said Ravenhide to Isabella. "I'm returning to the Spanish Main. Who knows if I will come back alive, but I will slay plenty of them before death claims me."

"You no have to go," said Isabella.

"But Ravenhide," I interrupted, "if you is sailing de great blue to de Spanish Main, you never tell me what me supposed to do in dat time?"

Ravenhide and Isabella swapped a long look. Quiet.

"What me supposed to do?" I said.

Ravenhide smiled. Isabella stared me as if she knew something that I did not.

"You can stay here with Isabella," he said. He took in a breath. "It's safe. No one will molest you here."

For a long moment, I didn't know how to respond. I thought of Marta and Gregory. *Me could never live here safe while dem ah suffer under Captain Tate's and Lyle Billings's lash.*

"Me cyan't stay here so," I said. "Me have to find plenty pieces of eight to buy Marta and Gregory's freedom."

"Nobody in Jamaica will pay anything to a Black girl," Ravenhide said. "Apart from food and water."

"You're ah Black mon," I said. "Me see white mon

paying you plenty money for your barrels and wood-work. And you tell me this Captain Morgan pay you nuff money to go to de Spanish Main. Let me sail wid you! Maybe me cyan do someting."

"Captain Morgan never invites women on his voyages."

"You cyan ask him," I challenged. "As your tongue know, me cook good."

Ravenhide thought about it. Isabella's gaze rested on me. Her eyes were curious.

"If me sail de great blue," I went on, "me could mek plenty pieces of eight. When me reach back to Jamaica, me could forward to Captain Tate's plantation and pay for Marta and Gregory's freedom. Me just hope Epo save me from dropping off de end of de world."

Ravenhide laughed hard.

"Don't laugh!" said Isabella. "Me hear that too."

I glanced and nodded at Isabella. She smiled back at me.

"If you sail close," she said to Ravenhide, "you drop off and cáete en el infierno!"

"Nobody is falling into hell," Ravenhide said.

I wondered what *infierno*, hell, was. *Maybe it's ah place where all de foolish dead people end up when they don't listen to good sense.*

Isabella's eyes grew big in indignation at Ravenhide. "Un fuego interminable," she said. *A never-ending fire.*

Ravenhide leaned against a barrel. He picked up a long blade of grass and pointed it at me. "Fortune might bless you," he said. "Your gods, Asase Ya, Nyame, and Epo, might grant you that. They have served you well so far."

"Me know me could get kill off quicktime," I said. "And me hear one bucko talk about fish big like ship ah swallow nuff people. Me cyan't stay here so. Me have to try."

Isabella looked at me as if she was about to warn me of a terrible danger. "Me see men on boat get skinny with tight face," she said. "You could see inside bones. First mate fling them in sea."

"One day we will all leave this cruel world," Ravenhide said. "I want to use my time to do something good after me see so much evil. Kemosha, this is a safe place for you to live. I ask, are you sure you want to follow me to the Spanish Main? If you say yes, you will witness bad things."

"Bad tings happen in Jamaica every day," I said. "Captain Tates are whipping Black people every day. Lillets are getting molested by buckos every day. Somebody rotting away 'pon ah gibbet every day. Me want to go to de Spanish Main."

Ravenhide held my gaze for a long while before he nodded.

Isabella prepared a meal of chicken, corn, yams, and the strange green fruit that she peeled and fried—Ravenhide called it *plantain*.

For a short moment the cruel world escaped my

mind as I tasted Isabella's dinner. My belly was full like it never had been before. I washed it down with spiced red wine. *Maybe one good day me will build me own liccle hut in a far, far land. But not until me free Marta and Gregory.*

We sat around two barrels that made a table. My drink loosened my tongue. I wanted to learn more about Isabella.

"Where you come from?" I asked her. "Your color nuh match your hair."

She glanced at Ravenhide before answering. "I come from Puerto Viejo," she said. "A good place. Mi mamá people live there many, many years. Mi papá was un pirata blanco inglés. He bring great shame to family."

I understood her words: her papa was a white English pirate.

"Mi madre cleaned fish by el mar," Isabella continued. "And her sisters too."

She told me the rest of her tale. English pirates continually raided her village and other settlements along her coastline of the Spanish Main. When she was fifteen, a first mate of an English ship had taken a fancy to her. But so did someone else. The first mate had to kill one of his crew members in a duel to claim her. She was brought back to Port Royal during a fierce storm. The first mate perished in the angry waters.

When they finally reached land, Isabella was sold into prostitution for ten pieces of eight. The men loved her light-brown skin and wanted to stroke her long black hair. She killed the first man who tried to have his way with her. Her hands were tied to a post and she was kept prisoner in a hog pen. She was told that she'd either spend the rest of her days in jail, or rot away nailed to a gibbet. Before the governor could hear her trial, she had bitten her way through her bonds and fled into the hills.

Ravenhide caught her in his backyard, scavenging for food one night.

"And you have been up here so for how long?" I asked.

"Me don't know," Isabella replied. "Me don't count days anymore."

"More than a year," Ravenhide said. "The governor himself declared that she is pardoned, and she can return to Port Royal if she wishes. The man who molested her hadn't paid her owner. Isabella had a right to defend herself."

"Nunca volveré!" Isabella said loudly. *I'll never return.* "Los hombres de Port Royal son demonios!"

I agreed with her. The men of Port Royal *were* devils.

"Me want to go home," added Isabella. "But me don't love el mar grande."

Ravenhide shook his head. "It's too dangerous in this time. The Spanish Main is plagued with English and Spanish ships. You'd only be captured again."

Isabella dropped her head. I'm not sure why, but I approached her and hugged her. It felt like we were fated to meet. *Maybe Nyame, Asase Ya, and Epo had ar-*

ranged it. Her forehead fell onto my shoulder, and she sobbed quietly. There she remained for a long moment. I thought of Mama, Gregory, and Marta. *At least de people me love are on this island. Life too cruel for girl-chile in this world.*

Isabella pulled away from me and wiped her face. I sensed she was trying to control her emotions.

"You ride sea with Captain Morgan again?" she asked Ravenhide.

"The last time Captain Morgan was in port, he said the next raid will be the biggest and most daring yet," he responded. "He'll be sailing in from his Firefly estates very soon. There will be untold riches to win. All will sign Articles of Agreement and everyone will get a share."

"Even somebody like me?" I asked.

"Maybe even a girl like you. All I can do is ask. You can cook, you can swing a sword. You can be of good service."

"Will you come too?" I asked Isabella.

She shook her head. "No. You have to kill me before me sail el mar grande. Last time, it come alive and want to eat me. Big wind and vex sea start big fight."

"If you want to leave this island," Ravenhide said, "one day you will have to brave the Caribbean once again. Maybe it will be safer in the future."

Isabella didn't say anything. I noticed the terror in her eyes.

"I don't intend to stay in Port Royal for too long if I return," Ravenhide said.

"Where are you going?" I asked. "To search for your people? Your family?"

"You ask too many question, Kemosha Black," Ravenhide snapped. "There are some things a man wants to keep inside and not speak about."

"He wants to go home too," said Isabella. "To the land of the Mandinka."

Ravenhide suddenly became angry. "Quiet!" he roared. He stood up abruptly and offered Isabella a brutal eye-pass.

Before he marched off into the bush, I recognized a sadness in Ravenhide's eyes. Isabella and I watched him disappear beyond the plantain trees. He cursed as he went.

"Me never mean to vex him," I said to Isabella.

"No worry," she said. "Him walk off plenty times when I say wrong thing. Him no like talk about home."

"Why?"

Isabella paused and gazed into the bush. I think she was deciding if she could trust me. "Españoles malvados killed his family."

"Bad Spanish men?" I asked, unsure of her words.

Isabella nodded. "He want revenge. That's why he follow Captain Morgan. That's why he joined ingleses ship. That's why he sail to Spanish Main. Him heart full of anger. Like fish full of seawater. Him no satisfy yet."

"The Mandinka. Where dem from?"

Isabella shook her head. "Him no like talk about family. One time I hear him talk about young sister in him sleep."

"Spanish men kill her too?"

She nodded again. "Sí. They came in the night. Ravenhide found her naked. They had their way with her then killed her. He blame himself for not being there. She was eleven years old. He cared for her."

"De English and Spanish are demons for true," I said.

"Demonios," Isabella nodded. "But no talk about him family when Ravenhide can hear."

Later, Isabella led me to a stream where we bathed ourselves, scrubbed pots, and rinsed out clothes. For a short while I forgot about my troubles and enjoyed being free. I closed my eyes and listened to the sounds of the bush. The birds sang so pretty. The breezes curled around the trees. I listened to the music of the leaves. The waters soothed my body. I so wanted to share the feeling with Marta and Gregory. *Working from sunrise to sundown on de plantation, me never get to love de prettiness of de day. Me have to free dem! Yes, me have to free dem for true.*

On our return, she showed me a variety of trees that bore strange fruit. We linked arms and didn't rush back. *This was meant to be.*

A pink sun dropped behind the western hills when Ravenhide returned. The rage had left his eyes. His brow had softened. "I have already seen that you have been blessed with courage," he said to me. "Come! We go to the Spanish Main and we shall return with enough pieces of eight to barter for this cursed island."

As we left, Isabella rushed up and embraced me. She held me for a long time. Water was in her eyes. *Maybe she feels we were fated to meet as much as I believe it.* "Que tu buen pie vuelva a honrar mi pequeña choza de nuevo," she said.

I understood her perfectly—*may your good foot grace me liccle shack again.*

CHAPTER 10

Captain Henry Morgan

When we hit the Port Royal Road, night had dropped like a black blanket. There were fewer stars in the heavens. The moon had lost some weight. Ravenhide had to remind the sentries at the gate that he was Captain Morgan's personal barrel maker. He showed them a letter that had a red seal on it. They allowed him to pass through but not without suspicious glances.

The cursing, cries, and yelps that came from the taverns and inns unnerved me. Someone screamed from the church as if they were being tortured. Ravenhide didn't stop to check who it was.

Ladies of the night did their business in shadows and alleys. Men drank themselves into sleep. Others gambled and fought each other. I heard the fierce barking of dogs and the strange screeching of long-tailed birds.

I was relieved to reach Ravenhide's shack and to see him lock his front door behind us. I went out the back and stood for a while, watching the bobbing shapes of the ships and boats in the harbor. A lone bucko far below chanted a new song:

> *"Sweet ole England*
> *We yearn for the ale in a tavern in London*
> *For too long I haven't seen your stony shores*
> *I am far abroad, fighting your wars*
> *I long to see you again*
> *My green country, my good ole friend*
> *I'll be back when I win my fortune*
> *It'll be so good to drink rum under an English moon."*

I peered far into the dark seas and wondered if I'd survive my next journey. *Epo, will you save me?*

My sleep was uneasy on this night.

I rose with the morning sun and peered into Kingston Harbour. A new ship was anchored there. It was taller than any other vessel I had seen. It had three long masts that reached out for the clouds. Hard breezes stiffened the flags. I couldn't imagine a big fish swallowing it.

Ravenhide joined me. He didn't say anything but just smiled. We watched men step off the ship and walk inland. I guessed Indika Brown would be selling plenty tankards of rum and whiskey on this day. *Misser Powell will have nuff mon to gamble wid.*

"He has come from his Firefly estates," Ravenhide said finally. He pointed to the big ship. "There she is. The *Satisfaction*. Isn't she beautiful for the eye to behold?"

"You call ah ship beautiful?" I said.

"We will eat well this morning. Then we go to Indika's tavern. Captain Henry Morgan always dines there."

I could hardly swallow my food. *This Captain Morgan might want to kill me for wounding Misser Marsh. He might want to trouble me woman parts. Him might not even want to tek ah girl to de Spanish Main. Him might want to test me sword.*

"Cyan't me just stay here so?" I said. "Maybe you cyan ask Captain Morgan if me cyan sail to de Spanish Main. Me will wait till you come back."

Ravenhide shook his head. "No, Captain Morgan likes to look into the eyes of anyone who sails the seas with him."

I ignored the food in front of me and took three glugs of spiced red wine instead.

"I have one bit of advice for you," he said. "When he gazes into your eyes, don't look away."

I nodded.

"Now we go!" he said.

Indika's tavern was empty apart from the dirty-faced white girl with swollen cheeks scrubbing the floor. The hogs out back squealed and grunted. I wondered where she came from and if she slept out back too.

"Where is everyone?" Ravenhide asked.

"Gone to the church," the girl replied. "Captain Morgan has come."

"Why do white people go to this place call church?" I said. "Cyan't they pray to dem god wherever dem foot land? What do they do in there?"

Ravenhide thought about it. "It's a place where many people . . . pray to Jesus. They like to do it together."

"Who is this Jesus?" I asked.

"That is a long tale. Come, Kemosha. Let's go and see Captain Morgan, the richest man in the Caribbean."

"This Jesus rich too?" I asked. "Him ah pirate too? Him have plenty gold and big house? Him counting him pieces of eight ah nighttime?"

"You ask too many questions."

When we left the tavern, mateys and buckos were making their way down the hill to the broadest building in Port Royal. The church. It had a white-painted wooden cross on the roof. Next to it was a white flag with a red cross. Stone steps led to the double-door entrance. I counted six windows that were taller and broader than me. It was like they built this church place for one of their gods to live in.

A huge crowd had already assembled when we arrived. Many were cheering and shouting. We jostled and barged our way through. Sea-riders recognized Ravenhide and offered him friendly greetings.

"King barrel maker!" one called out.

"Dark prince of barrels!" said another.

"Hail the rum protector!"

Two men stood on tables outside the entrance of the church. One wore a black hat. His mustache curled like a skinny wave. His brown hair fell below his shoulders. The sun had browned his cheeks and peeled his nose. Tied into a cross around his neck was a white cravat, and he wore a golden jacket and white slops. His boots were long and black, his belly was like one of Ravenhide's larger barrels. I guessed he was Captain Morgan.

The other man was dressed in a simple black frock. He was gray and bent, with whiskers that were white and long. Some sort of necklace hung from his neck. He held a thick book and looked like he had spent too long arguing with demons. I heard Isabella's voice in my head: *Demonios!*

Ravenhide and I squeezed in closer. I spotted Mr. Powell behind Captain Morgan and searched the crowd for Mr. Marsh but couldn't find him. I breathed a little easier.

"Avast, my gold-hungry buckos!" Captain Morgan began. He owned the same flavored tongue as Indika Brown. "Hear ye! Hear ye! Hear ye!"

The crowd hollered and roared as they waved their headscarves in the air. Captain Morgan held up his palms, gold rings sparkling on his fingers. The masses hushed. "On the next new moon," he said, "led by my *Satisfaction*, not one, not two, but *three* ships shall follow my sails to Porto Bello on the Spanish Main!"

I had never heard such shouting in my life. I covered my ears for a long moment until Captain Morgan silenced the hordes again.

"There are three castles in Porto Bello," Captain Morgan went on, "and the Spanish believe they are protected by God Himself. But by the grace of God, we will sack every single castle, fort, and house that we find in Porto Bello! And we will take their women too!"

They will tek their women? Me will play no part in dat.

Huge cheers rang out once more. I glanced at Ravenhide and even his eyes widened with excitement.

"And if they dare to put a Spanish sword in our way," Captain Morgan continued, "we will send their severed heads back to Queen Regent Mariana herself, and her lame son Charles."

"WE TRUST CAPTAIN MORGAN TO LEAD THE BRAVES! CAPTAIN MORGAN REIGNS OVER THE WAVES!"

Captain Morgan held out his arms wide and breathed in the acclaim. "There'll be enough gold and pieces of eight for everyone!" he bellowed.

When the crowd settled, Captain Morgan dropped to one knee and bowed. The old man in a black frock placed his hand on Captain Morgan's head. He closed his eyes and spoke words that were neither English nor Spanish.

The crowd hushed again as if a god walked among us.

"What de old man ah say?" I whispered to Ravenhide.

Ravenhide grinned. "He's speaking in an old language called Latin. He's probably saying, *Bring some gold back for the church and for me.*"

Captain Morgan stood up to yet more cheers and

applause. He took out papers from his breast pocket and waved them at the crowd. "Letters of Agreement!" he shouted.

It was then that he spotted Ravenhide. Suddenly I felt the ache of my legs and the boom of my heart. He nodded in our direction.

"Asase Ya," I whispered to myself. "Nyame, nuh let Captain Morgan chop off me good head."

"Come, Kemosha," Ravenhide said. "Let me introduce you."

I stood rooted to the ground like a stubborn sweet potato. Ravenhide tugged my arm. I almost tripped over but managed to regain my footing. Captain Morgan still stood on a table when we approached him. As we neared, I saw how his boots had gold buckles in them, and how spotless were his white slops.

"Captain! Captain!" Ravenhide called out.

Captain Morgan glanced down and seemed happy to see Ravenhide. He jumped from the table and the ground shook. He was a big man. His belly wobbled and his breath stank of rum. I backed away a step. Then another. I stared at the ground.

"By the cannons of Bristol!" Captain Morgan said. "And the sweet apples that grow beyond its shores. Ravenhide! I've been asking for your presence. I hope you're ready and able."

"I'm ready," Ravenhide replied. "And able."

"I have work for you to do before we set sail," Captain Morgan said.

"For a price," Ravenhide said.

"Am I not fair in what I pay you?"

"Of course. What is this work?"

Captain Morgan fingered his skinny mustache. "Canoes. I want you to check every one of my canoes before we sail on the new moon."

"I will make my way down to the harbor with my tools before sunfall," Ravenhide said.

"Good, good," nodded Captain Morgan. "I will get two buckos to prepare the black tar. I don't want these canoes sinking before they're paddled to their destination."

"If I tend to them, they will never sink, Captain."

"I trust your word." Captain Morgan paused and stared at me. I felt his eyes burn into my soul. *Asase Ya. Me hope you wid me.*

"And who do we have here?" he asked. I looked up. His eyes never left my face.

"Kemosha Black," said Ravenhide.

Captain Morgan stroked his chin and twisted his slim mustache. I felt the vibrations of my heart from my toenails to my brow. He leaned in closer and inspected me. His eyes were full of suspicion. Then a grin spread from his round cheeks. His teeth were the cleanest I had ever seen from a white man. "Are you the black strumpet who defended herself against my quartermaster, Antock Powell, for a count of a hundred?"

I nodded and swallowed air, backing away another half step.

"Speak!" he demanded. "You have a tongue!"

"Yeh . . . yes," I said.

"I have never heard of such a tale," Captain Morgan said. "Although a Spanish wench tried to split my heart with a dagger one night. She didn't live to boast of her deed."

"Captain Morgan," Ravenhide said, "she wants to sail with us to the Spanish Main."

Captain Morgan paused. I was thinking about changing my mind, but he stepped closer to me, searching my eyes once more. He didn't blink and neither did I. Suddenly, my legs were unsteady. *Too much spiced red wine! Asase Ya, me beg you to settle me heart before it punch through me chest.*

I remembered what Ravenhide had advised: *When he gazes into your eyes, don't look away.*

"Women can be a pestilence on board and a distraction," Captain Morgan said at last.

"They can also be good cooks and swift with the sword," Ravenhide said. "She has proved herself defending Antock Powell. No easy task. And she will assist me with my work."

Captain Morgan side-eyed me as he pinched his mustache again. "I see great anger and determination in your eyes. That is good. Anger can keep you alive. Determination is an asset for any matey."

I wanted to reply but couldn't think of what to say. I thought of Hakan at the plantation. He was angry every day. *Captain Morgan woulda loved him.*

"Will she pledge allegiance to the King of England?" Captain Morgan asked.

"Of course," Ravenhide responded.

"And can she sign her name?"

"I have taught her how to write," Ravenhide said. "When you have a moment, Captain, bring your Letters of Agreement to my hut."

"I will do. I want everything to be correct and in place for this journey. All who sail with me must be able."

"I will be able tonight," Ravenhide said. "Not one canoe shall sink. Not on my watch."

"This is the big one," Captain Morgan said. "The one I have been waiting many years for. There is more gold straining the chests of Porto Bello than the King of England counts in his palace. There will be blood, but let it flow from Spanish necks."

I felt my own life-flow surge up my throat. Captain Morgan watched me again. "If you play your part well," he said to me, "by the gray seas of Wales, there is a fair fortune to be won. I trust you are a better cook than my last. And if fate compels you, I hope you defend England like you fought against Mr. Antock Powell."

I nodded.

"She has a warrior's heart," said Ravenhide.

Captain Morgan turned to him. "Do not be late. There is much work to do."

CHAPTER 11

Articles of Agreement

For the next few days, I didn't see much of Ravenhide. I kept myself to his shack, and apart from trekking up the hill to fetch water, I didn't enter any inn or tavern. I was invited plenty times by rough-whiskered men promising fine garments and gold. Two wanted to buy me, but my heart felt good when I said, "Me ah free woman now and nobody cyan buy me."

Sometimes I peered through the crack of the front door at night to see if I could sight Lillet. I didn't spot her once.

When Ravenhide did return, his clothes were filthy and his face, hair, and forearms were covered in black stains. His sleeves were pulled up above his elbows and he cursed whoever built the canoes. Then he would collapse into his bed before he finished his dinner. His snores were louder than the tiny things in the grass. He was gone before I rose in the morning without so much as a bush tea.

Much of my time I spent peering out at the dark waters. I thought of Isabella and her shack in the hills. I remembered the stream where we bathed and the birdsong that kept us company on that good day. *It would be so nice if me could find ah liccle place somewhere far, far away where me could live. It would not be here so on this wicked island. And when me find me place me would invite Isabella, Marta, Gregory, and everybody else from de plantation. Yes. Even Lillet wid de one foot from Port Royal. Me have to find her sometime. Asase Ya and Nyame must smile 'pon her too. Vuela a casa. Me want to fly away to a new home, Mama.*

One cool evening, Ravenhide shook me awake. He had papers in his hand. "You have to learn to sign," he said.

He used a quill and wrote big letters on the paper. It wasn't neat.

"*K Black,*" he said. "This is what you must write when Captain Morgan calls."

I practiced signing my name for two days. Ravenhide wasn't satisfied until my words were neat and pretty. "Again!" he repeated, deep into the night.

Me wish me could show Marta, Gregory, Iyana, and Hakan what me could do. Me ah writer of English letters now!

***

It was late one evening when I was woken up by a cursing and a hollering. I climbed out of my resting place to find Ravenhide and Captain Morgan in a happy mood. They had their arms around each other's shoulders as they reeled and staggered here and there. They tottered into walls and bumped into tables and chairs. They shared a bottle of rum and almost fell over as they tried to sit on barrels out back. They steadied themselves, laughed at each other, singing a song under the skinny moon:

"We're gold hungry sea-riders married to the
Satisfaction
Robbing Spanish ships for the King of England
We'll sack ports
Cannon Spanish barricades
And count their pieces of eight
And find more women than a pimp can mention
To the Spanish Main we go
To Panama!
Under the full moon's glow
To Porto Bello!
May her chests be heavy
And the pretty women plenty."

Unable to keep their balance, they slid off the barrels and crashed to the ground. They didn't get up but seemed to sleep soundly. I picked up the empty bottle of rum and let them be.

* * *

I cooked a big breakfast the next morning. Corn dumplings, sweet potatoes, and hog meat blessed the plates. Captain Morgan licked his fingers when he finished. He seized me with a stare. *Asase Ya, why him ah look at me wid him big eye all de while?*

"Don't tell her I said so, but you cook a better breakfast than Indika Brown," Captain Morgan said. "That woman is to cooking what a cannonball is to swimming."

"Me try me best," I replied.

He wiped his hands on the grass. His gaze didn't leave me. "You really want to sail to the Spanish Main? To Panama? Porto Bello?"

I didn't hesitate. "Yes."

"You'll be in a man's world," Captain Morgan said. "Blood will be spilled. Men will be killed. The ocean bed will be filled. Those who lose will see their women violated."

I didn't know what *violated* meant, but I guessed it wasn't nice.

"The two-armed will become the one-armed," Captain Morgan went on. "The two-footed will become the single-footed. The one-eyed will be totally blinded. Your smile can be halved. Your head has more than a fair chance of being removed from its shoulders. I will not offer you any special favor just because you're a woman. The only thing you can truly trust is your sword and your courage."

I almost swallowed my tongue. I tried hard not to show my dread. *Kemosha, you're ah girl-chile. You have no*

*business sailing to de Spanish Main. And Mama's sea god,
Epo, don't even send you ah good sign. But how me going to
free Marta and Gregory?*

"She's as brave as anyone I know," Ravenhide said.
"You should have seen her fight Antock Powell."

Captain Morgan's glare remained fixed on me. "Yes,
Ravenhide. You have told me that tale six times now.
The seventh may send me to sleep. No doubt a man of
letters will write about the deed one day. It will entertain
the buccaneers on the wobbly stools in Bristol, no doubt."

I made up my mind. "Me won't let you down," I
managed.

Captain Morgan stroked his mustache. "We set sail
tomorrow at dawn," he said. "And if you can cook like
this every day, then welcome aboard."

"Thank you, Captain."

From his waist pocket, Captain Morgan took out a
scroll. He flattened out the creases on a barrel. "Letters
of Agreement," he said. "Ravenhide tells me you know
how to sign."

"Yes, me know how to sign."

"There are rules on this document. If you by chance
break any, your life will be mine to decide."

I swapped a quick glance with Ravenhide and
then nodded. Captain Morgan offered me a quill and
pointed to where I should sign. The writing above was
very pretty. I took in a breath and signed the scroll: *K
Black*. Captain Morgan rolled it up and put it back in
his pocket.

"If we win our fortune," he said, "your share will be equal to any cook, powder monkey, or scrubber."

I had no idea what a powder monkey did but I nodded all the same.

"If we lose," Captain Morgan continued, "then pray that the Spanish dogs do not keep you alive for too long. They have cruel devices that make your agony last as long as a sailless ship in the doldrums."

I gulped a sudden chill. I heard Marta's words in my head: *Foolish chile!*

"Too long I have stayed in your company, Ravenhide," Captain Morgan said. "But the rum was strong and so was your song. I go to check on the *Satisfaction*. It should be near enough ready. If it is not, I'll have buckos to torture. We sail on the morrow."

We watched him fix his mustache with some device he had in his breast pocket. He then took out a brush from his waist pocket and fixed his hair. Satisfied, he headed toward the front door. "Do not be late," he said before he left. "Arrive smartly."

I turned to Ravenhide. "Rules? What is rules?"

Ravenhide grinned. "Don't worry yourself about rules. Just cook good food, don't start fights with anybody, and don't steal from anyone. Nobody can molest you or challenge you on the ship once they sign the Articles of Agreement."

"That's not too bad," I said. "So me nuh have to sleep wid me eyes and wits open?"

"You'll be safe," Ravenhide assured me.

I breathed out and closed my eyes in relief.

"Oh, there is one more thing," he said. "Never refuse an order."

"Nuh worry about that," I replied. "Me follow orders all me life from Captain Tate. It kept me alive."

CHAPTER 12

The Satisfaction

The sun had yet to rise and moonlight brightened the northern skies. Ravenhide had woken me early. A horse and cart were waiting for us outside our shack—Captain Morgan had sent it himself. We even had a driver. Ravenhide loaded his tools and three barrels full of spring water. As I climbed aboard, I gazed toward the sea and wondered if I'd ever return to Ravenhide's hut. *Will me ever plant me good foot back on de plantation? Will me ever see Marta and Gregory again? Epo, me hope you won't fail me.*

The driver shook the reins and we trotted forward. Fifty paces down the hill, I heard a girl's voice call out, "Kemosha Black! Kemosha Black!"

The driver pulled up and I glanced behind my shoulder. Lillet hobbled toward us. I smiled as she approached. For a long moment she simply stared at me, unsure of what to say. Water was in her eyes and a bruise had swollen her chin. I glanced at Ravenhide and could see he was impatient.

"Is . . . is it true?" Lillet asked.

"What is true?" I responded.

"That . . . that you, ah girl-chile, sailing wid Captain Morgan to de Spanish Main?"

"Yes, it very true, Lillet. Me don't know which way is this Spanish Main or Porto Bello. But that's where Asase Ya is teking me. May She bless me good foot."

"And may She give you safe seas," Lillet said. "Me . . . me hope to sight you on your return."

The horseman shook the reins and we started once more. "I don't want you to be late," he said.

Lillet stood perfectly still on the Port Royal Road. She watched us as we made our way down the slope toward the harbor. *Maybe me shoulda asked Captain Morgan if me could tek Lillet wid me. Maybe not. How is she one foot going to manage riding de sea? Dat will be too much to ask of Epo to look out for her too.*

The shore was full of traders selling everything from tobacco to rolls of white sail. The sea was busy with small boats and larger vessels. Men hollered and cursed at each other. For a moment, I wondered what I was doing here. Marta's voice shouted loud in my head, *Foolish chile!*

Satisfaction, Captain Morgan's ship, had loomed above everything else from my vantage point at Ravenhide's backyard. Up close, it looked gigantic, the king of ships.

There were many levels. The outside of the upper decks was painted blue and white. The lower levels had the black tar pasted on them—the same substance that Ravenhide had used for the canoes. There was a ramp leading up to the ship. I imagined Isabella climbing a tree from her hiding place and looking down on us.

Bare-backed men wearing dirty slops and colorful headscarves rolled on barrels of all shapes and sizes and carried on containers, chests, and tools. Swords and daggers of all shapes dangled from their belts and cross-straps. Their arms were hairy, their lips were cracked, and their scars too plenty to count. Boys who seemed to be younger than my own years climbed the rope ladders and checked the rigging and white sails. Others checked the black cannons aimed out to sea. Each one was longer than Ravenhide was tall. "They are so loud," he had told me once. "They could rattle the ribs of Captain Morgan's grandfolks back in Wales."

On the upper deck, there was a man who peered at the seas through a spyglass. Beside him was a wheel that was fixed onto a platform and a broad post on the wooden deck. It was bigger than the cart's rollers. I wondered how it was used.

"Who is dat mon looking through de spyglass?" I asked.

"That is Mr. Edward Caspian, the navigator."

"And what is ah navigator?"

"The most important man on the ship," Ravenhide said. "He steers the ship by the stars. Make sure you give him the best food and ale!"

I recognized the man who joined Mr. Caspian on the upper deck—Mr. Antock Powell. "Mr. . . . Mr. Powell sailing wid we?" I asked.

Ravenhide nodded. "Of course. He's Captain Morgan's quartermaster."

"Will . . . will he trouble me? Him might want to test me sword again. He will kill me for true."

"No," Ravenhide said. "You're safe from him. Even Antock Powell had to sign the Letters of Agreement."

My next breath was long.

Mr. Powell spotted us jumping down from the carriage. He paused his conversation to side-eye me. *Oh, Asase Ya! Him still vex wid me! When him get de chance, he will surely plant him sword inna me belly when me sleeping.*

Men loading the ship offered me strange looks. They whispered and muttered under their foul breath. Their jagged teeth were dirtier than the mud in the hog pen. I tried to ignore them, but I kept my fingers close to my blade.

"Don't worry," Ravenhide said. "It's not every day they see a free Black girl boarding a ship."

"It's like they never see ah Black girl before at all," I said.

"Come, Kemosha. Let us walk across the gangplank, step along the gangway, and start work."

As we made our way across the ramp, I peered into the blue seas below. They were calm and quiet. I remembered Isabella telling me how vex water and big wind start fights.

"Cyan me go up to de upper deck and see how it look? Me want to tek ah close look at dat big wheel and see how it work."

"No," Ravenhide said. "We call it the poop deck and only the first mate, the navigator, the quartermaster, and Captain Morgan himself can stand at leisure up there."

He led me instead to a lower deck. There were canoes lining the gangways, tied to posts, each stained with Ravenhide's black tar.

The tiny cookhouse, if you could call it that, had plenty of chopped wood to start fires. Two big tar-painted barrels were three-quarters full of sand. Iron grills were fixed inside the barrels. Ravenhide pointed to them. "You cook for the captain's top crew on those," he said.

"What about de rest of de men?" I asked.

"You don't cook for them. You just serve them the cold salted beef and vegetables. Make sure you cut it up equally, otherwise they'll start fussing and fighting. They will take the ale themselves."

I sniffed hog meat coming from other containers. There was a recognizable stench emitting from another five kegs. It reminded me of Indika Brown's tavern. I had to suck in a deep breath and take a moment to settle my stomach. I coughed hard. "What is dat drink?" I asked.

"You don't recognize it?"

I shook my head.

"Ale," said Ravenhide. "Mateys prefer ale to water.

Dirty water can make you sick and kill you. It's not easy to keep drinking water clean."

Then I noticed many glass jars and smaller barrels sitting on shelves. They had corn and other vegetables inside them. I took off the lid and all kinds of powerful smells attacked me. Ravenhide laughed. "They put corn and vegetables in jars, and smaller barrels full of vinegar and spices. They do that to keep them fresh. When you sail on the seas, no one can guarantee that you'll return to land."

I couldn't help but think of a watery death. I closed my eyes and whispered a prayer to Epo. *Foolish chile! Kemosha! Is what you doing on this ship? It woulda been better if me stay wid Isabella. If broad sea swallow me, Gregory and Marta will never get to know. How dem going to look for me body? Only fish will sight me black skin turning blue.*

"We ... will return to land, won't we, Ravenhide? Epo nuh want me to drown when vex sea fight mad wind."

"I won't lie to you, Kemosha," Ravenhide said. "Bad things happen at sea. The bravest of men fight, fall, and drown. The biggest of ships sink. I have seen it."

"De whole ship get swallow up?"

Ravenhide nodded. "Bad things happen on land too. Just think about living for the day. Be glad that you see the sun shining when you open your eyes at dawn. Oh, one last thing. Make sure you put out the fire from the iron grill with the barrels of sand when you finish cooking. Put it out before you carry up the food to Captain's cabin."

"Where do me sleep?" I asked.

Ravenhide pointed to the floor at what looked like a piece of cloth with a skinny rope attached to it. "In a hammock," he replied. "When your work is done, you tie it up between two posts and sleep in it."

"Tie it up between two post?" I repeated. "Me never sleep in de air before. Me prefer de floor."

"Your choice," said Ravenhide. "And while you're making it, you best start preparing a meal for Captain's top crew. Apart from the navigator and Mr. Powell, you must satisfy the belly of the first mate. If anything be-falls Captain Morgan, he'll be your new leader."

"Who is this first mate?" I asked.

"Mr. Wilbur Jenkins. A Welshman. To your ears he will sound strange, like Indika and Captain Morgan."

"A Welshmon?" I repeated. "What is dat? It sound like him come from water."

Ravenhide laughed. "Mr. Jenkins is not as skilled with the stars like Mr. Caspian, but he is next in line. Serve him generous portions and you'll receive his favor."

Next to the cookhouse was a small cabin called the cable store. It was full of broken furniture, half-made barrels, and bits of wood. Ravenhide carried his tools in there and started repairing a chair. I didn't tell him so, but I was mighty relieved to know he wasn't too far away.

Once I found the pots and pans, I cooked hog meat, boiled sweet potatoes, and heated up pieces of corn and green beans. It was when I browned the last piece of meat that I spotted Antock Powell approaching. He ducked his head as he entered my workspace. It was difficult not to be intimidated by his hard one-eyed glare. He stood still for a short while. I felt for the handle of my sword and took my stance. There was barely any room to swing it. I checked where Ravenhide was, but I couldn't see him. I only heard the *tap, tap, tap* from his hammer. Panic rose in my chest. My fingers clamped on the handle of my sword. *Maybe he want another count of ah hundred to kill me off.*

"They tell me you're now to be called Kemosha Black," Mr. Powell said.

"Yes . . . yes," I stammered.

He searched my eyes. "You look more afraid of me now than when you defended yourself against my sword."

"Me . . . me afraid of de great blue," I managed. "It broader than broad."

He smiled. "You'll get used to it. Maybe in the end you'll love it as much as I do."

I tried to smile but my cheeks refused. My fingers relaxed.

"Now, avast!" he said. "Pay attention."

"Yes, me listening."

"Mr. Caspian loves his ale," he said. "And any other liquor he can find. Make sure he doesn't drink too much. We need his skilled eyes to read the charts and study the skies. Otherwise we'll end up on the Gold Coast of Africa rather than the Spanish Main."

"De Gold Coast of Africa? Where is dat?"

"Don't concern yourself where Africa is," Mr. Powell said. "Just make sure Mr. Caspian steers away from the ale."

"Me won't let him drink even ah teardrop. You cyan trust me."

Mr. Powell sniffed my cooking. "That smells good," he said. "It's well to start our voyage with a hearty meal."

"Yes," I said. "It soon ready."

Mr. Powell left. When I was satisfied that the meat had cooked through, I made sure I put out the fire with sand before I loaded a wooden tray with four plates of hot food.

"Ravenhide, cyan you show me de way?"

He led me up to the poop deck. We passed the big wheel before we ducked under a short doorway and stepped down a staircase to Captain Morgan's cabin. I felt the waves rise and fall beneath me. Tiredness crept into my bones. Captain Morgan sat around a table with Antock Powell, Mr. Caspian, and an orange-whiskered, fat-bellied man who I guessed to be Mr. Wilbur Jenkins. They studied charts, maps, and papers. Paintings of well-dressed, long-haired white people hung from the wood-paneled walls. A red and black patterned rug covered most of the floor. There was a chest in a corner with a padlock attached to it the size of Captain Morgan's fist. Next to it was the broadest bed I had ever seen—Marta, Gregory, and myself could have all slept in it without bumping into each other. In another corner was a small barrel of rum, which Mr. Caspian continually glanced at. The smell of it filled my nostrils.

I remembered what Marta and Mama used to say when they brought meals for Captain Tate and his wife. "Dinner is served," I said.

They looked up, licked their lips, and cleared the table.

I placed the plates down in front of them and backed away to the door. I stood next to Ravenhide until they tasted the food. They had their own knives and forks, bottles of liquor, and mugs. My heart banged like Ravenhide's hammer.

Captain Morgan sampled my food first. He chewed, then paused and considered something. He munched again and tilted his head to the side. He then raised his eyebrows and hunted his food down with a long glug of rum. The hammer inside my chest doubled in size.

"Ahhhhhh!" Captain Morgan finally said. "A fine meal to start a voyage."

The other men nodded before they attacked their own plates.

Thank you, Nyame. At least dem won't kill me or fling me over into de deep blue today.

By the time I returned to my kitchen, men had already formed a line for their meals. They came with their own dishes and homemade spoons. Some ate with their hands. I served them salted beef, green beans, and corn.

A bare-footed mulatto boy introduced himself as Tenoka Sinclair. He said thank you and asked for my name. He explained to me that most of the other boys who had checked the sails and rigging had remained ashore. "Why dem choose ah girl-chile to cook?" he asked me.

"Becah me cyan cook good," I replied.

"Cyan you cook ah liccle someting for me?" he said with a smile.

"You want to get me fling off into de deep blue? Go'long wid your cheeky self."

Tenoka was the last to be served so I followed him out on deck. His job was to climb the rigging, check on the sails, and stand high up in a cage to watch what the birds could see. He called it the crow's nest. "They would have to chop off me good head before they mek me climb up there," I told him.

I returned to my kitchen and scrubbed my pots. When I finished, I wanted to rest but it wasn't too long before I heard someone cry, "*Avast, mates! All on deck!*"

"The captain wants us to assemble below the poop deck amidship," Ravenhide called from the cable store.

"Do me have to go?" I said. "Me foot well tired and me eyes begging to close. Me want to lie down somewhere and rest me bones till de next moon."

"Everybody has to assemble," Ravenhide insisted.

I dragged my weary self to the upper deck.

I was one of the last to arrive. Captain Morgan stood on the poop deck beside the big wheel. He looked smart in a red jacket and white slops. His long hair blew in the soft breezes. Antock Powell, Wilbur Jenkins, and Mr. Caspian were with him.

Tenoka Sinclair watched everything from high up in

the crow's nest. Another boy fiddled with a sail that got snagged in rigging. The sound of the sails flapping and flopping drowned out the carking from the white birds above. A new day spread its yellow light from the east.

I had to stand with my legs apart to keep my balance.

"Avast, my mateys," Captain Morgan started. "I will not lie to you. The booty from our last visit to the Spanish Main wasn't as bountiful as expected. And our next task is perilous. There will be numerous Spanish devils and guns to navigate. They are most treacherous, and they will be most desperate to kill you. If they can't do that, they will happily maim you."

"And we are desperate to kill them!" shouted a man.

"But the prize is bigger than any of us have ever seen or counted," resumed Captain Morgan. "They will not expect us to attack Porto Bello. They are sure that their cannons will defend any English ship approaching Porto Bello's harbor. But good fortune favors the hearty souls who face down peril. I have a most devious and brilliant plan. And I have yet to fail you. Are you with me, my brave buckos?"

The crew hollered and whooped their approval. Even Ravenhide raised his sword. I was too exhausted even to raise a hand.

Captain Morgan pulled out a curved dagger from his belt and held it above his head. "To Porto Bello!" he roared. "And her riches!"

The rope securing the gangplank was untied and pulled ashore.

"Weigh anchor!" cried Captain Morgan. One of the men reeled in this net full of stones that had been sleeping on the seabed. When it was hoisted on board, Captain Morgan yelled again, "Take the helm, Mr. Edward Caspian!"

Edward Caspian stood behind the wooden wheel, looked up, and checked the wind and sails. He turned the steering circle halfway. The sails caught the breeze and we started to move. I felt a cramping in my stomach and almost lost my footing. Everyone raised their swords and daggers once more.

"For King Charles the Second of England!"

"And all of his mistresses!"

"And may he keep his merry head!"

"And not lose it like his father!"

"A merry ole king is he!"

"With mistresses a-plenty!"

"For Spanish gold and pieces of eight!"

"We will storm the Spanish gates!"

I had to hold onto the side of the ship as we pulled away from the harborside. It was only then I realized there were three more ships in our wake. They were smaller than the *Satisfaction*, but they all carried canoes on their gangways.

Slowly, the island of Jamaica appeared smaller and smaller. Its green hills became a squiggly line beneath the horizon. I thought of Mama, Marta, and Gregory and wept.

Ravenhide pulled my arm and whispered into my

ear, "Kemosha, dry your tears and look busy. Captain Morgan does not favor idlers. Return to your kitchen."

Before I went back to the lower deck, I retched and vomited over the side of the ship. I felt dizzy. Vexed sea and angry wind had made their way to my stomach. *Epo has failed me.* Ravenhide shook his head but I wasn't finished. Three times I had to empty whatever was in my belly into the frothing sea.

Eventually, I got back to my kitchen on unsteady feet. I had to rest for a while. I felt very weak.

"Boil some water," said Ravenhide.

I did what I was told. He offered me a mug with bush tea. I sipped it slowly. I had barely enough strength to raise the tankard to my lips. *Only Asase Ya know how long me going to last on this journey. Foolish chile.*

"Ravenhide," I said, "please tell me again. How long this ship tek to reach de Spanish Main?"

"Depends on the trade winds," he responded. "Maybe four to six days."

My heart dropped below my belly button.

A short time later I felt a little better after I ate a corn dumpling. The air was stale around me. The stench of ale, vinegar, spices, and raw meat attacked my chest. I decided to make my way to the upper deck where I could catch fresh breezes.

I arrived on the gangway. I climbed onto a canoe and looked out to sea. *Asase Ya! Where de land there? Me nuh see no land! Me going to fall off de broad blue!* I checked port and the starboard side. *No land, no green mountains.*

No hills. Just de long, wide blue! Why de men nuh worried?

In a frenzy, I ran down to my workspace and into the cable store. Ravenhide was repairing a table.

"Ravenhide! Ravenhide!" I screamed at him. "De land gone! Maybe it sink to de deep blue bottom? De navigator turn wrong way! There is nothing but blue seas all about. We're going to surely dead! Me nuh want to drown! Epo never listen to me!"

"Kemosha," Ravenhide said, "you have to calm yourself."

"Calm meself? Calm meself? How cyan me calm when me cyan't sight no land? Me have to tell Captain Morgan. Him better find ah next navigator and fling Misser Caspian into de sea! Him no good! Him cyan't see ah damn ting!"

I ran to the gangway and was about to make my way to the poop deck. Ravenhide caught me, wrestled with me before he bundled me back to the cookhouse. I punched and slapped him in the face and belly. I tried to wriggle and squirm myself free but his forearms were powerful. "Leggo your hand from me! Tek your big self off ah me!"

"Kemosha," he said, "you have to calm yourself. We will see land soon enough."

I puffed out hard. "But all me cyan see is blue water. We're lost, we're lost! Why me ever put me good foot 'pon dis damn ship?"

"We're not lost, Kemosha. Trust me, you will see green trees again."

I didn't believe him.

* * *

For the rest of the morning I busied myself scrubbing pots and serving men mugs of ale. I gave them generous portions for I guessed it could be the last drink they'd ever tip down their necks. Tiredness licked me. I could barely keep my eyes open.

Tenoka Sinclair watched me as he sipped from his mug during his break. His calf muscles were round, and he wore nothing on his feet. His toenails were black, and his top garment was too big for his frame. I could see scars below his neck. "Where you come from?" I asked.

"De Old Harbour plantation," he replied. "Misser Gerald Moggins used to own me but him gone back to England now. Misser Wilbur Jenkins, who was ah pirate, come to buy me. Him mek me work 'pon him ship for food and ale. Me glad now becah me sign me Letter of Agreement for de first time for Captain Morgan. Me not much older than fourteen years, but dem now call me a privateer and me will get ah liccle share of de booty."

Someone called for him then, and he was gone.

It was nice that someone talked with me. *If me soon dead, at least me will die wid two friends.*

CHAPTER 13

The Navigator's Tale

I couldn't remember when I had fallen asleep but Ravenhide shook me hard as I lay on the cook-house floor.

"Kemosha! Wake up! Open your eyes!"

"What? Where?"

"Kemosha!"

"Where me is?"

"Aboard Captain Henry Morgan's ship, the *Satisfaction*."

"De what?"

"The *Satisfaction*."

I rubbed my eyes and shook my head.

"You never see him come in and drink?" he asked.

"See who?"

"Mr. Edward Caspian," Ravenhide said. His eyes were wide. "He's been down here. I was coming out of my store and I saw him leave. It seems he's been down here for a while. His feet looked like they were walking the waves."

"Me never sight him," I said.

"You didn't see him because *you* were asleep!"

"Ravenhide, me sorry but me so tired dat they coulda lash me back and me woulda still carry on sleeping. It's ah great wonder me wake up at all."

Someone sang above. Though I wasn't sure if "sang" was the right word. It was sore for my ears. Ravenhide glanced up and shook his head. I'd never seen him look so scared. "Oh no," he said, "that's our navigator."

I heard crew members laughing. I recalled what Mr. Powell had instructed—*make sure Mr. Caspian steers away from the ale.* I swapped a panicked look with Ravenhide.

"We better go up to see what damage ale has done to Mr. Caspian."

We made our way to the upper deck. My heart kicked my ribs once I rested my eyes on the navigator. Edward Caspian danced on the poop deck with a stretched grin on his face. His hair was as wet as his tongue. A tankard was held loosely in his right hand and he tipped ale all around him. His cheeks were very red. His steps were clumsy, and he kept dropping to his knees. No bird in the world could ever be challenged by Mr. Caspian's singing.

"I want to lay down with my virgin Marie once again
To caress her smooth skin beyond her hem
Too long we have been parted
She has slept alone for too many moons in her bed

I should've married her in Bristol
Wed by a bishop in a cathedral
But Captain Morgan, my dear ole friend
Who once saved my life from robber men
He called me to the Caribbean
On my eyes he leans on
To steer the Satisfaction *to the Spanish Main*
But, oh, I want to lay down with my virgin Marie
again
And to caress her smooth skin beyond her hem . . ."

Captain Morgan and Antock Powell emerged from their cabins. If eyes were able to stab hearts, Edward Caspian's chest would've been full of holes. The crew stopped their laughter and hushed. Mr. Caspian ceased singing. He reeled to the left and to the right. He tottered on his toes and heels. He swayed forward and sideways. He almost fell over backward before dropping onto his chest, his right cheek bouncing off the deck with a loud thud. His tongue was brown, and it tasted sun-kissed wood.

Oh, Asase Ya, no! Ale kill off Edward Caspian!

Ravenhide and Mr. Powell went to assist Mr. Caspian. *Him alive! Just about.* Ravenhide carried him below. I was getting ready to head back to my cookhouse, but Captain Morgan called me over: "Kemosha Black!"

Cold seawater found its way into my veins. He wasn't smiling. His fingers groped for the handle of his dagger, its blade glinting beneath the Caribbean sun.

Oh, Asase Ya, no!
I didn't bring my sword with me. *Foolish chile.*
I looked around. There was no land. *Could me fling meself overboard? De water must be mighty deep. Big fish will surely swallow me. Me hope me dead quick. Mama, me coming to you. Epo, mek sure me reach me mama.*

"By the leaky barrels of Tiger Bay," Captain Morgan shouted at me, "do *not* keep me waiting, Kemosha Black!"

Slowly, I made my way to the poop deck. Captain Morgan held his hands behind his back. His long sword scraped the floor. His eyes followed me. His red nose snorted as I approached. My heart smacked against my insides. I sniffed salty air and it almost made me sneeze.

I stopped three paces from him and kept very still. "Yes . . . Captain?"

He stared at me hard for a long while. I felt the swelling waves beneath me. I spread my legs apart to keep my stance. The breezes puffed into the sails as I sensed all eyes on me.

"Wasn't you ordered to keep a watch on Mr. Caspian's drinking?"

"Yes . . . yes. Mr. Powell did ah tell me."

Captain Morgan took one long stride toward me. Mr. Powell had a hint of a grin upon his lips.

"If I see Mr. Caspian in this condition again, you will be swimming in Davy Jones's locker."

"What . . . what is Davy Jones's locker?" I asked.

Captain Morgan didn't answer me. Instead, he

turned and marched back through the doorway and down to his cabin. Mr. Powell followed him. I breathed out long and hard.

"Davy Jones's locker is the sea's graveyard," Tenoka Sinclair called down from the crow's nest.

I imagined flailing in the ocean as my throat and lungs filled with seawater. I sucked in a long mouthful of air before I went back to my kitchen. When I reached there, Ravenhide had tied Mr. Caspian to a post with rope. The navigator's cheek was swollen but I didn't think he felt any pain. He had a strange grin spreading from his lips.

"Throw some water over him," Ravenhide ordered.

I did what I was told. Mr. Caspian burped, blinked, and shook his head. He attempted another song, but the ale had killed whatever was left of his voice.

"And again," Ravenhide said.

This time I emptied a whole pot of water over Edward Caspian's head. He cursed some vexed curses that I had never heard before.

Ravenhide secured the rope and tied his hands. "Watch him closely," he said. "When he's a bit more sober, give him some bush tea and maybe some food—it'll soak up all the ale."

Ravenhide went back to his work. I sat on a barrel and watched Mr. Caspian for a long while. It was better for me to watch a man than peer out to the seas where there was no land. *Even when this journey finish, me have to do it again to return to Marta, Gregory, and Isabella. How me going to survive?*

* * *

A red sun had almost dipped into the ocean when Mr. Caspian awoke. He shook his head, blinked, and scratched his chin. His left cheek was red, and his top lip was fat. His gaze settled on me. "So, you're the one," he said.

"De one?"

He laughed hard before he settled himself. "The female one who defended Antock Powell's sword for a count of a hundred. Captain Morgan told me that entertaining tale."

I nodded. "Yes, dat is me. Kemosha Black."

"Miss Black," he said, "my bonds are tight. Can you untie me?"

I hesitated.

"Ravenhide!" I called. "Ravenhide! Misser Caspian open him eyes."

"Good," Ravenhide replied. "Give him some bush tea."

"I can't drink tea with my hands tied . . ." said Mr. Caspian.

I thought about it again. "I will untie you, but if you even tek ah single drop of ale, me will slice your belly open like me preparing ah young hog to cook."

Mr. Caspian smiled. "You have tough words for a woman so young."

"Me live ah tough life," I said. "Tough women grow me. It hard for all of de people who grow wid me."

I loosened the rope, then quickly started a fire and

boiled water. Edward Caspian's eyes watched me closely. As I poured the bush tea, he put out the fire with sand. He accepted my mug and stared into it like it offered him the answers to his life.

"Who . . . who is de Marie you ah sing about?" I asked.

He stared into space.

"Your wife?"

He shook his head. "Not yet. The Lord has not granted me that yet. She is my intended, but Captain Morgan wanted me to follow him to the Caribbean. We have won our fortune, but I fear I'll be forever marooned on this vessel. I hope Marie still waits for me but maybe she's with someone else now. A fine lady will not wait for too many moons."

Silence.

"You hungry?" I asked, wanting to change the subject.

He nodded.

I cooked a small portion of beef and a sweet potato and warmed some green beans. It didn't take him long to finish the plate. He licked it clean.

"That's better," he said. "With God's grace, I'm ready to resume my duties."

"Mek sure you steer de ship good," I said. "Don't sail we off de broad blue. Me nuh want to drop off de world."

He stood up to leave, but then paused and turned around. "Miss Black . . ."

"Me don't know if me should give you extra food,"

I cut him off. "Captain Morgan, Mr. Powell, and de big belly man—"

"Mr. Jenkins," Mr. Caspian said.

"They might want me to cook for dem too but me well tired."

"No, no," said Mr. Caspian. He offered me a long look. "I'm sorry."

"Sorry for what?" I asked.

"For . . ." He took three steps toward the gangway before speaking again. "Sorry for what . . . for what your people have suffered. For . . . for . . . And still . . ."

He paused, touched his wooden cross that hung around his neck, and went about his business.

Was him apology for teking de ale or for someting else? Me nuh sure.

Later that night, somebody else interrupted my sleep. The decking creaked as a man crept toward me. His short steps were unsteady. He wore a black bandanna and lusted at me with green eyes. Gold earrings dangled from his left ear. His neck was red. I remembered his name was Callaghan; he swabbed the deck and kept the cannons dry.

Thankfully, I had strapped my sword about my waist.

The waves soared and dipped below us. The image of Oliver Marsh gate-crashed my mind. Rum poisoned Callaghan's breath. I stood up and automatically took the stance that Ravenhide had taught me.

"You have to be punished for your sins today," Callaghan said. "You can pay with your body."

He lunged toward me. Before he could molest me, I drew my sword.

"You place one dutty finger 'pon me body and me will rip out your throat first and chop off your man parts second. Go 'way wid your dutty self!"

Callaghan hesitated. I pushed the tip of my blade under his nose. He stared at it.

"You want to test me?" I challenged. "Me ready for you. Come try!"

Callaghan backed away. I exhaled.

I couldn't capture sleep again that night.

CHAPTER 14

Vexed Sea and Angry Wind

’m not sure how much I had slept on the first few nights, but my body was awakened by rolling and crashing against the salted beef barrel. My back was bruised, my left knee cut, and I had to pick out splinters from my shoulder.

Everything was dark. One side of my cookhouse was higher than the other. The floor was no longer level. It rose and fell and spun to the left and to the right. My pots and pans clashed against each other. There was a howling outside. I tasted salt in the air. I heard curses and raised voices. I tried to stand up but fell over again. I may as well have drunk a barrel of ale.

"Ravenhide!" I yelled. "Ravenhide! Me did tell you! We have dropped off de edge of de world! Everybody going to dead! Only Epo cyan save me now. Me hope your god smiles 'pon you."

Ravenhide emerged from the cable store. His tools slid this way and that. He made his way toward me by gripping the posts and the walls. Grim determination marked his jawline. "Don't worry, Kemosha, it's just a storm."

I could barely hear him.

"It's just a storm!" Ravenhide raised his voice.

"Storm don't mek de world turn upside down," I said. I wrapped my arms around the barrel of sand and closed my eyes. "Epo, you cyan tek me now. Me beg you look after Marta, Gregory, Iyana, Hakan, and everybody else at de plantation. Oh, and look after Lillet too, de girl wid one and ah half legs back in Port Royal."

"It will pass," Ravenhide said. "I have survived evil winds more powerful than this."

"Worse than this? There cyan't be no worse than this. You don't see the floor turn into the ceiling and the ceiling turn into de walls?"

I hooked my leg around the nearest post and closed my eyes. At any moment I expected the great blue to drown me. I pressed my lips together—I didn't want any seawater to fill my lungs. *Epo, me nuh want to dead inna blue water and cough it out when me see me mama. Cyan't you fling me to land?*

The air hissed and spat. The barrels crashed and tipped onto their sides. The walls rattled and creaked. Jars fell to the floor. Smells were released. Memories of my mama filled my head.

I remembered coughing hard one night. I was four

years old, maybe three. She stroked my head and held me close. I felt the sweat on her neck. I recalled her words: "Le canto a Asase Ya pa' que te vengan cosas buenas"—*I sing to Asase Ya, better will come to you.*

Then I heard her scream as she gave birth to Gregory. Marta helped deliver him as I watched in a corner of our shack. Sometime later, she wept long tears as she breastfed my new brother. She looked over him and whispered, "Lamento mucho haberte traido a este mundo cruel"—*I'm so sorry for bringing you into this wicked world.*

A sudden jolt brought me to my knees and out of my memories. Something snapped above. Seawater flooded the deck. I relaxed my hold and accepted my fate. I fell onto my back, closed my eyes once again, and waited to see my ancestors. There I lay for a long while. Death was slow. Death was loud and death was wet. I heard urgent voices above. Maybe they were last prayers.

"*Edward damn Caspian! You steer we off de wide blue. You cyan't read de stars no more than I.*"

"*It woulda been no worse if dem let fat hog steer de damn ship. We shoulda kept you tied up and let somebody else upon dat big wheel.*"

Death didn't come. I opened my eyes.

I heard a voice, but it wasn't Epo or Mama. It was Ravenhide. "Just hold on tight," he said. "Don't let go."

I did what I was told. I summoned all my might to cling onto the sand barrel once again. My nails dug into the panels. My arm muscles strained. I retched out seawater, but I held onto that keg like it was my firstborn.

Sometime later, the floor leveled again. Barrels stopped sliding. I felt the waves recede beneath me. The wind stopped howling. I relaxed my shoulders. I tried to stand up, but my legs hadn't got used to the sudden calm.

"You all right, Kemosha?" Ravenhide asked.

"Me nuh sure. Is this what death feels like?"

Ravenhide grinned. "I don't know what death feels like but you're alive. Be thankful for that." He managed to climb to his feet. Then he lifted a fallen barrel and turned to me. "You survive your first storm. Before long you will laugh in the face of a hard wind and be refreshed when the cold blades of rain hit your cheeks."

He helped me restore my kitchen and mop the floor with old torn sails. As we worked, I heard frantic footfalls resounding from the gangways and upper decks. We sat down and paused for a short while with our thoughts.

"Ravenhide," I said, "where do you people come from? You don't talk like ah slave. Me beg you tell me."

He didn't answer for a long moment. Instead, he stared into space. I was about to stand up, but his lips finally moved. "I mentioned before that I come from the Mandinka," he said. "We had to move north. A long journey. To a town by the sea called La Mamora. A busy place full of Spanish people and much wickedness. The sands near that town stretch out forever. I have seen things there that a small boy should never see. It's north of Casablanca. That's where my family lived . . . that's where they died. Where I learned to make barrels . . . from where I had to escape."

"Where . . . where is La Mamora? Casablanca?"

Again, Ravenhide didn't reply for a long while. A painful memory filled his eyes. "A long, long way across the seas. The west coast of Africa."

"Will you go home one day?" I asked. "To La Mamora? Or to Mandinka land? You t'ink me mama come from de same place?"

"Kemosha Black!" Ravenhide suddenly raised his voice. "You ask too many questions."

He spoke no more of this matter and returned to his cable store. He picked up a hammer and started banging with it. I didn't think he was repairing anything.

I was sitting up against a sand barrel when I spotted Antock Powell approaching again. I was too tired to stand up in his presence. He looked down at me with one-eyed contempt. I was about to mention that the deckhand, Callaghan, had wanted to have his wicked way with me. *Would Misser Powell believe me? Would he tek me word over ah word from ah white mon? Maybe Callaghan won't trouble me again after him have ah long look at me sword. No, Kemosha, better hold your tongue.*

"Captain Morgan, Mr. Caspian, Mr. Jenkins, and I would enjoy a hot meal to settle our stomachs after the storm," Mr. Powell said.

I didn't reply. Instead, I half closed my eyes and turned my head away.

"We do not wish to wait too long," Mr. Powell added, then left.

I went to Ravenhide. He sat in a corner twirling his hammer. "Only Asase Ya know how to ketch ah fire when everyting wet up," I said to him.

Ravenhide grinned and shook his head. He glanced at the ceiling. "You have to cook dinner with wet wood, and I have to fix the ceiling with the wrong wood. Such is our fate."

CHAPTER 15

⚔

𝕷𝖆𝖓𝖉 𝕬𝖍𝖔𝖞

ive days had passed, and I had yet to see anything green apart from what sickness came
out of my mouth. When I rose from my rest, I
would immediately run to the gangway only to be met
by an endless blue. No breaking waves. No land. No tree.
No bush. Just the wide, wide blue that stretched out to
meet the bright skies. Some waves frothed white here
and there. Others swelled higher. It felt like the crew of
the *Satisfaction* and the mateys of the three other ships
were the only living beings in the world. *We must be near
de end. Where de waters finish. Where we drop off.*

Three times I had hard words with Edward Caspian,
but he would smile away my curses and thank me for his
recent meal. He was the politest white man I had ever
heard.

*Me must give thanks to Asase Ya for keeping me good
self alive, and stopping mon like Callaghan visiting me at
nighttime.*

I spent my mealtimes with Tenoka Sinclair. He told me he had two older sisters and a younger brother. His mama was still alive. Her name was Moneka. Like me, he didn't know where his papa was.

"Me getting me share of de booty for de first time after this mission," he reminded me. "After this voyage, me want to go back to Old Harbour and buy de big house. And me want me family to live in it. Yes, Kemosha. That's why me want to go to de Spanish Main. To mek me pieces of eight."

On the sixth night, Edward Caspian ordered Tenoka to the crow's nest. The stars were plenty and the moon had ate well. I sat on a canoe and peered out to the dark seas. They were very calm. The night was warm. Sweat covered my forehead and dripped from my armpits, but my belly had grown used to the rise and dip of the waves.

Captain Morgan and his top crew had retired to their cabins. Men had finished their work for the day. Some ate their meals and others sipped their ale. I spotted two of them sharpening their swords as the man beside them slept. I had asked Ravenhide to keep a watch on the kitchen. I was about to retire when I heard Tenoka cry, "Land ahoy! Land ahoy!"

Tenoka must have eyes like night birds becah me couldn't sight ah damn ting.

Everyone assembled below the poop deck. I passed Callaghan on the way. For a short moment he paused. He said nothing but his eyes promised to violate me. I ignored him and moved on.

Lamps were put out. It was a strange sensation being at sea in near total darkness. The moon shed a pale light. Our three sister ships looked like long shadows. I heard distant voices on the sea breezes. Captain Morgan appeared with Mr. Jenkins, Mr. Caspian, and Mr. Powell on the poop deck. The crew fell silent.

"Drop anchor," Captain Morgan ordered.

The anchor was released. The ship trembled as the stones hit the seabed.

"Untie the canoes and take up your paddles," Captain Morgan demanded.

His will was done.

"Mr. Caspian has assured me that Porto Bello is about seven miles away along the coast," Captain Morgan continued. "A day's march. We will leave the *Satisfaction* anchored here and paddle to the shore. No man or woman will stand in our way. We will attack the first castle from the rear and then take the rest of the town. Their defenses inland are weak and vulnerable. They will not be expecting us."

Loud roars and shouting bruised my ears.

"Lower the canoes!"

The crew went about lowering the canoes with ropes and dropping them in the seas. They loaded them with supplies; they took the barrel of salted beef and jars of vegetables. Ravenhide grabbed my arm and whispered into my ear, "I will follow Captain Morgan's lead. You stay with the ship."

"But me want to go wid you," I said.

"No, Kemosha," Ravenhide said firmly. "You stay with the *Satisfaction*. Keep a good watch. Tenoka and a few others will be with you. Make sure Mr. Caspian doesn't drink himself to death. We need him sober if we have to make a swift getaway."

"But me want to get off this damn ship and plant me good foot on land again. Me cyan't stand it no more! Me have to get off or de smell will soon kill me!"

"No, Kemosha!" Ravenhide shouted. "Do as I say!"

"You're not my master! You never buy me. You cyan't tell me what to do!"

Raising his right hand, Ravenhide slapped me hard. It snapped my head to the right. The pain spread from my face to my neck. In a quick moment I remembered the beatings Captain Tate and Lyle Billings inflicted on me and others at the plantation. A hot rage burned in my chest and reached its way to my hands. I went for my sword.

"Kemosha." Ravenhide softened his voice. He placed his hand over mine. "Don't be foolish. We have both signed Articles of Agreement. A fight will be the death of both of us. I'm sorry, but you must stay here. Defending Mr. Powell for a count of a hundred is one thing but fighting for your life against Spanish devils is another."

I relaxed my grip and rubbed my face. I said nothing. I offered him a brutal eye-pass and walked past him to the gangway. *Me will beat him on land! Articles of damn Agreement have no say there!*

The crew, including Callaghan, gripped the rigging

and lowered themselves down to the canoes. They took their weapons with them. I didn't admit it to anyone, but I hoped one of those Spanish devils that Ravenhide spoke about would cut out Callaghan's eyes. *Demonios*, I heard Isabella in my head.

Before Captain Morgan stepped down to his small vessel, he addressed the crew once more from port side: "This is our moment. Our time. The fight before us, and the brave deeds we are about to commit, shall be written down for the ages. New Shakespeares will create plays out of our courage and blood. Kings and queens will watch them."

He raised his dagger and sword to the heavens. "To Porto Bello! None shall stand in our way!"

"To Porto Bello!" the crew shouted as one.

They chanted a new chant. Ravenhide joined in. His throat muscles bulged and danced.

> *"Rally around to the English flame*
> *We lay claim to the Spanish Main*
> *If they stand in our way*
> *They will be slayed*
> *And the seas will belong to us again."*

Wilbur Jenkins and Antock Powell descended to their own canoes. A few men carried lamps. They silently paddled to an invisible shore. When they reached a distance, they looked like fireflies skimming across the dark waters.

Tenoka joined me on the gangway. We both peered into the deep night until the lamps faded.

"Maybe big fish swallow dem," I said.

"Me nuh t'ink so," replied Tenoka.

"What . . . what if de Spanish beat dem and cut off dem heads?" I asked. "What do we do?"

Tenoka didn't hesitate. "We beg for ah fast wind to carry we back to Port Royal. But we cyan only leave if we know Captain Morgan and Misser Jenkins dead."

"What do we do while they're gone?"

"Rest up," he said. "And eat good."

"Eat good? De hog meat start to smell bad and de corn running out. De sweet potato not so sweet. It beginning to spoil. De green beans finish. If we don't get fresh food quicktime, we'll be eating wet wood and tough rope."

"They will send back food supplies," Tenoka said.

"You sure? Me not going to linger too long 'pon this stinking ship wid me belly empty."

"Just enjoy your time," said Tenoka. "We nuh have to worry weselves about fighting Spanish people."

"Me cyan't do that. Not while Ravenhide clashing swords wid Spanish mon. Him teach me to fight wid sword. If me see him again him better be careful becah him teach me too good!"

"We have to stay here so," insisted Tenoka. "If everybody left, who would mind de ship?"

CHAPTER 16

The Spanish Main

Four days had passed.

I had risen early. My best part of the day was catching the rising sun. It blessed the waters in a long amber streak that reached out to the horizon. I watched the coastline and listened to the sounds of birds who flew above. Some were white, others black, and all the colors in between. Sometimes they visited us on deck when we ate, singing their songs and chirping their chirps. In quiet, rare moments, the world could be peaceful and beautiful. I longed to step ashore.

There hadn't been any sign of Captain Morgan, Ravenhide, or anybody else. *Maybe dem dead. Maybe Spanish mon ah cut off dem heads. They will need one mighty big sword to cut off Captain Morgan's headtop. Ravenhide did ah tell me dat Spanish mon have plenty cruel devices. Me have to look for him. Yes, Kemosha. Asase Ya and Nyame never mek your foot to stay 'pon ship and sit down all de while.*

I walked out to the gangway and looked out to shore. Green trees and bushes fringed the coastline. The waters close to the beach were a brighter shade of blue. The land curved to the right and thinned out into the distance. The hot sun blurred the horizon. *Me could drink from a water coconut right now!*

I lifted my gaze and I made out gray-blue mountains over yonder. I longed to sit beside something green while eating fried plantain. I thought of Isabella and her warm hug. Her soft hands. Her black hair. Her kind smile. *Maybe if me keep me foot on this ship, me will end up chanting ah love song like poor Misser Caspian.*

Me have to get off this damn ship.

There were only six men on board including Mr. Caspian and Tenoka. *Four of dem should be able to watch him good.*

I found Tenoka on the starboard side of the vessel. He was tying knots in the rigging.

"There are two canoes 'pon de gangway on port side," I said to him. "Me going to tek one of dem and mek me way to shore. Me want to find Ravenhide. Me want to mek sure him still living. And if him still living me going to t'ump him hard for boxing me. Me nuh forget dat!"

Tenoka looked at me as if I drank a barrel of spiced red wine. "Stay here so, Kemosha," he said. "By paddling ashore, you might bruk your agreement if Captain find out. You might lose all your pieces of eight."

"Captain Morgan might be dead," I countered.

"Right now, Spanish mon could be marching here so to kill all of we."

"Captain Morgan never lose ah battle," Tenoka said. "Spanish mon fear him. If they have swift legs dem better use it to run away. Him merciless!"

"Me fear Spanish, English, and all of dem," I said. "Me going to find Ravenhide. Nuh bother try and stop me."

"But you don't know which way to find him," Tenoka argued. "De Spanish Main long and it'll tek many moons and years to walk one side of it."

"If me cyan't find him then me have to look for some food," I said. "There's ah whole heap of empty food barrel. And when you shake de jars, nothing ah rattle inside."

I returned to my kitchen and picked up my sword. I paused as I ran my finger down its length. I strapped it around my waist. "Time for work."

I made my way to deck and cut the rope that attached a canoe to a post. I was trying to lift it over the side of the ship when I spotted Tenoka again.

"Are you sure you cyan paddle?" he asked.

"Me nuh sure," I replied. "But me soon learn. If me don't jump off this damn ship me will kill meself!"

Tenoka hesitated. He looked out to shore then back to me. "Me will come wid you," he said. "To mek sure you don't do anyting foolish."

"Me nuh want anyone to come wid me," I said. "You don't ketch yourself in any big trouble wid Captain Morgan yet. Him already holler at me and promise to fling me overboard inna Davy Jones's locker."

"Kemosha Black!" Tenoka roared at me. "Sometime your head too thick and your tongue too busy to tek in good sense. Me coming wid you and dat is de end of dat. Captain Morgan cyan't fling *everybody* overboard."

I offered Tenoka one of my fiercest glares. "If you want to come wid me, you better help me wid this boat!"

Tenoka climbed down the rigging and I released the canoe. He held onto it before I threw down two paddles. I picked my way down and hopped into the boat. I almost tipped into the sea as I lost my balance. I sat down, took up a paddle, and smiled. It felt so good to be off that damn ship. I sucked in a lungful of good air.

The waves seemed gentle, but it was more difficult than I had imagined rowing the half mile or so to the coast. White seabirds circled around me. I prayed that there wasn't anything underneath to swallow me.

By the time we reached shallow waters, my arms were spent. When the sea was knee deep, we jumped out of the canoe and dragged it ashore. Seaweed collected around my calves. The water was cool. My feet sank into the soft sand. It was hard work heaving the boat to dry land.

We spotted two buckos sitting on barrels on the beach. I was glad to see that Callaghan wasn't one of them. They were roasting something on a spit. Whatever it was made me well hungry. Dozens of canoes were camouflaged farther inland with broad leaves, bush, and branches.

The men recognized us and stood up.

"Are you not ordered to stay on board the *Satisfaction*?" one said.

I had to think fast.

"Yes," I replied. "But we're running out of food and ale. Me must find Captain Morgan and tell him. Remember, de navigator, Edward Caspian, is on board, and me nuh want him to ketch sickness."

"We would go with you, but we have been ordered to keep watch on the canoes," the other man said. "We want to stay in the captain's favor."

"We all want to eat good when we return to Port Royal," I said. "Me want to remind Captain Morgan dat pieces of eight and gold is fine, but you cyan't eat shiny metal. Dem nuh good for de belly and it will bruk your crooked teet'."

"So please tell we which way dem go," said Tenoka.

The first man pointed toward the trees. "Go through the woods and then follow the coastline," he said. "The castle is that way."

"T'ank you," I said. "Me hope to come back wid plenty food."

We picked up a trail of footprints through the woods. The ground beneath us was wet and yielding, the grass long and green. Tenoka warned me to look out for snakes. When he described how long they were to me, I picked up my good foot and ran for my sweet life.

The soft ground sapped my energy, but we soon reached drier land. I puffed hard. The light between the trees grew brighter. The air cleaner. Fresher. It was nice to hear birds singing in the treetops once again. Small creatures scratched and scrambled here and there. I was surrounded by rich green and light browns. I thought of Isabella and yearned to see her again.

"You want to rest?" asked Tenoka.

"No, mon," I said. "Let we go'long."

The land opened out to swerving green fields. They rose steadily inland and fell again into shadowed valleys. They climbed once more until they met the blue-gray mountains in the distance. The smell of the grass was pleasant. Several times I sneezed hard. I guessed my body wanted to rid itself from the stench of the ship. I stared at the ground, not quite believing the broad blue wasn't underneath me anymore.

CHAPTER 17

The Killing Sands

My eyes followed the footprint trail. It wriggled this way and that before bending again toward the sea. I made out a small settlement. Spiraling above it, smoke stained the perfect blue sky. I started toward the village, but Tenoka stood still, his eyes staring straight ahead.

"You not coming?" I said.

"Yes," he replied. "But me eye tell me we not safe 'pon this land."

"If we not safe, then Ravenhide cyan't be safe. Come, let we sight what is burning."

As we approached the village, I sensed something terrible. Death was in the air. A foul breath entered my nostrils. The breezes blew quicker as we neared the sea, but it couldn't shift the aroma of rotting bodies. The waves soared waist high and crashed on a smooth, sandy beach. I shortened my stride. There were about twelve or thirteen huts made of wood and stone. Some were smaller than others. I couldn't see any fire, but smoke billowed from six of them.

Tenoka spotted the first dead body. He almost tripped over it. Spills of blood framed it and reddened the ground. It was a brown man with long black hair, about twenty-five years old. A hammer rested beside him. His left arm had been cleaved horribly. Four fingers were missing on his right hand. He had been stabbed through the heart. One eye was closed and the other open, and his black beard was painted scarlet. Half of his nose had been chopped off. Flies buzzed around and drank on his wounds. Something tiny and many-legged crawled over his knee. A crab investigated his foot. I had to cover my nose and hold my breath.

I retched and brought up what I had eaten for breakfast.

I wanted to return to the *Satisfaction*, but something compelled me forward. There were fifteen more corpses, three of them women. Maybe more: two came in and out on the tide. We found a boy younger than Tenoka, his throat slashed, his face mutilated.

I heard a dog bark. I glanced to my right. A small, long-haired hound, no more than knee high, woofed at us then sniffed the ground. It seemed confused: I wondered if it was looking for its master.

"Me want to find food," said Tenoka. "One of these huts must be ah cookhouse."

I gave Tenoka a hard glare. "You going to look for some food and there's death all about?"

Tenoka shook his head and went about his business. *He's probably seen wasting bodies before. So, it don't trouble him so much like it trouble me. When Captain Tate killed ah Black mon at de plantation, we buried de body quicktime. Me could just about deal wid dat. But this is evil 'pon evil. There must be ah whole shipload of dead body at de castle. Me nuh want to see it. Me nuh want to sniff it.*

Suddenly I heard a high-pitched shriek. I turned my head toward the cry and saw a girl. Dressed in rags, she looked no older than twelve. She rushed toward me in a mad fury, carrying a short sword in front of her. Her eyes were fixed on me, full of pure revenge. Her mouth was wild, her tongue danced, and her cheeks were tight. Her black matted hair flew behind her.

"Mataron a mi familia!" she screamed. *They killed my family!*

For a short moment, I stood in shock. Then I remembered Ravenhide's teaching. Stand sideways on. Right foot in front. Stay calm. Only have eyes for her sword.

She tried to cleave my head off my shoulders, but I easily parried her. She swung from the right and the left. I blocked her. She hacked at my knees and I denied her again. She gritted her teeth and cried out once more. She grabbed her sword with both hands and attempted to split my head and to halve my body. I avoided her vertical slice and cross-whacked her blade out of her hands.

Thrannnngggg!

She fell to her knees and dropped her head. She lifted her arms as if in prayer. I stood over her, but I stayed my hand.

"Matame," she said. "Matame ahora!"

I shook my head. "Me nuh wish to kill you."

She didn't understand my words.

Leaking tears, she managed to climb to her feet and walked into the ocean. There she stood perfectly still, gazing out to sea. I watched her, unsure of what to do. She threw her sword into the waters and fell to her knees once more. "*Aaaaaahhhhgggh!*"

It wasn't a scream that came out of her mouth. It wasn't a wail. It was something more primal than that. It must have raged from her heart, torn her throat, and blistered the inside of her cheeks. Something from her ancestors. I thought of Mama and all who came before her.

Guilt overwhelmed me. I considered tossing my sword into the great blue too. I wanted to wade into the waters until the Caribbean swallowed me.

I heard a sound behind me. Tenoka. I had forgotten he was with me.

"What . . . what shall we do wid her?" he asked.

I didn't reply.

Instead, I pushed farther into the rising waves until I was abreast with her. The sea was lukewarm. I managed to attract her attention and pointed to the gray-blue hills.

"Largate de este lugar," I said to her. *Leave this place.* "Busca un lugar seguro." *Find somewhere safe.*

No response. She peered out to the seas as eye-water dripped down her cheeks.

Mama's sad face grew large in my head.

"Abandona este lugar," I raised my voice.

No reaction. She stared into the clear water as if she wanted it to engulf her.

"Me find some salted fish inna barrel," Tenoka said. "In one of de smaller huts. It might be still good to eat. Come help me bring dem back to de ship."

"Do what you must do, Tenoka."

"When we drop off de fish, we could look for Raven-hide after dat."

"Me nuh want to look for Ravenhide anymore," I said.

Ravenhide help to do this. Him and mon like Antock Powell, Captain Morgan, and Callaghan.

"If him dead, him dead," I added.

"There's some potato there too and a basket to carry it."

"As me say, do what you must do."

I stood in those soaring waves for a long while. The sun roasted my head and shoulders. Every now and again, I splashed myself. The girl didn't look at me until she turned and made her way back to shore. Her eyes were empty, as if all the emotions that once filled her had drained out.

She made her way to the cookhouse and emerged from it with a basket of scallion, salted fish, and potatoes.

"Leave her be," I said to Tenoka. "Let her tek what she must tek."

We watched her walk inland and across the plain. She didn't turn around once. She crested a hill before disappearing into a valley. My heart begged me to follow her.

I turned to Tenoka. "This wrong. Asase Ya, Nyame, and Epo know this is wrong. Why do de gods mek this happen?"

Tenoka nodded. "Maybe it is wrong. And only de gods know why they mek it happen. But her people would do de same to we if dem get de chance."

"Maybe her people just want to fish and mind dem business," I said. "Maybe dem want to just let people live."

"Maybe some of her people get tired of ketching fish and step aboard Spanish ship and kill whoever dem come across," Tenoka replied.

"Me nuh want to step back to de ship," I said. "Everyting is evil all around me. Death breathing all over we. Me going to stay here so. Maybe me will find ah quiet place so me cyan live."

"And let Spanish mon find you. And dem will brutalize you and have dem way wid you. And then kill you. Your body will get lashed by de waves. Dem won't even bury you. Dutty crab will eat out your good foot."

I didn't reply.

"Don't you want to get back to Marta?" Tenoka said. "Your brudder Gregory? You forget about dem?"

I couldn't stop my tears. I collapsed into the waters as grief and frustration overwhelmed me. I wanted to scream like the girl with the black matted hair. I allowed the waves to ride over me. Salt water itched my lips.

Tenoka splashed his way toward me. He lifted me up and placed an arm around my shoulders. "Don't forget why you come here," he said. "To mek your pieces of eight to buy your people's freedom. Just like what me want to do."

Tenoka was right, but my soul commanded me to follow the young girl and see how she was.

"Come, Kemosha. Let we start walk back. Buckos will love de fish and de potato."

"Why does one group of people want more than de next group of people?" I asked. "Why cyan't everybody be happy wid what dem have? Why does one have to conquer de other? Why does one have to be de slave and one have to be de masser?"

Not answering me until he had filled a basket with food, Tenoka came back out to the waters once more. "When me working on de plantation," he said, "sometime mon would try to eat more food than other mon. It would cause plenty arguments. Sometime, fight would bruk out. Me sight mon get stab up and t'ump down. Masser had to holler someting and tek out him flesh-scraper."

"Maybe if women mek all de decision," I said, "and if women decide how everybody get served, there would be less fussing and fighting. And less of mon wanting more than de other."

"Women mek decision? And get dem to decide how tings go?" Tenoka chuckled.

I didn't laugh with him. I offered him a violent eye-pass and made my way back to shore.

"Kemosha!" Tenoka called. "Don't look 'pon me like dat. You cyan't blame me for how de world ah run."

Ignoring him, I entered the cookhouse. This hut hadn't been charred by fire. I thought about the women who worked here and their day-to-day lives. I imagined them giving birth to their children and telling them stories about their ancestors.

There were baskets made of twigs, reeds, and thick grasses. I hesitated before I placed the food in one of them. *Asase Ya, me beg you forgive me.*

Then I started up the hill, thinking again of the young girl with the matted hair. "Asase Ya," I prayed out loud, "me asking you to look after dat girl-chile. Mek sure she find good food and mek sure she find somewhere safe to rest her young head."

CHAPTER 18

𝔊uilti𝔫ess

I wanted to wander farther inland in no particular direction. I didn't want to serve men who committed such wickedness. Tenoka had to run and pull at me twice to persuade me to return to the *Satisfaction*. At one point, he threw me to the ground. I lashed out, punching him in the face. I kicked him on his shin. He held onto my arms and tried to dodge my feet.

"You're too wild!" he yelled at me. "Keep your damn foot still! Me not your enemy!"

"Let me go!" I shouted. "Tek your hand off ah me and let me go where me want to go."

"Kemosha! You cyan't just give up on life. When we reach back to Port Royal you will t'ink different. But you cyan't stay here so."

"Watch me!" I yelled at him. "Me cyan stay anywhere me damn well please. It nuh matter anyway becah there is evil here and evil in Port Royal."

He picked up my sword. "There are people depending on you," he said, pointing my blade at me. "And if me return to de ship widout you, Ravenhide will kill me two time and then ask me to walk de plank. Come, Kemosha, me beg you."

"Ravenhide is just as wicked as any of dem," I said.

"But Ravenhide give you ah chance. If you never met him, you'd be dead right now. Dem would have brutalize you and nail you to de gibbet."

I sat down and thought about it. Tenoka glared at me as he pulled up his slops and rubbed his shins. His leg was bruised. Isabella grew large in my mind. So did Marta and Gregory. *Cyan me really free dem? Ah foolish quick-tempered girl like me?*

We stared at each other for a long while. The rage in my chest faded. The need to wield my sword died.

I stood up. I sheathed my blade and adjusted my belt.

"Come mek we go," I said. "Let we see if this fish good."

We stopped at the beach and roasted the food with the watchmen. The fish was spoiled but we had quite a feast because the watchmen had caught a rabbit. They thanked us for cooking the meal and helped us pull our canoe out to sea.

As I sat in the boat and grabbed my paddle, my belly was full, but guilt tied itself around my heart. It weighed me down like an anchor net full of stones.

We reached the *Satisfaction*. As I climbed the rigging, I hesitated. I wanted to let go and fall into the deep waters. I closed my eyes. I imagined the salty waters filling my throat and lungs. Marta, Gregory, and Isabella spoke to me. I saw their faces. They were waiting. *Vuela a casa.*

I climbed aboard.

CHAPTER 19

Booty

Mr. Caspian and the mateys who had kept watch on the ship loved the potatoes and scallions I roasted for them. They licked their fingers and scraped their plates clean. They claimed it was the best meal they had ever had. They offered me broad grins and made up a new chant.

> *"The potato queen of the Spanish Main*
> *Meals cooked by Kemosha we never complain*
> *No more maggots in hog meat*
> *No more chicken claws in my wonky teeth*
> *Hail Kemosha, queen of the pot*
> *The only cook we know who serves our food hot!"*

Tenoka laughed and was merry with them. My smile only reached my lips. My stomach begged to be fed but with every bite I took, I thought of the beach girl with the matted hair. Her agonized cry echoed inside my head.

She was still in my thoughts when two days later, ten canoes returned to the *Satisfaction* loaded with chests and barrels.

They had won their battle. Many of them had been killed. None seemed sure of the final count. Some lost fingers, hands, and eyes. Their bandages and rags were purple, and their stitches were crude and ugly. A few were loud and victorious, but most were relieved to find their feet standing on the deck.

I wasn't sorry when I learned that Callaghan hadn't survived. But Ravenhide wasn't among those who had returned either, and my heart dropped like *Satisfaction*'s anchor when I learned this.

I whispered a quick prayer to Asase Ya before I asked about him.

"He's still alive," a bucko replied. "He has killed a number of Spanish swines with his swift blade. He's as good a swordsman as I have ever seen. He's with Captain Morgan. They have taken up residence in the richest house in Porto Bello. Others are still in the castle and the town looking for gold, treasure, and women."

"Me nuh care if him living or if him dead," I said. "Me just want to go back to Port Royal."

It wasn't the pure truth. Of course I wanted to know that he was safe.

The bucko gave me a hard look. "We have lost fourteen men so far," he said. "Some say sixteen. The battle at the castle was fierce. But once we claimed victory, Spanish men fled into the hills. If they regroup and march here, you will depend on us to defend you."

"Me cyan defend meself," I said.

The man shook his head and walked away.

Five days later, Ravenhide returned with another twenty mateys. Relief washed over me like a mighty wave, but I didn't want him to see that. I watched from the gangway as they lifted barrels of different sizes on board. They brought bright-colored garments, Spanish curved swords, gold rings, long boots, gold-buckled shoes, coins, silks, and hats. They sang songs and bantered with one another. They shared deeds of bravery, killing, and crushing Spanish barnacles. I had no idea what these were.

Men cheered, hollered, knocked their tankards together, and stamped their booted feet. I shook my head and went back to my small kitchen.

Ravenhide found me later; he rolled a barrel up to me. His grin was wide, but his forehead was gashed. He wore new yellow breeches and a fine red jacket with shiny copper buttons. New black boots hugged his calves, a skinny orange scarf decorated his neck. "For you," he said. "The best spiced Spanish red wine I could find."

I turned my gaze away from him.

"Kemosha," he said, "didn't you hear me? I've brought you a gift."

I turned to face him. "How many women did you kill? How many children?"

Ravenhide's lips moved up and down but no words came. He narrowed his eyes.

"How many?" I repeated.

"Not one," he finally answered.

"Lie you ah tell!"

"Yes, I did kill," he admitted. "Seven was my count. But none of them were women or children."

"Don't lie to me, Ravenhide! Me see what your cruel sword work ah do 'pon de shore."

"That wasn't my doing," he protested.

"Didn't you forward in dat direction? Me sight your footprints! De people just live by de sea and all dem do is ketch fish? And you killed all of dem. Isabella come from ah village just like dat! You forget dat?"

"I didn't take part in it."

"Lie you ah tell!" I yelled at him.

Silence.

I stabbed him with my gaze.

Ravenhide dropped his head and closed his eyes. My right hand touched my sword. It itched to grab hold of it and wield it. The beach girl's wail rattled through my head once more. Her shriek could have split her throat. It bruised my ears and my mind.

"We stopped on the shore near the woods and made camp there for a little while," Ravenhide explained. "Captain Morgan didn't want to waste darkness, so we pushed on. We came upon the village when the moon still hung high."

"And you decide to kill ever'body in it!"

Ravenhide shook his head. "Captain Morgan wanted to march on to the castle immediately. But some of the crew, Callaghan and others . . . became . . . excited . . ." He trailed off. He didn't need to tell me any more.

"You never stop dem?"

He didn't answer me.

"Me find ah whole heap of dead mon, dead women, and dead boy-chile!"

"It . . . it was just . . . Captain Morgan ordered us to march to the castle. I didn't check to see what the men left behind."

"You never hear any screams?"

No response.

"You never see de blood painting de water and turn yellow sand purple?"

Ravenhide stared at the floor.

"As soon as me get off this damn ship me never want to see you again!" I said.

"Kemosha, this is the world we live in. Would you rather live out your life on a plantation? Where the lash is just a complaint away? At least we have some kind of life."

"No!" I snapped. "But if me fight, me want to fight for someting important."

Ravenhide started to reply but couldn't find the words.

"If me have to raise me sword again," I continued, "dat you give me, it'll be for someone's freedom, not someone's pieces of eight and pretty garments."

He turned from me and went inside his cable store.

We didn't share another word for more than ten days. I'd hear him tap-tapping his hammer repairing this and that. I'd serve him his meals, but I refused to meet his eyes.

Chickens were brought on board and lived around my kitchen. Ravenhide built a wooden coop for them but there was no space for me to sleep. For the next few days the men enjoyed boiled chicken, potatoes, and corn. They made themselves merry with drink and told tales of dead Spanish folk. I only cared about reclaiming my sleeping space and offering Ravenhide angry eye-passes. My dreams were invaded by the beach girl with the matted hair.

"Kemosha! Kemosha! You all right?"

I opened my eyes. Ravenhide stared at me with deep concern. He went to touch my forehead but I slapped it away.

"What do you care!" I shouted at him. "It's your sword dat cause me dreams to be unsettled!"

"How many times do I have to tell you?" he said. "I didn't kill a living soul on that beach."

"Lie you ah tell!" I spat.

Ravenhide shook his head. My accusing eyes wouldn't leave him alone. Finally, he retreated to his room.

CHAPTER 20

A Silent Conversation

Captain Morgan, Antock Powell, and Wilbur Jenkins returned on board with yet more caskets, chests, and wooden crates and boxes. Their sun-lashed cheeks were tired from grinning.

The *Satisfaction* sank a little lower into the waters. Ravenhide had told me to save a chicken for them for their meal before we set sail. I didn't answer him but did what I was told. I could hardly move in my kitchen for barrels of ale, spiced red wine, and new supplies of hog meat and vegetables. My jars were refilled.

Captain Morgan and his top crew enjoyed my feast. He even told me to reward myself with a tankard of spiced red wine. So, I did what I was told. I drank two tankards. I wanted to rid the image of all those slain souls on the beach. The blood, the wounds, the faces. The crabs. The stillness. The flies. Death.

Oh, Asase Ya, Nyame, Epo. Please nuh let dat happen to me.

Sometime later, I struggled to my feet. My toes had an argument with my ankles. In my attempt to stay upright, pots and containers fell to the floor. Ravenhide may as well have been repairing one of the barrels inside my head. I had to sit back down again. I held my forehead in my hands and prayed to Asase Ya for my headache to stop.

"Miss Kemosha Black."

I didn't bother opening my eyes to see who had addressed me.

"Miss Kemosha Black."

"Ravenhide!" I said. "Me still nuh want to talk to you! Tek away your sword-happy hands and go 'way from me!"

"Ravenhide is on deck," someone replied. "I'm Mr. Caspian. Your navigator."

I opened my eyes. My headache banged harder as brightness hit my gaze.

"Oh, Misser Caspian," I said. "Me sorry. Me nuh feeling too good. Not good at all."

Edward Caspian smiled as he glanced at the spiced red wine barrel. His wooden cross dangled in front of me. "Ravenhide told me you enjoy an occasional tankard of red wine."

"Me t'ink me enjoy it too much," I said. "If you come for more food you might have to wait ah liccle while. Until me good foot feel like it want to walk again."

"No," he said. "I have come to thank you for the meal you cooked. It was divine."

"To t'ank me? Ah white mon t'anking me? It was just ah skinny chicken, corn, scallion, and potatoes. Me used to cook dat up every day back in de plantation."

"Maybe," Mr. Caspian said. "But, by the Lord's grace, it's never tasted so good."

"Me glad to be of service," I said.

"Will you allow me to have a tankard of red wine?"

I wasn't sure. *Captain Morgan might still fling me over into Davy Jones's locker if Misser Caspian drink too plenty. Maybe it'll be all right if me watch him drink. Everybody else flinging rum down dem necks and Misser Caspian drinking nothing but stale water.*

"Just one tankard," he insisted. "They'll never forgive me if I get drunk and they get lost at sea with all this booty on board."

I laughed. "Yes, mon. Take one tankard of wine. It's de best me ever did taste."

Mr. Caspian served himself. He sat down beside me and sipped his wine. He nodded and licked his lips. "Tell me, Miss Kemosha. Will you return to the Spanish Main on this ship if Captain Morgan commands you? He will give you a purse of more than a hundred pieces of eight when we arrive at Port Royal."

I shook my head. "No, mon. Me want to stay 'pon good sweet land. Me want to bless me eyes on green again. Me want to go to ah place where me could live and nobody tell me what to do. You know any place like dat?"

Edward Caspian pondered my question. After a while, he nodded. "Yes, I have been in the Caribbean for many, many years. And I have seen small islands where no human foot has fallen, and no human words are spoken."

"These small islands big enough to grow plenty corn, raise chickens and hog, and build ah mighty house?"

"Big enough for ten mighty houses."

I sat up and leaned forward. I grabbed his shoulder. "Cyan you tek me there? To one of these small islands? How many days sail from Port Royal?"

"Three days, maybe two, if we get fair winds and the grace of the Lord. But I can't take you there on this ship."

"Me could tek four or five canoe," I suggested.

"You will need something bigger than canoes. You need a sail."

"If me could get someting bigger, will you tek me to ah small island?"

"It depends."

"Depend on what?" I asked.

"On Captain Morgan. He will want me to be aboard his next mission. He never sails without me."

"But him sailing back to Port Royal to rest him foot and count him pieces of eight," I said. "And him will tek time trying on all of him new garments. And he has more pretty boot to try on than me cyan count. Him won't even realize you gone for ah liccle while."

"I . . . I will have to think about it. I will pray to the

Lord and ask for his advice. And you will have to buy a small boat."

"Nuh worry about dat," I said. "Me will get me small boat."

I served myself another tankard of spiced red wine. I downed half of it in one go. I wiped my lips with the back of my hand and smiled at Edward Caspian.

"You promise you will tek me?" I said. "And me good, good friend Marta. And me have ah liccle brudder, Gregory. Him so sweet."

"Who would adjust your sails and work on the rigging?" Mr. Caspian asked. "A navigator can't do everything."

"Me will learn," I replied. "And ask Tenoka. Him know everyting about mast, rope, and rigging. You must promise to tek we. Don't me cook you nice dinner? Don't me boil you bush tea when you drink too much?"

Edward Caspian scratched his cheek. He drained his wine once more and side-eyed me. "I have to learn what Captain Morgan's plans are when we arrive at Port Royal. Usually, he sails to his Firefly estates and takes his rest. But not always."

"Where is Firefly?"

"On the north coast of Jamaica," Mr. Caspian said. "Near Port Maria. Where the sands are wide and long. Where the birds have many colors and sing pretty songs. Where the fish are skinny and have many bright colors. The view over the ocean is a blessing for this lonely Welshman's tired eyes."

"Let Captain Morgan enjoy him nice look over the seas for plenty moons," I said. "Let him sit down and get him belly fat wid plenty hog, chicken, and cow if him cyan find it. While him doing dat, we'll be sailing to ah new land. Ah land where sweet potato and plantain easy to grow. Ah place where the waters grow fat fish."

"But you still have to purchase your vessel," said Mr. Caspian. "And that'll be at least six hundred pieces of eight for a ship with cabins and storerooms."

"Me nuh want anyting too big. If we all have to sleep 'pon ah skinny deck, then let it go so."

CHAPTER 21

In the Shadow of the Blue Mountains

The voyage back home was a peaceful one. My belly didn't erupt its contents out of my mouth. The sea had settled its quarrel with the wind. I closed my eyes and thanked the mercy of Epo.

The blue sky won its battle with vexed clouds and cheerful buckos sang plenty songs as they worked.

> *"I'll buy me a fine woman in Jamaica*
> *Her bosom must be ample, legs sailing on forever*
> *But if she wants to be a wife*
> *I'll run away for my life*
> *And I'll be back riding the water."*

I was also thinking of a fine woman. Isabella. *Maybe me is de first woman inna de world to have feelings for ah woman. How cyan me ever tell anyone? Marta would nuh understand. Ravenhide would laugh. Mama might have cussed me till she cyan't cuss no more. But me feel how me feel. Me pray she thinks de same way about me. And when me bless me eyes 'pon her again, me will never leave her sight again.*

When I wasn't cooking, scrubbing, and cleaning, I studied Tenoka and his work in my waking hours. I listened to the conversations he had with Antock Powell and anybody else who gave him an order. Soon I knew the difference between a mizzenmast and a boom horizontal, and that they called the steering wheel of the ship the helm. I worked out that the wooden thing beneath the boat that steered the ship was called the rudder.

I offered to help Tenoka when he worked on the rigging and sails. I even climbed up to the crow's nest. I didn't stay there long as the swaying and the rocking unsettled my stomach and bruised my bravery. If I looked down, it caused a quake in my heart.

When I made it back to deck, Tenoka was waiting for me. He wasn't concerned about my wobbly legs.

"Kemosha," he said, "why do you want to do me work? If Misser Powell find out and t'ink dat you doing some of me work, me could find meself inna big trouble. Me nuh want to walk de plank and end up inna Davy Jones's locker! Keep your good foot inna de cookhouse!"

"Me want to learn what you have learned," I said. "When me reach Port Royal, me going to buy meself ah liccle ship."

Tenoka looked at me as if I had turned into a fish. "And what you going to do wid ah liccle boat?" he asked.

"Sail to ah land where nobody plant dem dutty foot!"

Tenoka shook his head. "Same Kemosha, always dreaming big dreams."

"So Marta always tell me."

He climbed up to the crow's nest quicker than I had stepped down.

"Land ahoy!" cried Tenoka, hours later.

All crew came on deck and peered out to the horizon. I could make out the narrow strip of land that made up Port Royal. The semicircle of Kingston Harbour opened wide next to it.

"Move up on deck!" ordered Antock Powell. "Move up on deck!"

We made our way amidships below the poop deck. Captain Morgan, Wilbur Jenkins, and Antock Powell were already there. They were dressed in smart jackets, clean white slops, and shiny boots. They stood behind a table laden with hogskin bags. Excited faces were all around me, some even started chanting. Captain Morgan soon hushed them.

"We have won a famous victory," he said. "It'll be written in the pages of history. The Spanish will fear us whenever they see the cross of St. George. They are a foolish people who still haven't learned their lesson from the Armada. We are the masters at sea. We are the gods of the Caribbean. And always will be."

Gods of de Caribbean? Me will never close me good eye and pray to you.

I wondered what the Armada was. *Maybe it was ah big fish dat swallow up ah Spanish ship?*

"Hail Captain Morgan!" someone cried. "The Spanish destroyer!"

"Captain Morgan rules the waves!"

"Cry for King Charles the Second, the Merry King of England!"

"Cry for my wife and nine children! Long may I serve Captain Morgan!"

"Cry for my mistress in Portsmouth—but don't tell my wife!"

Captain Morgan calmed the roars and cheers. "My officers," he continued, "my crew, my family, come to collect your just reward. Don't spend too much of it on loose women, damp tobacco, and stale rum. Don't venture too far from Port Royal. There are still plenty treasure chests to be emptied on the Spanish Main."

"Hurrah!"

Everyone formed a line.

I was one of the last to collect my heavy hogskin bag. I untied the strip of leather and opened it to find shiny coins. I smiled.

I imagined returning to Captain Tate's plantation and offering him twenty pieces of eight to free Marta and Gregory.

"You have earned your share of the booty," Captain Morgan told me. "Not once did I find a worm, a maggot, or any other creature in my dinner. A rare treat indeed. Don't take your cooking hands too far from Port Royal. I'll have need for you. There'll be more strikes on the Spanish Main. There'll be more pieces of eight to collect."

"T'ank you, Captain."

I placed my bag beneath my undergarments and went looking for Tenoka. I found him in my cookhouse pouring himself a mug of ale. I took out my bag and emptied the contents onto the top of a closed barrel. "How . . . how much is there?" I asked him urgently.

"Kemosha," he replied, "give me ah chance to count it!"

Tenoka took his time in counting my reward. "Thirty one . . . thirty-two . . . thirty-three. Misser Jenkins teach me how to count."

"So, you get ah bag of money too?" I asked.

"Yes, me very first bag. One hundred and sixty pieces of eight!"

"Mek speed," I said. "Me nuh want to spend de rest of me day listen you count money."

"Seventy-one . . . seventy-two . . . seventy-three . . ."

He stopped at one hundred and twenty.

"Asase Ya, Nyame, Epo—bless me!" I said. "But me shoulda been paid de same as you."

"Same as me?" Tenoka raised his eyebrows. "But you ah girl-chile."

"Ah girl-chile who as rapid wid ah blade as any mon! Anyway, me hope me cyan buy Marta and Gregory freedom."

* * *

There wasn't a cloud in the sky when we docked at Port Royal. The sun was high. The breeze had taken its rest, and white birds circled above. Midday. The blue mountains looked magnificent. The hills soared into the distance. It felt so good to bless my eyes on green again. Then I remembered the long days and aches of Captain Tate's plantation.

Ravenhide fared me well. I ignored him. Tenoka hugged me tight before he ran along the gangplank and up the dirt road, his pieces of eight jingling in his pockets. He headed toward the inns, taverns, and night women of Port Royal.

I waited for Edward Caspian to leave the ship and approached him. "Me will look for you soon," I said.

"Don't be too long, Miss Kemosha," he replied. "I still don't know how many days Captain Morgan will rest at Firefly. He has plenty riches to count. Be swift in your doings and may the good Lord guide your steps."

"Me going to buy ah liccle boat."

"I'm sure you will, Miss Kemosha."

"And me want you to steer it."

"Perhaps."

"Where cyan me find you?" I asked.

Edward Caspian rubbed his chin. "In church," he finally answered. "Great sins have been committed. I have to ask the good Lord for forgiveness. My soul feels heavy."

"What is forgiveness?"

"You don't have to worry about that, Miss Kemosha. You pray to a different god than I."

"Nuh worry, Misser Caspian. Me will sight you soon."

"Be careful, Miss Kemosha. You are no longer protected by the Articles of Agreement. You're on land now. Don't trust anyone. Port Royal is still a town where there are more daggers than Bibles. Evildoers are plentiful here."

"Me sword ready if anybody want to trouble me."

"You should find shelter with Ravenhide," he advised. "No one will harm you if you're under his roof. Even *I* am not safe walking the byways and backways of the wickedest town on God's earth."

I shook my head. "Me will be all right, Misser Caspian. Nuh worry youself."

He fared me well.

For a moment, I thought about seeking Lillet.

Maybe find Lillet later, Kemosha. You have to buy ah horse and cart.

All the available horses were at the service of Captain Morgan and his men. The trader who sold me a donkey and small cart looked at me with strange eyes. He studied me hard as he slowly counted his twelve pieces of eight.

I didn't care. I had my beast.

I named my donkey Freedom and hitched the small cart to his back. He had big dark eyes. I led him away with his nose close to the ground.

190

I also bought a curved Spanish sword with its sheath and belt, a barrel of water, a small keg of spiced red wine, and vegetables.

Starting on the harbor road, I spotted Ravenhide standing on a hill. My heart banged my ribs. I fixed my gaze on Freedom's neck, but I felt the heat of Ravenhide's glare just as much as the high sun. I wondered if I would ever see him again.

Forward to Isabella, Kemosha. Me hope nobody trouble her. Me hope she still safe. Me hope she hug me good when me sight her. Me hope she feel de same way to me as me do to her. Asase Ya, you know me journey been tough. You mek me survive all de troubles life fling at me. Captain Morgan have him gold, Ravenhide have him shiny garments, Misser Caspian have him Jesus. Cyan you bless this feeling me have for Isabella?

I pulled Freedom along the dirt track that led to the green hills. It was hard work. I stopped three times to take in water. Freedom licked it up greedily. It took awhile for my ears to get used to the shrieks and calls of the bush again; several times I flinched and jumped. *Maybe me shoulda ask Ravenhide to guide me.*

Sweat collected on my back and between my breasts. The mud road quit. The grass grew wild. After another hour I spotted two white men building a mighty cabin just off my route. They had already constructed a fence around their property. I pulled Freedom into a trot and hoped they didn't see me.

Isabella have neighbors.

I pushed on until half of the sun was hidden by the western hills, when I recognized the flattened grass and the trees that led to Isabella's cabin. My heart pounded like Ravenhide's biggest hammer.

Kemosha! What you going to do if she nuh there?

Tiredness licked me. My calf muscles felt tight and my soles were bruised. My top garment was drenched. I wasn't sure how many hours I had been trodding. I swapped a long look with Freedom. He blinked, shook his head, and swished his tail. I stopped again for water, this time pouring it over my head. Freedom brayed before we started again. The scent of broad leaves invaded my nostrils and caused me to sneeze.

Finally, I blessed my eyes on Isabella's cabin. The leaves of the trees hung over it, protecting it from angry weather.

I thanked Asase Ya, Nyame, and even Edward Caspian's Jesus.

"Isabella! Isabella! Where you there?"

No response.

"Isabella!"

Dread crept into my veins. *Maybe de two white mon down de hill find her and have dem wicked way wid her. Maybe dem kill her!*

"Isabella!"

Then I spotted her.

My heart danced.

She ran toward me. She was swift over the grass. Naked feet. Her long black hair trailed behind her. I couldn't stop leaking tears. But she was troubled. I was confused. *Why her face look so scared?*

When she reached me, she placed a hand over my mouth. "Callate," she said. "Callate."

My mama used the same words to me when I was small: *Still your tongue.*

"Englishman build cabin downhill," she said. "Not far. Me move soon. Go higher."

She took my hand and led me to her hut. I tugged Freedom's reins and he followed. He drank from Isabella's water trough as I secured him to a post.

Once inside the cabin, Isabella felt my face with her fingertips. It was as if she was checking if I was real. She touched my cheeks and my forehead. She ran her thumb over my lips. She caressed my palms and forearms. She stared into my eyes. She picked the grit and dust out of my hair. Capturing her gaze for a long while, *now* I knew she felt the same as I did.

She leaked tears before I wept. It was a glorious moment when she finally pulled me into her warm hug. No words were spoken.

It was meant to be.

She placed her palms on my cheeks and then cradled my chin. She kissed me tenderly on the forehead and stared into my eyes again. I wondered if Asase Ya and Nyame were watching me. *They must t'ink it's all right becah they have kept me alive and Isabella too. We cyan show how we feel for each other. The gods have willed it. They have answered my prayers.*

Her fingers dropped to my neck. She caressed my collarbone as I searched her cheeks with my lips. I found her mouth. She slowly removed my garment. It dropped to the floor. I wanted her to have her wicked way—and any other way—with me. She led me to her bed.

My body had experienced the agonies of a fierce lash, hunger, and thirst. I had never imagined that it could savor such pleasure. It overwhelmed me.

When we finished making love, she smiled at me while kissing away my happy tears. She eventually got up, as my being tried to understand what had just happened to it.

She cooked me plantain, corn, and sweet potatoes. For a second course, she offered me mango and soursop. I felt awkward and couldn't find words for a while. I tried to avoid her gaze. She simply smiled at me.

When I had finished eating, she asked, "Where Ravenhide?"

I hesitated. I had to admit to myself that I missed him. "Inna Port Royal," I eventually replied. "Drinking him drink and celebrating Captain Morgan's victory."

I chose not to tell Isabella of our falling out, nor the slaughter on the sands. I thought of the girl with the matted black hair. They were *her* people.

Before the sun dropped, she led me to the stream. I made sure that my hogskin bag of money was tied around my sword belt. She bathed me and washed my hair. We made love again. She kissed my scars and I caressed hers. I wanted to feel her touch forever.

As the half moon climbed the sky, I sat on the bank of the stream with my feet in the rushing waters. Isabella rested beside me with her arm around my shoulders. We peered through the gaps of the branches and leaves. We marveled at the emerging stars in the young night. Invisible creatures in the grass seemed to voice their approval.

But Marta and Gregory were never far from my mind.

As we lay close together that night, I whispered, "Me have to leave you soon. Me have to go back to Captain Tate plantation. Me have to use me pieces of eight and buy freedom for Marta and Gregory."

She gently cupped my jaws and searched my eyes. "Ya no quiero estar solo." *I don't want to be alone anymore.* "Nighttime," she said. "Tan solitario. La soledad me matará." *I'm so lonely. Loneliness will kill me.* She shook her head, crossed her arms, and gripped her shoulders. "I go with you," she said.

I considered it. *If me have to wait for Isabella while she teking her foot to plantation, de days and nights will mek me turn me into ah damn fool.*

"Sí," I nodded. "Ven conmigo." She could go with me.

Her smile showed me all her teeth. She held me in a hard embrace, and I felt her cheek against mine. We kissed. I closed my eyes, but I still feared losing her.

"We have work to do," I said.

* * *

The next day, I led her outside, picked up the curved Spanish sword from the cart, pulled it out of its sheath, and offered it to her. She looked at it as if it were an enemy. Slowly she reached out and grasped the handle. She studied the blade and checked the sharpness of the cutting edge and held it aloft. She hacked the air this way and that.

"Tengo que volver a matar?" she asked. *Do I have to kill?*

"Tal vez," I replied. *Maybe.* "Tal vez no." *Maybe not.*

She placed the sword back in the cart and hugged me tight.

"No se puede confiar en los ingleses," I told her. *Englishmen not to be trusted.*

I remembered how Ravenhide had first schooled me in the ways of the sword. And so, beneath the shadow of the blue mountains, I taught Isabella for four days and four nights. I worked her hard until the sun dipped below the trees. Her palms blistered, bruises darkened her arms, and her calf muscles screamed. Not once did she complain, not even when I pulled her out of bed before the sun opened its eye.

Edward Caspian's words nagged me. *Do not wait too long, Kemosha. Captain Morgan will want his navigator for his next sail to de Spanish Main. You don't know anybody else who cyan read de sky.*

On the fifth night, I whispered to Isabella, "Tomorrow, we fill up barrels wid water and fruits. We go."

"Sí," she replied. "Quisiera haber podido salvar mi gente." *I wish I could have saved my own people.*

CHAPTER 22

Return to the Plantation

I woke before Isabella. I had hardly slept. For a long moment I simply watched her. She looked so peaceful, breathing in and out. I felt an urge to brush her hair. I didn't want to bring harm to her. I didn't want to bring war to her. I kissed her gently on the forehead. She twitched but continued sleeping.

Maybe me could go'long now and leave her here? Yes, Kemosha. At least she will wake up and be safe. She living ah good life up inna de hills. She nuh have no hog or chicken to eat but she have plenty fruit and vegetables. She have shelter. She have water too. She nuh suffer from any English or Spanish lash. As long as dem nuh find her, she be all right. Me could nuh forgive meself if dem find her and have dem wicked way wid her. Me will always have de time me had wid her. Nobody else need to know.

I sat up slowly and dressed as quietly as I could.

I went outside. It was a cool morning and the ground was damp. I untied Freedom and led him to a patch of fresh grass. I stroked his head and cleaned the night matter that had collected in the corners of his eyes.

"Me will leave you wid Isabella," I said to him. "There is plenty-plenty grass for you to eat here so. Isabella will look after you nice. And if she want to climb de hill, you cyan carry her."

"Kemosha! Kemosha!"

I turned around. Isabella stood under the doorframe. She was naked, her sun-browned skin glistening in the Jamaican dawn. "You leaving for water widout me?" she asked. "Ya voy, espérame." *Wait for me, soon come.*

My heart sank like a fallen soursop. Her fate was now tied to mine.

"No," I said. "Me just wanted to see if Freedom all right."

We bathed in the stream together. We splashed water at each other, pushed our heads under, and pulled each other's legs. The fresh waters didn't feel so good on my body as before. My cuts and bruises stung. It was unspoken but I guessed we both knew it could be the last time we spent good time together.

Kemosha, forwarding to de plantation is mighty dangerous. Captain Morgan's Article of Agreement cyan only protect you 'pon de ship. And you don't know de way too good. Long time since you ride away from Captain Tate plantation.

Our return to the hut was a slow one. I stared at

the ground as I went. I dragged one foot after another. At some point, Isabella stood in front of me, placed her fingers beneath my chin, and lifted my head.

"No te preocupes, mi negra bella," she said. *No worry, Black beauty.* "You survive el mar. You survive Spanish Main. You survive anyting."

As we neared her cabin, I felt my spirits soar like Tenoka climbing the rigging of the *Satisfaction*. I missed him too. *Me wonder if him will tek him foot from Port Royal and go'long to see him own people.*

I kissed Isabella on the cheek and wrapped my arms around her neck. "Sí," I said. "Me cyan survive anyting."

I heard a strange sound. It wasn't the carking of a bird nor the call of a small grass creature. I looked at Isabella and pressed a finger to my lips. I crouched and crept forward. There was another horse and cart outside Isabella's hut. My blood throbbed in my veins. Worry rang hard in my head. The horse was drinking out of the water trough, Freedom looking nervous beside his much bigger cousin. I yanked Isabella's arm. Her eyes spoke of dread. I guessed it was the Englishmen who were building a big house down the hill. *Whoever it is could kill me for true. Dem might want dem wicked way wid me too. If they find us here so, there will be no new land to sail to.*

"Wait!" I said.

We listened.

Voices.

There was more than one.

Male voices.

I stood up and drew my sword. It trembled in my grasp. I felt my heartbeat pulse from my headtop to my foot-bottom. Sweat dripped from my temples. We only had one weapon—Isabella hadn't taken her blade to the stream. *If there are two mon roaming 'pon Isabella's land, me will have to kill both of dem. Dem cyan't go back to Port Royal and tell everybody about Isabella's place. Me cyan't hesitate. Me cyan't show no mercy.*

"Espera aquí," I said—*wait here.*

Isabella took a backward step, and another, and hid behind a bush. I made two paces forward. The tip of my sword trailed in the grass. I picked it up a little. I trod as quietly as I could. A sudden breeze disturbed the treetops. A bird squawked somewhere above. Freedom turned his head and spotted me. He brayed and pawed the ground with his foreleg. The horse continued to lick the water. I stepped on a sharp twig and had to suffer the stabbing pain and not let it escape from my mouth.

I gripped my sword tight, closed my eyes, and said a quick prayer to Asase Ya and Nyame. For a long moment I stood still, trying to breathe in as much courage as I could. The sun felt hot on my head. With my blade held horizontal in front of me, I ran around to the side of the cabin. "*Ayaaaaahhhhh!*"

I was about to strike a mighty blow, but I recognized the broad shoulders and big hands of the first man. A Black man.

Ravenhide.

I snapped my head to my right and spotted Tenoka.

I tried to make sense of it all, but nonsense flowed from my mouth. Tenoka laughed hard.

"Is this de way you greet me after we spend so much time together?" said Tenoka. "Maybe next time you should forward wid Captain Morgan to ah Spanish castle. Spanish mon will flee from you for true."

Ravenhide didn't move. He side-eyed me as if I still might use my sword on him. I turned away from his gaze and called Isabella. When she turned the corner, Tenoka stared at her for a long moment as though she were a duppy raised from the dead.

"Are . . . are you de same Isabella taken from the Spanish Main?" he asked. "Who wore ah red frock but never could be tamed? And you kill ah mon wid ah dagger beneath your undergarment?"

"Sí," Isabella replied, looking away as though it was painful to remember.

"We sing ah song at sea about you," Tenoka said. "Me never believe it when Ravenhide tell me you still living. Me t'ink lie him ah tell. De song don't lie about how pretty you is."

Isabella smiled. I blushed but I didn't think Ravenhide and Tenoka noticed.

"What you're doing here so?" I asked Ravenhide. "Why you follow me here so? And you, Tenoka. You get tired from drinking ale and rum?"

Silence.

"We . . ." Ravenhide began. "We . . . we want to fight for something important."

"And what is important to you?" I said. "Isn't pieces of eight, Spanish garment, and long black boot important to you? Why you nuh fight for dat?"

Ravenhide paused and stared at the ground. I guessed my words hurt him. *Good!*

"To go with you to fetch your good friend Marta and your brother Gregory," Ravenhide said. "No more are we in the service of Captain Morgan."

"Me have me pieces of eight to buy dem freedom," I said. "Me hope me never have to draw me sword."

Ravenhide stared into the distance, but Tenoka shook his head. "Do you really t'ink white plantation mon would tek money from one of him own slaves? Him might tek everyting you have and send you back to de cookhouse. Wicked dem ah wicked."

I thought about his words as all eyes aimed at me.

"Me have to try," I said. "Me nuh want to kill anyone. But if Captain Tate force me to draw me sword, then me will."

"We will go with you," said Ravenhide. "The overseers will pick up their weapons against you. As much as I know, no Black man or woman has ever left a plantation and walked free with pieces of eight in their pockets."

"You might have to kill dem all," said Tenoka. "And if you do, Captain Morgan will see you as an enemy. Buckos tell me him own ah plantation too. Him de richest mon inna Jamaica and him nuh want anyting to change dat. He will hunt you down like him hunt down de Spanish. And when him ketch you ..." Tenoka didn't finish his words. Instead, he shook his head.

"Are you ready for that?" Ravenhide asked. "That is what awaits you. He will make sure that your death is a slow one."

I sucked in a long breath and swapped glances with Isabella.

"Yes, me ready for dat," I said. "Me want to leave dis land. Go to ah place where you nuh have to look behind. Go to ah place where me could just ... live and be free. Vuela a casa."

"Then we go now," Ravenhide said.

"Now?" Tenoka said. "Me cyan't stay to drink ah liccle water and eat ah liccle someting? We trod ah long way from Port Royal. Me foot tired. Me hear good tings about de plantain dat grow here so."

I turned to Isabella. "Tenoka belly begging for someting. Let we mek him someting before him belly get vex."

Isabella nodded. "No hay problema," she said. "Man always think of belly."

I helped Isabella cook a meal of plantain, corn, potatoes, and a chicken that Ravenhide had brought with him. As I stirred the pot, I whispered to her, "Dem don't need to know how we close. Me nuh sure what dem might say. All me know is dat Asase Ya and Nyame bless we."

Isabella smiled. "Entiendo," she replied in a hush—she understood. "A quien yo me entrego bajo la luna no es asunto de ellos"—*but who me give meself to under the moon is not dem business.*

We both chuckled. Ravenhide and Tenoka wondered what amused us. We didn't tell them.

No meat of our meal was left on the bone. Not a scrap. We washed it down with a tankard each of spiced red wine.

"Nuh drink too much," said Tenoka. "Me know how it mek you walk strange."

"It could be de last red wine me drink," I responded, draining my mug.

"Maybe it's best that Tenoka and I travel a fair distance behind you," Ravenhide said. "It's a rare thing for two or more Black folks to walk in this island without the white man's permission."

I agreed with Ravenhide on this.

"And we want them to be surprised," added Ravenhide. "Surprise can be our friend."

Soon after, we fed and watered the beasts. I was glad for the delay before we set off because the spiced red wine made war inside my head. I had an hour or so for my feet to stop quarreling with my knees.

I made sure I secured my hogskin bag of pieces of eight around my hips and under my garment before we departed. I hated the thought of giving it all to Captain Tate.

I led the way with my right hand close to my sword. Isabella guided Freedom. Ravenhide and Tenoka started two hundred paces behind. By now, the angry skies had cleared. The sun grew strong but Asase Ya blew nice breezes in our faces.

We kept close to the sea and only trod together inland when the ground became soft and marshy. My feet collected mud and my legs felt heavy. Ravenhide showed us the best way. Tenoka described crocodiles to us—I had never seen one.

"And their teeth long and sharp like pirate dagger," Tenoka told me. "Their tail more terrible than any masser's flesh-scraper."

The mosquitoes were too many to count. I spotted wheel tracks and hoofprints, but we didn't encounter a single soul on the open track. The breath of the ocean added a calming sense to the song of the birds. I felt as if we were being watched. *Maybe Nyame is smiling 'pon we.*

We stopped in a small wood where we drank water, fed our beasts, and sank our teeth into soursop. I gazed at Isabella and wished we were back at her stream, making love. Fear for my life and everybody else's entered my head and spread through my body like a disease.

"Vendrán días mejores," Isabella said. *Better days will come.*

"Sí," I replied. I groped for the handle of my sword. At this moment, it was my comfort.

We set off again.

This time Ravenhide and Tenoka were four hundred or so steps behind. The land opened up. High green hills rose to our right. The ocean rippled and sparkled to our left. No ship or boat rode the waters. The breeze blew soft and the grass creatures were loud. My feet ached and my knees creaked. The horizon was a blur.

In my head, I prepared for confrontation. I wondered how Captain Tate carried his sword and how he took his stance. *Could me best him? Could me defend meself against him mighty blade?* I glanced at Isabella and she seemed well.

As the sun reached its highest point, we passed a tree with a sign on its trunk marked in white paint.

"We close," I said to Isabella. "Very close."

She took my hands into hers and closed her eyes.

"Qué los dioses nos protejan," she said. *May the gods protect us.*

Isabella secured Freedom to a tree where he stood, swishing his tail as flies buzzed around his eyes. We sat down with our backs against the trunk and awaited Ravenhide and Tenoka, clutching our swords tight to our chests.

Ravenhide will know what to do, Kemosha. Tek him good words. Him and Captain Morgan raid de Spanish Main. Dem have killed plenty mon.

CHAPTER 23

Blades of Death

"Leave your beasts here," Ravenhide said as he joined us under the tree. "Don't follow the track. Cross the field. The grass is long and will offer us cover for a short while."

I climbed the tree and peered across Captain Tate's land. Slaves toiled in the cane field. Others chopped wood, tended vegetables, and washed clothes in barrels. A woman I didn't recognize beat a carpet hanging on a rope on the front lawn. Young children ran about naked. Boiling sugar drifted on the breeze and black smoke puffed out of the cookhouse. I sniffed hog meat.

Marta. How me have missed your complain ways. Me wonder if you working alone or Captain Tate find somebody else for you to cook wid. Gregory, where you there? Me promised you me would do me best to return.

I jumped down from the tree, Isabella watching me. I picked up my sword and started for the field. Isabella took out her curved sword from her sheath. Determination stiffened her lips. She followed me. *If we're going to dead, then we dead together. Dat's how it was meant to be. Asase Ya will collect we. Our spirits will live forever. Maybe de gods will set we down near ah wide stream wid trees of fruit hanging over we.*

"One more thing," Ravenhide said. "You're on his land. Captain Tate won't hesitate to kill you. Remember, on land there aren't any Articles of Agreement. If in doubt, strike him down first. We'll be close behind. Remember what I taught you."

"Yes, me know, Ravenhide," I replied. "Always keep calm. Never lose your temper, keep sideways on, and step wid ah light foot."

"We'll take care of any overseers," said Ravenhide. "Whatever happens, we're fighting for something. Remember that of me."

I stared at him hard. "Yes, me will remember dat of you. Many more tings me remember too. Me mighty glad you're wid me."

I took in a long breath and started for the front lawn. Isabella walked with me. The grass was pale and high.

As I neared the big house, several slaves paused their work, stood up, and watched our approach. Two or three whispered to each other. Another pointed. Someone ran in the distance as if carrying urgent news. I spotted a few faces that I recognized, but I didn't stop and talk with any of them. My stride shortened, my eyes fixed on the big house. I only had thoughts for my blade and Captain Tate's.

The woman beating the carpet stilled as she watched us. Her eyes were marked with suspicion. She had lighter skin than any slave I had known. I guessed she was a mulatto.

"Misser Tate!" she called. "Misser Tate! Some dutty Black girl stepping up to de big house!" She picked up her rug and carried it inside.

I glanced behind me. Ravenhide and Tenoka had vanished.

Where dem there? Oh no!

A white overseer emerged from a side door of the big house. I stood still and tugged Isabella's arm. For a long moment he stared at us. Then he walked toward me, his stride long.

My shoulders tensed. I heard Isabella take in a mouthful of air.

I recognized the overseer. Misser Lyle Billings. His long brown hair was tied in a ponytail. His cheeks were red, and his beard grew wild. I had watched him whip Hakan many times. He had ripped the flesh of others too. I had seen him have his wicked way with our women. He had grinned as he went about his work. I had spat in his dinner plenty times: I stirred it in. I served it with dead ants, crushed spiders, and the blood of cockroaches. I had begged Asase Ya to turn him into a creature with more than five legs.

Every muscle in my arms tightened. I glanced over my shoulder again. No Ravenhide. No Tenoka. *Cyan me do this?*

I felt my pulse in my wrists and within my hands. It vibrated in my temples. My hogskin bag of pieces of eight seemed heavier.

"Where is your master?" Lyle Billings asked me. He stank of stale sweat and hot rum.

"Me have no masser," I answered.

He gave me a long glare. "What plantation do you come from?"

Him nuh remember me.

"Me come from this one," I said. "Me was born here so. Me good mama dead here so, and Nyame now looking after her. Me good brother live here so too. Me want to talk to Captain Tate."

"Who owns you?" he demanded.

"Nobody own me. Me defended ah blade for ah count of ah hundred to win me freedom."

Lyle Billings sniffed and squinted. "Freedom? There is no freedom on Captain Tate's land! No mule or animal will roam free here. And the same rule applies to Negroes." He pushed out his lips and angled his head. He glared at me so hard I felt he was studying my skull.

Now he switched his attention to Isabella, leering at her from foot to headtop. Rage surged in me like a soaring wave. *If him place one dutty finger 'pon her!*

Isabella narrowed her eyes and lifted her chin in defiance.

"Captain!" he called out. "Captain Tate!"

As we waited on the front lawn for Captain Tate to appear, Lyle Billings returned his stare to me. I held his gaze and managed to control the anger spreading from my chest.

"Captain Tate!" he called again.

Another overseer came in from the field. He gripped his back-ripper in his left hand. I stood still but shifted my eyes from right to left.

Finally, Captain Tate emerged from the double front doors, ambling from shadow into the sun's rays. His white breeches were loose. He wore his black boots, but no garment covered his torso. Brown and gray hairs grew thick on his chest and his neck was red. He stopped in front of me and held his hands behind his back, confident. His sword dangled from his belt.

"Kemosha," he said, "it's disobedient to approach my house without permission. Do you remember the punishment for that?"

"No, Captain Tate."

"Where is your master—Mr. Powell?"

"Him nuh masser no more," I said.

"Is that his sword you carry?"

"It's me own sword. De road from Port Royal to here so is ah dangerous one."

"If he has been lost at sea then you belong to his lady, Indika," Captain Tate said. "Has she sent you back to me?"

"Me nuh belong to lady Indika," I said. "Me's ah free woman."

"You are *somebody's* property."

"Me nuh nobody's property."

He laughed for a short moment, then Isabella caught his attention. His skinny cracked lips bent into a smile. My right hand tickled the handle of my sword. He took a step toward Isabella, who gave me a quick glance before retreating two paces. "There is no need to fear me," he said.

Lyle Billings looked on.

Isabella placed her fingers on the handle of her curved blade. The veins in my wrist stretched my skin. My fingertips turned red. My pulse boomed inside my dry throat.

"Me . . . me come to buy Marta and Gregory's freedom," I stuttered. "Me will give you twenty pieces of eight. Ah fair price dat."

Captain Tate ignored me. He reached out a hand and touched Isabella's cheek. He gazed at her like he wanted his wicked way with her. He answered me but didn't turn around to face me. "I don't know how you got here but you belong to Antock Powell and his intended, Indika. You will stay here under my ownership until he or Indika claims you. Your pretty friend will work in my house. And she will warm my bed. Now, give me his sword for safekeeping."

"Me nuh bring Isabella or meself to work for you," I said. "Me come to buy Marta and Gregory's freedom."

Captain Tate leaned back and laughed hard, an ugly sound to my ears. "I will not trade with a Negro," he sneered. "Your body, your labor, and whatever you own is mine. That's the law!"

Without hesitation, I drew my sword. He pulled out his. In a diagonal strike, I aimed for his neck. *"Ayaaah!"* He defended my attack; his eyes spoke outrage.

I heard movement and shouts behind me and to the side. Suddenly another overseer appeared to my left. Many sets of feet bruised the ground. I had to keep my eyes fixed on Captain Tate's blade. He lunged forward, his right foot climbing high in the air as he made a long stride. He slashed at my head, tried to rip my chest open and hack off my arm. I just about defended his counter. My sword rattled in my grip. Baring his teeth, he launched another attack, ferocious, infuriated and determined. His long skinny metal sliced the air this way and that.

"You dare to challenge me!"

His sword was quicker than Antock Powell's. He swiped for my legs, stabbed at my heart, and tried to take off my arm. I took four rapid paces backward. It was then that I noticed fighting all around me. Ravenhide, Tenoka, and Isabella: all wielded blades. A clash of metals. The air was filled with swipes, yelps, hollers, and curses. It was hard not to stop to check how they were faring.

Keep your eye 'pon his sword, Kemosha. Never let dat go. This won't finish wid ah count of ah hundred.

Captain Tate grunted when he made his next strike at me. His right foot stamped the ground as he forced me back. Dust flew up. I deflected a blow aimed for my throat but my grip loosened. I almost dropped my sword, my fingers throbbing and stinging.

I managed to take my stance again. Right foot forward, left arm behind. Sideways. Light of foot. He jabbed at my eyes and tried to split my head. He darted to my left and then to my right. A flurry of strikes almost lost me my head. I found myself on my back. I got up as quickly as I could and kicked him back. He took his stance again and came forward once more. Fury stained the gap between his eyebrows. He slashed at me from all angles. I stood my ground and deflected his blade, keeping my wrist strong. Suddenly he blew hard. Sweat covered his neck. His cheeks reddened. He wiped perspiration from his headtop.

"*Ayaah!*"

I charged forward. He parried my thrusts aimed at his head and crotch. For a short moment, I forgot Ravenhide's teachings. I gripped my sword with two hands and hacked and cleaved as much as my waning strength allowed.

"*Ayaaarrgghhhh!*"

He stumbled. His left foot gave away. To correct his fall, his arm reached for the ground, and so he left himself open.

I didn't hesitate. I drove my sword through his ribs, two-handed. I twisted and pushed again. His eyes widened, mouth opening. He blew his last breath. Slowly, his mouth closed. It took a mighty effort to pull my sword out. His face was painted with shock as he hit the ground. He fell at my feet and rolled over to his side.

I lifted my blade and was about to strike him again—

There was no need. He was very still. Dead. I raised my sword, thinking of the lonely girl with the matted hair on the beaches of the Spanish Main. In my head I could see her disappearing beyond the valleys. This was for her as much as anyone else.

"*Ayaaaaaggghhhh!*"

Isabella.

I spun around.

Bodies on the ground. Spilled blood. Isabella and Ravenhide. Four dead overseers.

Isabella! Asase Ya. Nuh tek her from me.

I ran to Isabella first. She lay on her side. Her legs were at a strange angle.

But now she was moving. My heart sang. In a short moment I closed my eyes and thanked Asase Ya.

Isabella used her hands and pushed herself up to her feet. She only bled from a cut behind her ear. She wiped the dust and mud from her face, and our eyes met. She smiled. "Tu escuela de espadas me enseñó bien," she said—*your sword school teach me good.*

I returned her smile, but something caught my eye. Ravenhide. He had been gored under his left armpit. Blood pooled around his shoulders. His eyes were closed. Four dead overseers were close by.

He didn't move. No flicker.

Something cold gripped and squeezed my heart. The chill spread to my fingers. My pulse banged the sides of my head again. I couldn't take a step toward him, I didn't want to.

Tenoka went over to him and placed a hand on his neck. There, he rested it for a while, checking. I sensed my brothers and sisters of the plantation closing in, several running inside the big house, carrying weapons. My eyes were fixed on Ravenhide.

Tenoka placed his hands beneath Ravenhide's head. His eyes remained shut. I willed them to open. He seemed to be at peace.

I couldn't bear it. I turned my gaze away. *Asase Ya, Nyame, if you want to sacrifice somebody, then sacrifice me. Nuh kill Ravenhide. Him free Isabella. Him free me for true. And through me, him free everybody.*

I felt an arm around my shoulders. Isabella. "Debemos enterrarlo pronto, antes que el sol pudra el cuerpo," she said—*we must bury him soon before the sun spoils his body.*

"Is there more overseer?" Tenoka wanted to know.

"Two of dem run off," Hakan replied, coming up. "Dem never have nuh belly for de fight."

"But their tongues cyan carry news," Tenoka said. "We cyan't stay here so. We must all leave here quicktime."

"Not before we lay Ravenhide to rest," I said. "We must prepare him so we ancestors cyan tek him. We must do dat."

With Tenoka and Isabella, I carried Ravenhide from Captain Tate's land. We laid his body behind the tree where Freedom and Ravenhide's horse grazed.

As we prepared his body for burial, I spotted Marta and Gregory. They had followed us off Captain Tate's land. I stood still for a moment as emotions swirled inside of me.

"You're late!" cried Marta. "Foolish chile! But better come late than never!"

I approached Gregory first. He stopped walking, his face spelling disbelief. I held his shoulders and looked into his eyes.

"Me did tell you me was going to come for you," I said.

He seemed too shocked to speak, tears fell down his cheeks. New scars marked his neck. He had grown half a finger in all this time.

"You have nothing to say, Gregory?" I smiled. "Your big sister come back for you." I wrapped him in a tight hug. We held each other for a long while and I refused to let him go. I whispered into his ear, "Me going to tek you to freedom."

He pulled his head away from my collarbone and finally smiled. "What is freedom?" he asked.

I shook my head and cried.

Brothers and sisters who had recognized me watched me with big eyes and even bigger wonder. I told my story and adventure to them as best as I could. I wasn't sure if they understood it all, but they cheered me when I concluded my tale.

Someone sang a song that I remembered my mama singing. Long tears fell once more.

*"Los abuelos se lo llevarán
Llevarlo a casa*

Le darán agua y lo cuidarán
Volverá a ganar su lugar."

It was beautiful to listen to.

Yes, *the ancestors will carry him home*, so the chant went. *They will water and nurse him. Ravenhide will take his stance again.*

I wanted to wail, and I wanted to sing. I wanted to curse the gods for allowing Ravenhide to die. Then I wanted to chant Asase Ya, Nyame, and Epo's names for keeping me alive. I wanted to join Mama wherever she was. "Muchos más tendrán que sufrir," she once said to me. "Muchos más tendrán que morir—no me preguntes por qué." *Many more will have to suffer, many more will have to die—don't ask me why.*

Suddenly exhaustion and emotion licked me. I fell to my knees. Marta and Gregory lifted me to my feet and set me down against a tree. They stroked my face and dried my tears. They brought me water. They hugged me, kissed my forehead, and held my hands. They laughed and cried, cried and laughed.

Hakan walked over to me, Iyana with him. "Not one of we dared to believe your good foot still walking," he said. "The ancestors must ah protect you. You is de one who carry de fire, de fire to start revolution." He raised his hand and gazed at the heavens. "*Asase Ya!*" he chanted.

"*ASASE YA!*"

"*Nyame!*"

"*NYAME!*"

"*Epo!*"

"*EPO!*"

Men came with spades and forks. I watched as they dug the grave behind the tree. I took Ravenhide's keys from his pockets, and Iyana washed his wounds and cleaned his face one last time. She took particular care of his hands and feet. They danced around his body and urged the gods to protect him through to the next life. As they lowered him in, Marta and Hakan sprinkled his flesh with water. They said chosen words about our ancestors and the tree gods. They chanted Nyame's name. Finally, they called on Asase Ya to accept Ravenhide's spirit.

"Who was he?" asked Hakan. "Where him come from?"

"They called him Ravenhide," I said. "Him mama give him de name of Souleymane. Him come from the Mandinka people."

Hakan nodded. "The Mandinka! Ah mighty people."

"Him save me life," I went on. "Spanish people kill him family. He sailed to the ends of the broad blue waters. Through me, him will save plenty more life. Him was de best barrel maker inna Port Royal. Him was a fine swordsmon, so even Captain Morgan say so. But more important than dat, him fight for someting good."

"All it teks is for one somebody to get up and stand up to dem, then others will follow," Hakan said. "Me run quicktime to join de battle. Me sight Ravenhide kill two of dem. Him sword rapid and fierce. But de next one tek him from behind before me could reach."

* * *

Brothers and sisters returned to the big house and took whatever pleased them. Men fought over Captain Tate's clothes. They drank his rum and ale. They chopped up his cupboards and tables. They placed their bare feet on his pretty chairs and rolled and bounced on his bed. They hacked his paintings, ripped up books and charts, and pulled out the flowers from his garden.

They killed the fair-skinned woman I had seen beating the carpet. I tried to stop them, but they wouldn't listen to me. I learned she was Captain Tate's mistress: they said that she had taken the place of Captain Tate's first wife.

"Evil had grown in her since she start sleep in Captain's bed," Hakan told me as he pulled me away. "She cause many back to get lash."

Her screams echoed around the plantation. A sudden chill charged through my veins.

They tossed Captain Tate, his light-skinned woman, and his dead overseers into a deep ditch. Flies and mosquitoes fed on them. Their vacant eyes reminded me of those dead faces on the sands of the Spanish Main. I had to walk away.

I made sure Freedom and Ravenhide's horse were watered and fed before I headed back to Ravenhide's burial place.

"Me cyan't stay here so for too long," I spoke to the grave. "Me hope you're back wid your family. Asase Ya, Nyame, and Epo will mek sure of dat. Me will never forget you, nor will me allow Isabella and Tenoka to forget you. No, sah. Sleep good. You're de papa me never had. One good day we'll be drinking spiced red wine again. Me sure de gods will save some for you and me."

CHAPTER 24

A Parting of Ways

Many of the freed slaves slept in the big house, but I decided to sleep in my old cabin. It reminded me of Mama. I could almost smell her: I sensed her touch, her embrace, her gentle words. Her smile. I wished she could have seen this day. Or maybe she did—perhaps she had watched from her high place beside the gods.

Isabella rested with me. We were alone. We made beautiful love before she fell into a deep sleep, her head nested beneath my chin. It was a comfort to listen to her breathing pattern. A half of me wanted to chant to the world about my love for her, but my other half wondered how Hakan, Iyana, and the rest of my brothers and sisters would react to me loving a woman.

I thought of Ravenhide and tried to imagine his parents. I wondered if they offered him words of comfort when he was small, when the grass creatures cussed and the moon was high. *Maybe they wanted him to fly away home too.*

Twice I got up in the night to check the cart path. A few of my brothers and sisters, Tenoka among them, were still drinking and eating. They danced, chanted songs, and banged their tools against barrels and tree trunks.

I knew I had to depart before the sun opened its eye. I left Isabella and looked for Hakan.

I found him in Captain Tate's bedroom with Iyana. They were asleep and naked. I watched them for a while. *No need to keep ah look out for masser.* There was something beautiful about a Black man at perfect rest with his Black woman. I couldn't remember Mama, Marta, or any other Black woman I knew ever experiencing that.

I nudged Hakan. He didn't move, so I pinched his shoulder.

He sat up in a rush as if he was about to be attacked.

"It's me," I said. "Kemosha."

"Kemosha," he said. "De sun still sleeping. No slavemaster here so. No overseer here so. What's troubling your forehead?"

"Me have to leave here so," I said. "And you have to go'long soon too. Me going to buy ah boat and sail to ah land where no white mon ah trod."

Hakan looked at me strange. "But white mon everywhere. There is no land where de white mon don't plant dem foot and build ah big house."

"There is!" I insisted. "And dat's where me foot teking me."

"And how cyan you buy ah boat? You nuh have no pieces of eight. We search all over de house and cyan't find nothing."

"Me . . . me might have ah liccle someting," I said.

My hogskin bag was still tied around my hips under my slops. Only Isabella had seen it.

Hakan shook his head. "You need ah whole heap of someting."

"Nuh worry yourself, Hakan. Me will buy me boat. Even if it only two mon long."

"Better we stay together," he said. "When de sun open its eye, me leading everybody to de hills. Some of we people are already there. Come wid we, Kemosha. Dem cyan't find we inna de hills. Their foot get plenty tired chasing we. And their horses stumble when they try to climb up there."

Iyana stirred. She picked the matter out of her eyes and sat up. She stretched her arms and yawned. Her scarred cheek didn't look so bad in the night. "We have to move now?" she asked.

"Me would nuh leave it for too long," I said. "White mon will come here so. The governor might even come here so. War they will bring. Terrible and brutal war."

I remembered the slaughter on the sands of the Spanish Main once again. This time I could smell the rotting bodies, the blood, and the empty eyes. I saw the ants. The crabs.

Hakan turned to Iyana. "Kemosha don't want to follow we to de hills."

"Then you will soon dead," said Iyana. "They will ketch you, molest you, lash you, put you inna cage. Rip your back open wid dem flesh-scraper. Best we stay together where de land hard to trod and white mon leg get weary."

"No," I replied. "Me done wid fighting. Me tired of sighting dead people all about."

"But we have to fight," said Hakan. "De white mon don't give we no choice. And me know where to go. There is Black mon inna de hills. De Maroons, some people call dem. We going to find and join dem."

"And wid dem," Iyana added, "we will back de wicked white mon to de sea. So Asase Ya tell me so!"

"Me want to find ah green land and live," I said. "Dat's what me mama wanted too. 'Quiero encontrar una tierra verde para poder vivir allí.'"

"Sí," Hakan nodded. "She tell me de same ting. But there is no such ah place. We have to live here so, up inna de hills. Behind de cover of de bush and where de clouds rest. And we will fight dem till de last one of dem is dead."

"Hakan, you quarrel wid Captain Tate and Lyle Billings for as long as me remember," I said. "Maybe dat is what Asase Ya want *you* to do. *Me* have to go where Asase Ya send me. And dat is to ah green place dat is free from war."

We shared a long look. He recognized my determination and nodded. He reached out his hand and gripped my shoulder. "So dat's how it must be," he said, narrowing his eyes. "Marta and Gregory walking wid you?"

"Me going to look for dem now."

"Walk good," he said. "And may we ancestors guide your strong foot."

"And may they smile 'pon you too."

"Me will never forget you, Kemosha," Hakan said. "Freedom walks in your heart and you carry it to release us. Our pickney will chant your name."

Iyana climbed off the bed and hugged me tight. She rested her chin on my shoulder for a short moment. "We could use your mighty sword in we fight," she said. "De same blade dat strike down Captain Tate. Me never believe it possible. Asase Ya gave you de heart of ah warrior. But forward to your green land, if you must. May de gods look after you."

"And may they keep your hand strong under de moon."

I left the room and searched for Marta and Gregory.

Marta wasn't in the big house nor any of the cabins. I found her in the cookhouse, scrubbing pots and plates in a barrel. I watched her for a short while. Memories of rising in the morning with Marta and cooking with her hit me with a rush. *Foolish chile, Kemosha! You don't do it dat way! Nuh burn de ham! Nuh leave de chicken claw 'pon de plate!*

"Marta!" I called. "Is what you doing? No slavemaster to cook for inna de morning."

"Somebody have to clean up after everybody eat big," she said. "Me and me sisters cook ah big feast."

"Yes," I said. "All belly full. But everybody must leave here so quick."

"Me could nuh sleep," Marta said. "Me nuh know what to do wid meself."

"Where Gregory there?" I asked.

"He's wid your friend who you come wid."

"Tenoka?"

"Yes, dat him name."

I snatched the pot from out of Marta's hands and placed it on the floor. She was outraged, but before she cussed me, I spoke first: "Me want you to listen to me, Marta. And listen to me good."

"Listen? Foolish chile! What madness you want poor Marta to carry on wid now? Me sight de shine in your eye!"

"Me want you to come wid me," I said. "Everybody must leave here before de sun wake up. Plenty white mon will soon come here so. And they will bring brutal and terrible war wid dem."

"Maybe de white mon who come here so won't be so bad-minded as Captain Tate?"

I shook my head. "You ever meet any slavemaster or overseer dat treat you good and speak nice wid you?"

Marta paused and glanced into the hills. "No."

"Me leaving as soon as me find Gregory and Tenoka."

"And where your foolish foot teking you?" Marta asked.

"Across de seas," I said. "To ah green land where plantain tree grow long and de chickens are fat."

Marta side-eyed me for a long moment. "Me cyan't come wid you," she said finally. "If me must leave this place, me going to follow Hakan to de hills. Me hope me old foot cyan carry me. Dat plan is ah good plan."

"You must go'long where Asase Ya tell you to go'long," I said. "But white mon war will follow you every step you tek. No long hill or high bush will keep dem from you."

"They won't follow we to bush and hilltop," Marta argued. "So Hakan and Iyana tell me so."

"Yes dem will! You nuh want to live inna place where white mon nuh trod, plant your own food, and rest where you want to rest?"

"Dat is ah dream dat your mama talk about plenty time," Marta said. "'Vuela a casa.' Her dream kept her living for many moons. She was sick well before she give birth to you. But it was just ah dream."

Mama appeared big in my mind. Her kind face, her compassion. Tears formed behind my eyes. I sniffed them back.

"Marta," I pleaded, "white mon tek me and want to have dem wicked way wid me. Dem nearly chop me up like sliced scallion. Dem send me 'pon long boat where me never see nuh land. Me sick more times than me eat. For one long moon all me sight was de broad blue waters and de endless sky. Me survive all of dat to come back to you and Gregory. And now you want to tell me you're teking your old foot to de hills."

"This is all me know, Kemosha," she responded. "Me

never could really t'ink about your mama's dream. At least me cyan see de green hills over there so."

We shared a long moment of silence before she stared at the floor. Something emptied from my heart.

Marta picked up the pot and started scrubbing once again. I shook my head, turned, and looked for Tenoka and Gregory.

I found them on the front lawn. Gregory held a sword in his hands and Tenoka schooled him as he swished it this way and that. I remembered how Ravenhide first instructed me in his backyard in Port Royal. It seemed so long ago. I watched them for a short while before stepping forward.

"De sun soon rise," I said. "White mon war will soon turn de green grass red. And me have sighted what dem brutality cyan do. We leaving now."

Gregory stood still and inspected his blade. "But me want to fight dem, Kemosha. Let dem come!"

I recognized the same defiance in him that Iyana and Hakan shared. His eleven-year-old eyes had fire in them. They promised violence. *He will have to wait till he's plenty taller than de sword.* I shook my head. "Gregory, your bravery big but your size too short," I said. "And even if you do kill dem, more will come. We're going to ah place where nuh white mon ah trod."

"And where is dat?" Gregory asked.

"Ah place across de broad seas."

He looked confused. Then I realized he had never seen the great blue before.

"Come, Gregory," I said. "We have to find some food to carry wid we before it done."

"Marta coming wid we?" he asked.

I hesitated. "No," I said.

Gregory's head dropped. "We walking to your freedom? Where is dat?"

I lifted his chin with my fingers and gazed into his eyes. "Freedom is waking up ah morning time and teking time over breakfast. Freedom is growing food for yourself wid nobody standing over you wid ah long lash. Freedom is bathing yourself in fresh waters and nobody telling you to come out. Freedom is teking time to listen to de pretty bird singing. Freedom is spending good time wid de people who love you in dis world."

Gregory thought about it and nodded. "Dat sound like ah good place."

Before I returned to the cookhouse, I went to Mama's cabin and woke Isabella. "Hora de irse," I said—*time to go.*

"Al mar?"

"Sí."

She looked at me hard. "You no want to follow your people to de hills?" she said.

"No."

"Estás segura?" She wanted to know if I was sure.

"Me want to go to ah place where we don't have to look over we shoulder. Ah nice green place where me cyan walk free and easy. Ah safe land where there are no more Captain Tate to fight."

Silence.

Isabella seemed to know what troubled me. "Did you look into his eyes when Captain Tate's life gone?"

I didn't want to answer. I turned the other way.

"Did you?" Isabella repeated.

"Sí," at last I replied. "Me nuh want dat same feeling again."

"Y yo tampoco," she said—*and neither do I.*

I had forgotten that she had taken a life too—the man who tried to molest her in Port Royal.

"Me want to fly away," I said.

"Is that your dream or your mama's dream?"

She trapped me with her brown eyes. I stared at the ground.

I wasn't sure how to reply. *Yes, it was me mama's dream. But me dream too. Me nuh want to live inna de hills and fight all de while.*

"At nighttime, Mama would always talk about flying away home," I said. "She would wake up inna de morning and watch de bird dem fly. Free as anyting. Maybe me will never reach there but me want to try to find ah home for meself."

Isabella held my gaze for a moment before she smiled. "Estaré feliz de ir contigo." *I am happy to go with you.*

CHAPTER 25

A Choice of Paths

I left Ravenhide's horse with Hakan. He and Iyana promised to look after the animal well. Hitched to a small cart, Freedom had to bear the load of fruits, vegetables, a barrel of water, and a salted piece of hog meat that Marta provided. I could barely meet her eyes as she handed it over.

The darkest hour had passed, and in the skies I saw shades of blue and the outline of clouds. Birds announced the coming morning.

Gregory led Freedom. Isabella and I walked behind the beast, and Tenoka, his eyes looking here and there, took up the rear. His sword was ready. Mine was clutched tight in my right hand. Tears formed behind my eyes, but I managed to hold them back. *Ravenhide dead! Marta following Hakan to de hills.* It was hard to accept.

We had traveled three hundred strides or so when I heard a call from behind. I couldn't see who it was, but I recognized the voice.

"Kemosha! Kemosha!"

Marta.

"Kemosha! Why you gone and left me! You're too damn fast! Wait for me nuh!"

My heart lifted.

She emerged out of the darkness, hitching up her frock and running as hard as she could. When she reached us, she bent over and placed her hands on her knees. She blew hard before she spoke.

"Now me is ah foolish woman," she said. "You see what madness you mek me do? If you find ah nice place, you going to need somebody to cook nice."

"Me cyan cook nice," I said. "Captain Tate and Captain Morgan never complain. Buckos of de *Satisfaction* were well happy wid me cooking. Dem chant ah song about me."

"But, me sorry to say, your cooking not as good as me own," Marta said. "Yes, me will go wid you, but give me some water before me tek another step. Me old foot tired already."

I gave her water to drink. I could have filled the mug with my tears.

We had trod for two hours. The sun had opened its fierce eye. No clouds were above, and the breeze slept. The wild grass was alive with the chatter of small creatures. Marta's hard puffing and panting provided a wordless chant for our journey.

Gregory said he wanted to see the great blue, but

Tenoka was against it. "Better we get to Ravenhide place as soon as we cyan," he said. "No time to linger."

"Marta old bones need rest," I reasoned. "And Gregory foot still young. Come, let we rest by de broad seas and cool we foot inna de waters. We'll eat ah liccle someting."

We passed through a wood of skinny trees and long leaves. We picked our way through thick bushes and leaped over wide ditches. Finally, our feet met soft, golden sand. Bright blue waters spread out to the horizon where it touched the sky. There was little breeze to stir the waves. No ship rode the seas. The tide came in gently, as if it didn't want to wake anyone. For a short moment, I dared to be happy: the people who I loved in this world were with me. And we were *free*. My heart sang a song from the ancestors. I imagined Mama looking down on me. *Vuela a casa*. I smiled the biggest smile I could remember.

Gregory watched in wonder. "So much water," he said. "It broader than anyting me ever see."

"Yes it is," I said. "Broad like de sky when no cloud trouble it."

Gregory walked slowly up to me. He spoke just above a whisper: "Kemosha, you really t'ink there is ah land where no white mon walk?"

I peered out to the horizon before gazing into Gregory's eyes. He reminded me of Mama. "Yes," I said. "Somewhere out there is ah land for we. We cyan't see it here so but believe it."

"It hard to believe it true when me cyan't see it," said Gregory.

"Was it hard to believe you ever see me good self again?" I asked.

Gregory dropped his head. "Me did lose hope," he admitted. "Every morning me would look out for you. But after ah while me stop do dat. Me stop speak your name to Marta becah she would bawl long tears."

"But me here now," I said. "Asase Ya, Nyame, and Epo mek it so. And they will mek we find this new land."

Gregory lifted his head, turned to me, and smiled. We hugged and I shed more eye-water.

"Nuh light any fire," Tenoka warned, coming by. "We just stop off here so and eat some fruit."

After we ate, Isabella waded into the waters up to her knees. Then she stopped, crossed her arms, and stared into the horizon, standing very still for a while. I caught up with her. The ocean was so clear, we could see our feet on the sand.

"Me pregunto si el gran cielo se lleva a nuestros muertos," she said. *I wonder if the great sky takes our dead.*

I looked up to the heavens. The sun felt hot on my cheeks. "Sí, me sure Ravenhide, me mama, and anybody close to you is looking down on we."

Isabella smiled. "Come," she said. "The sun strong today."

"Tenoka," I called. "Gregory. Let's tek up our good foot and forward to Port Royal."

We took on water before starting through the woods again.

As we were making our way, I suddenly sensed something beneath my feet. The ground shook and vibrated. It was as if Asase Ya had come down to earth and walked the land.

We swapped worried glances. "Gregory, Marta," I said, "stay here so wid Freedom. Nuh let go of him. Tenoka, Isabella: come let we see what bruise de ground."

We crawled through the trees, keeping our bodies low to the ground. Isabella took the lead. She could move along the hard earth quicker than any of us. Agile. Nimble. I forgot that like me, she had escaped from the English too.

She led us down a gully before climbing a ridge. Hard mud collected beneath her fingernails and stained her forehead.

"Callate," she said. *Still your tongues.* "Blancos a caballo." *White men on horses.*

I pulled myself up to see.

Fifteen mounted horses, maybe twenty. More men marched on either side of them. They were wearing expressions of brutality. They wore three-pointed hats, pale breeches, and long boots. I thought of Hakan, Iyana, and my brothers and sisters at the plantation. *Me have to tell dem. Let dem know white mon ah come wid dem terrible war. Me must go back. Give dem warning.*

"We must return," I whispered. "Let Hakan and Iyana know what coming to dem."

"No, Kemosha!" Tenoka said. "We cyan't turn back now. Dem riding big horse. How we supposed to reach back to de plantation before dem?"

I sprang to my feet. "Nuh, mon! We have to tell dem!"

With a hard tug, Tenoka pulled me down. I fell on my left elbow. He glared at me with fierce eyes as I rubbed my arm. He covered my mouth with his hand and shook his head. I dug my nails into Tenoka's wrist and he let go of me. "We have to do *someting*," I said. "Brutal war coming to Hakan and Iyana. Dem must know. Nobody else cyan tell dem."

"Hakan nuh foolish," Tenoka said. "Him know him have to leave de plantation. At first light him woulda tek up him foot and lead him people to de hills. De Maroons will give him ah good welcome."

"But say him don't tek up him foot and gone?"

"We have to trust him to do dat," said Tenoka.

"We have to—"

I felt another hand on my shoulder. Isabella. She held me in her gaze and spoke softly: "Tus hermanos y hermanas tienen su camino, nosotros temenos el nuestro." *Your brothers and sisters have their path. We have ours.*

I stood up but Isabella and Tenoka pushed me down again.

"Stay here so!" Tenoka demanded. "You want dem to kill all of we? And remember, Gregory and Marta back over there so. Dem cyan't run so hard as we."

Isabella nodded. I accepted defeat.

Me beg you, Asase Ya, give speed to dem good foot and mek dem trod quicktime to de hills.

We started again. Fearing more white men on horses, we kept to the coastline as well as we could. We climbed over rocks, threaded through trees, and splashed in marshy puddles where our feet disappeared. Tenoka looked out for crocodiles. I didn't admit it, but I'd rather have taken my chances with white men on horses than long beasts with dagger-like teeth. Freedom didn't complain. He plodded along with his nose close to the ground, though the flies wouldn't leave his eyes alone.

We stopped once again for water and fruits in a small cove. The trees were tall there and the leaves were broad, offering us cover. Bright-colored birds in high branches looked down at us and shrieked their comments. The soursop delighted my tongue and went down well.

Marta and I made a fire, roasted the hog meat, and boiled sweet potato. It was good. As we ate, the sun fell to the west and the near-full moon lit the ocean with a shimmering silver path. The strengthening breeze licked our cheeks and we heard it sailing through the leaves. I wished we could have stayed here but knew white men would eventually discover us.

"When we reach Port Royal," Marta asked, "what we going to do next?"

"Forward to Ravenhide's place," I said. "Me have de key. We will rest our foot there so. Then me have to find ah mon."

"And which mon you have to find?" Marta wanted to know.

"Ah mon call Edward Caspian," I replied. "Ah navigator. Him cyan read de skies and steer big boat. Ah good mon. But him love him drink."

"Ah white mon?" Gregory asked.

"Yes, ah white mon."

"We just kill plenty white mon back at de plantation," Gregory said. "How cyan we trust this Edward Caspian? Me never know ah white mon who nuh want to beat me."

"This one won't beat you," Tenoka said.

Gregory side-eyed me. "This Edward Caspian might want to beat me too. Dat's all Misser Billings want to do to me."

"Edward Caspian will steer we boat," I said. "To de land where we foot cyan walk free."

Gregory turned away. He sat on the sand and peered toward the seas. I hated it that he didn't believe me, but in his eleven years he had yet to meet a clean-hearted white man.

I decided to lie on the beach until the sun took its rest. I didn't want to appear in Port Royal when the sun was king. I hoped Edward Caspian would prove to Gregory that there are good white men in the world.

CHAPTER 26

Unholy Counting

The moon climbed the southern sky. Avoiding the merchants and traders of Kingston Harbour, we finally reached the narrow cart path leading to Port Royal. The long and winding strip of land was muddy and soft. The night breeze was strong, salt was in the air. Waters on both sides lapped our feet. I glanced skyward and what clouds I could see moved quickly in the heavens. Freedom took his time, but he managed to keep straight. The ebbing and frothing seawater didn't seem to bother him as much as it did Marta. She hopped and danced whenever the broken waves approached her feet. But Gregory only had eyes for the lights of Port Royal. "It look mighty pretty," he said.

"You rode de great blue in one of dem?" Marta asked, pointing to the ships in the harbor.

"Yes, me did," I said. "And it mek me belly feel like somebody wid big spoon ah stir me insides."

We came to the gate. I had forgotten about the two

men who guarded its entrance. Their swords were long and forked at the tip. I felt a crunching sensation in my stomach.

What do me say to dem? Oh, Asase Ya! Nyame! Dem going to send me back to de plantation where white mon will bring war to we.

They sat on a well-worn bench, enjoying a chicken leg each. A lantern shone between them. One owned a wild beard, and the tip of his nose had been sliced off. The other was bald and clean-shaven, brown grease dribbling down his chin. I sniffed the ale in their tankards. They looked like they wanted to be somewhere else, anywhere else.

The bald man looked at us and stood up, with plenty of questions in his eyes. He went for his sword and held it in front of Tenoka's nose.

"Halt!" he said. "Where is your master? And that master better not be a Spanish swine."

Tenoka struggled for words, raising his palms in submission. Gregory retreated a step. Marta froze.

"We . . . we masser is de quartermaster Misser Antock Powell," I stuttered. "Misser Powell send me to collect more slave from de plantation. Mr. Powell soon building ah new tavern. And him need help to build dis new place and slave people to cook and work in it."

"Whose swords do you carry?" the bearded man demanded.

"They belong to Misser Powell," I replied. "Him tell we dat de Port Royal Road is ah dangerous road, where bad people might want to trouble we. Misser Powell tell we him don't want to lose him property."

The two men looked at each other. I didn't think they bought my tale, but now they fixed their eyes on Isabella. She backed away a step, fingering the handle of her sword as if she wanted to wield it. I hoped she wouldn't.

"And you'll be serving behind the counter of Mr. Powell's new tavern?" the hairless one said to Isabella. "There are ladies of the night plying their trade in Port Royal, but none have hair and skin like you. You will make a welcome addition."

"Captain Morgan's quartermaster will ask a high price for her," said the man with a beard.

"I will pay a fair price for her," responded the bald man. "Her hair alone earns it."

"Your fingers will not caress her hair before me," said the bearded man.

Isabella didn't move but she returned their gaze. It was full of hatred and contempt. "Déjame pasar," she said. *Let me through.*

The two white men swapped another long glance.

"Go on through," said the bald man. "We fare you well, and we will visit you soon. I cannot speak for my friend, but I'll be gentle!"

We passed through the gate and didn't look behind. The taverns and bars had long ago opened. Curses, threats, and insults fouled the air. We did our best to avoid the reeling rum-drinkers and two men who had found a bed of puddles.

A short while later, under spitting skies, we arrived at Ravenhide's cabin. I heard the waves rolling in, far below. I picked out the key from my pocket and, whispering a quick prayer to Asase Ya, pushed the key into the lock and turned it sunwise. The door refused to open.

All eyes arrowed at me.

I pushed the door with my shoulder, but it resisted me. I cursed the gods. Tenoka glanced up and down the path. Marta sat on the cart and dropped her head into her hands.

I turned the key to my left. There was a clicking sound. *Thank you, Asase Ya!* I kicked it open. The hinges wailed, ripping the cobwebs that had collected in the high corners.

"Go in," I said.

As they entered, I held back to refresh Freedom with water and carrots. I stroked his flank as he licked the water. I couldn't help but think of Ravenhide and the time I spent in his cabin. Now, I released my tears, remembering how he offered me shelter on my night of escape. I took time to compose myself before I went inside and closed the door.

Marta was already stretched out on the bed. Her eyes were closed, and her snores were heavy. There were more bright garments, hats, neck scarves, and shoes in Ravenhide's chest than I could remember. Sawdust had blown in from the rear and covered most of the floor.

I stepped out to the backyard. It was full of unfinished barrels, lengths of wood, chippings, and Ravenhide's tools. The tears behind my eyes pushed again but I held them back.

The others enjoyed the view that overlooked the harbor. Asase Ya stirred the seas, sudden ripples of white crisscrossing the leaping waters. Lanterns lit up the shore and the many ships anchored below. I made out young men of Tenoka's age repairing the rigging and sails. Traders still did their business alongside the harbor road despite the late hour. But no ship was as impressive or as tall as Captain Morgan's *Satisfaction*. I was relieved it wasn't in port.

"You sailed in one of dem ships, Kemosha?" Gregory asked. I saw he had pulled on one of Ravenhide's bright yellow shirts.

"Dat shirt is drowning you," I laughed.

"Me will soon fill it out," replied Gregory. "Me will grow broad and long like Hakan. Tall enough to work on any wide boat down there so."

"Me sail inna ship plenty bigger than anyting you see in the harbor," I explained. "They called it the *Satisfaction*."

I remembered my sickness and wobbly legs.

"To get to this green land we're going to sail in one of dem down there?" asked Gregory.

"Ah smaller one," I said. "It only have to carry six of we."

"And who do we buy this small ship from?" Gregory asked.

"Misser Edward Caspian will tell us dat. Me better go and find him."

"And where you going to find him?" Tenoka asked.

"Dat big place call ah church."

"De *church*?" Tenoka repeated.

"Yes, mon. Come mek we find him. Isabella, Gregory, stay here so."

Isabella looked at the barrels as if they reminded her of a memory. She picked up one of the smaller kegs and twisted off the lid. She sniffed its contents. "Before you go find sky reader, can we drink first?"

I walked over to her and snatched the barrel from her. I pressed it against my nose. Spiced red wine.

My grin was wide.

Isabella smiled too. "Necesitamos celebrar nuestra llegada segura." *We need to celebrate our safe arrival.* "Ravenhide would like that."

I found two tankards on a shelf in Ravenhide's small cookhouse and filled them with wine. We thanked and honored the gods before we drank. I shared my mug with Isabella; Gregory tasted after Tenoka enjoyed a sip. He tipped it down his neck like he downed water. He creased up his face and spat it out. "It will help you ketch sleep," I told him. "Sip it slow."

"Nuh drink too much, Kemosha," warned Tenoka. "We have to find Misser Caspian and me nuh want to look for him when you walking strange."

Everyone laughed again. It was a nice moment, and we forgot our worries.

Taking Tenoka's advice, I allowed myself two sips

before returning my mug to Isabella. "Come, Tenoka," I said. "Let we find Edward Caspian."

"Espere," said Isabella. *Wait.*

"You want to come wid we?" I asked.

Isabella shook her head. "Me don't want to see ingleses," she said. "Demonios!"

I understood. Nobody English had treated her well. At least Mr. Caspian showed me kindness.

"Córtame el pelo antes que te vayas," Isabella said. She wanted me to cut her hair before I left.

"You sure?" I asked.

"Sí."

She collected her hair, twisted it into one long thick braid, and held it up so I could make a clean cut. I took out my sword.

"Córtalo," she said—*cut it.*

I hesitated. I swapped a quick glance with Tenoka. He nodded.

I found it harder to slice Isabella's hair than kill Captain Tate. I watched her black locks fall to the ground. I'm not sure why, but a deep sadness filled me. She urged me to crop it shorter, and I did what I was told. When I had finished, her scalp looked like the setting sun. I couldn't stop my tears.

"Gracias," Isabella said. "Ahora los ingleses no me desearán tanto." *Now the Englishmen won't desire me so much.* She offered me a broad smile. "Estaré segura."

I stared at her dead hair for a long moment before turning to go. "Nuh open de door to anyone!" I ordered.

I gave the key to Isabella and after we left, she locked the door behind us. When we passed Freedom, he neighed and fidgeted as if he wanted to accompany us. I stroked his forehead and fared him well.

"Tenoka," I said, "me cyan't remember which way is de church."

"Come," he said. "Me will show you."

"Me want to look for Lillet too. De girl wid de one leg."

"You sure she still about?" Tenoka said. "Girls of de night don't last too long inna Port Royal. Sometime buckos buy dem and tek dem away."

"Don't say dat, Tenoka."

Soon, we stood at the bottom of seven wooden steps that led to the church entrance. It was built on a rise and it offered us a generous view of the harbor below. The lights were pretty. The rain had stopped but it left pools of still water in the holes and divots in the ground. Flies and mosquitoes buzzed around my ankles, the water-logged grass singing of small creatures.

The building was now painted white, the same color as the big cross fixed upon its roof. There was even glass in the windows. But I couldn't see any lanterns or any sign that someone was inside.

"You sure Misser Caspian here so?" Tenoka asked. "Him love him drink, so he must be inna tavern."

"Him say to me to look for him in church."

"At this time?"

"Him might sleep here so," I said.

"Me nuh t'ink so," said Tenoka.

"He would nuh lie to me."

"You trust de word of ah white mon?"

I thought about it. "This one white mon," I replied. "Yes. Nobody else."

We climbed the steps and stopped at the thick double doors. We shared a glance before I tried the handle. The skies started to spit again, the breeze more alive here than it was outside Ravenhide's cabin. In my head I heard Marta call me *foolish chile*, but I turned the handle. The door opened with a long squeak and we stepped inside. I wiped rainwater from my face and stamped my feet. It was very dark inside. I sniffed sawdust, paint, and rum. The windows rattled and the wind hollered.

I could just about make out benches on either side of a central walkway. At the top of the aisle was a long table dressed in white. A single high-backed chair stood behind it.

"Him not here," said Tenoka. "Misser Caspian must be drinking inna tavern somewhere. Come, mek we go. White mon nuh like Black people in this place. This is where they pray to their white god Jesus."

Curiosity won the battle inside my head. With soft feet, I made my way to the table. It had a white-painted wooden cross sitting on it that was circled by six candles. There was an empty tankard. It stank of rum and so did the tablecloth. A painting of a white man with long hair and blue eyes hung on the back wall. Wrapped in white robes, he wore a crown of wild grass.

Tenoka didn't follow me. He stood by the door shaking his head. "Foolish chile," he said. "Dat's what Marta call you. She have good cause."

As Tenoka spoke, I heard something to my right.

I squinted: there was another door. A smaller door. I spotted a crack of light around its frame. There was a *chink, chink, chink* sound.

Maybe Edward Caspian inside of there. Let me check.

I crept my way over to this other entrance. I'd have to duck to get inside. There was no handle. Only a keyhole. A thin arrow of light shone through it. I pushed the door open. The candlelight momentarily blinded me, but I still noticed the long sword held in front of my eyes. I tipped my head back and raised my palms. My heart woke up and banged my ribs.

"Me . . . me just come here so looking for Misser Edward Caspian."

The man who held the blade was old and bent. Gray whiskers framed his cheeks. He was the same man who stood next to Captain Morgan when I had first met him. His eyes were sunk back into his head, his nose was red and crooked. He wore gray slops and a colorful jacket that I recognized from the Spanish Main. His toes were twisted and pointing in different directions. Behind him was a room with a bed, a table, and a chair. Sitting in a corner was a small barrel of rum. Pieces of eight were piled in neat rows on the table beside a thick book with a cross on it and a long candle.

"How did you get in?" the man asked. His hand trembled as it held the blade.

"De ... de door was open."

"Did you break it open? This is the Lord's house."

"No. Me nuh bruk it open. Truth me ah tell you."

Tenoka's feet scrambled to join me.

The old man stepped forward two paces. I retreated, not wanting to turn my back on him. He pushed the door closed behind him.

"I am the Lord's servant," he said. "But I will not take confession or anything else at this hour. Nor will I be disturbed. Especially not from your kind. Now *go!* Or I'll report you to the governor himself. My word to him could nail you to the gibbet! And death comes very slow on a gibbet. *Go!*"

"Me just want to know where Misser Edward Caspian there so," I said. "Captain Morgan's navigator."

The gray man slowly lowered his blade. "He was here," he said. "He confessed and prayed with me for a few days. He donated pieces of eight for the upkeep of my church. A holy man indeed. But he's gone."

"Where him gone?" Tenoka asked.

"That is not my affair," the old man replied. "I have done my godly duty. I have blessed the navigator and his ship the *Satisfaction*. They will sail with Godspeed. Now go!"

He pointed to the front door with his sword. We didn't need to be told twice.

CHAPTER 27

The Buccaneer's Elbow

Tenoka and I made our way to Antock Powell and Indika Brown's tavern. There wasn't a spare seat in the house nor any leaning space on the walls. Men hollered and chanted, smoking short pipes. It was a wonder that they could see what they were doing. Through the cloud, I spied men sitting in corners kissing and fondling their ladies of the night. There seemed to be as much ale on the floor as in the men's tankards. They sang a song that I recognized from my time aboard the *Satisfaction*. It made me smile.

> "As the dark raven crows
> This is how the tale goes
> There was an old matey from Bristol
> Whose mother called him Saul
> He made his fortune from tobacco

And sailed his young wife to pretty Tobago
She could drink, she could puff
She was very, very tough
And she could mark her fist on a pirate's eyebrow
She couldn't read a book
She wasn't the best cook
But Saul did truly love her so

Little did Saul know
She had a bucko on the go
And the father Saul thought he was
Wasn't actually so
Her children were sired by the bucko Joe
He heard a pirate spreading his news
Joe's fist delivered the devil's own bruise
Saul didn't listen to the clues
Never did Saul suspect the bucko Joe
Before fever killed him in pretty Tobago

The widow and the bucko
Had another three children
Spent Saul's pieces of eight
On a big house and a wide garden
Never mistreat a bucko
You could lose your wife
To buckos like Joe
As the dark raven crows
That is how the tale goes."

Roars of hollering and laughter filled the tavern. I even spotted Tenoka mouthing a few words of the song.

Indika Brown and a mulatto girl served drinks and hot food behind the bar. I recognized buckos and mateys from the *Satisfaction*, and they raised their tankards when they spotted us.

"Kemosha! Queen of the pot!"

"Hail the potato queen of the Spanish Main!"

"Tenoka! Young master of sails!"

"Hail the rig-walker!"

I checked the dark corners and coves of the tavern, yet Edward Caspian wasn't to be seen. Indika Brown glared at me and cursed my name, but I ignored her and approached the mulatto girl behind the counter. She looked younger than me. A red swelling colored her left cheek.

She reminded me of someone else. "Have you seen de one-legged girl?" I asked her. "They call her Lillet. She ... she sometimes comes in here so wid ... wid men who buy her company."

The girl shook her head, then leaned over and whispered into my ear, "A bucko kill her after him had him way wid her. So it go."

I paused, not wanting to believe her. *Why should me be walking and living and Lillet suffer and die?*

"You sure?" I said.

"Me sure. Me help to bury her in de patch of land behind de gibbet. She had red marks 'pon her neck. Someone say de man nuh intend to kill her. Dem say an accident."

"Who is this mon?"

"Ah bucko who come to Port Royal for two days from across de seas," the girl said. "Him had plenty pieces of eight and buy nuff drinks for him mateys. Him gone now. Sailing de great blue inna long ship. So it go."

For a moment I couldn't move. Another piece of my heart dropped out, and a ball of hot fury swelled in its place.

Me shoulda tek her wid me to de Spanish Main. Me shoulda beg Antock Powell or even Captain Morgan himself. Asase Ya, Nyame, Epo, why you never look after her? Me have to leave this wicked place.

As I cursed the gods once again, Tenoka asked seafolk if they had seen the drunken hide of Edward Caspian. No one seemed to know where the navigator was.

When we left the tavern, the rain landed hard on my head. We ran to seek shelter. "Maybe Misser Caspian drink himself to death," Tenoka said.

"No, mon," I replied. "Him *must* be about somewhere."

We checked five more taverns and two brothels. By now even I began to lose hope.

"Did you know de one-legged girl?" I asked Tenoka.

Tenoka stared at me for a short while. "Yes," he finally replied. "Me did know her. Me used to sight her from time to time."

"Did you buy her company?"

Tenoka didn't answer at first, he just looked at the ground. Puddles formed around our feet. "Kemosha," he said, "we cyan't save everybody. We cyan't tek everybody wid we."

"We cyan try," I said.

"Better to save de people who we know."

"Me did know Lillet!" I snapped.

"Me sorry, Kemosha. Sorry for all de wickedness inna Port Royal. Sorry for all de Lillets. We should go back now. Isabella, Marta, and Gregory will wonder where we there."

"There is another place," I said. "Me hear mateys on de *Satisfaction* talk about it. Ah dangerous tavern. Where buckos gamble their pieces of eight to try and mek more. They don't put any limit on what they cyan bet wid. The Buck, or someting? You remember where it there?"

"De Buccaneer's Elbow," said Tenoka. "Ah gambling house. Dat place is at de bottom of de fort. It well dangerous. Plenty sea-folk lose dem life in there."

"We not going to gamble and mek war wid anyone," I said. "We going to find Misser Caspian."

"All right," Tenoka nodded. "But if me lose me life, me duppy going to come after you, Kemosha Black!"

"Stop talk and let we go'long to this place."

Tenoka led the way. Rain bounced off my head and soaked my headscarf. We trod uphill toward the fort as the path turned muddy and slippery. We made a right turn at the stream and stepped down the steep hard steps behind the fort. Black cannons, longer than me, were aimed out to sea. A man in uniform wearing a three-pointed hat stood on the battlements, peering through a spyglass. Apart from the tossing waters, I couldn't imagine what he could see.

Down and down we went. Rainwater dripped along the solid walls. The staircase was narrow and winding.

We reached the ground and found ourselves close to the seafront. The waves crashed onto the shore. We crossed a strip of sodden grass. There was a short, cobbled street with a row of three stores built on it. The nearest one was a goldsmith's, which had iron railings in front of its entrance. Its padlock was bigger than a sea-rider's dinner plate. In the middle was a store that sold shoes, boots, and shiny buckles, and the place at the end was a tavern. It had to be the Buccaneer's Elbow: a sign with a strong arm clutching pieces of eight and gold nuggets hung above its entrance. It swayed whenever a gust of wind caught it. We stood outside, the rain lashing our faces. Dark shapes bobbed up and down in the vexed seas.

"You sure you want to go inside?" Tenoka said.

"If we don't find Misser Caspian, what are we going to do?" I replied. "We have to leave this place. Look what happen to Lillet."

We entered the tavern, going down three steps. There were candles on tables instead of lanterns, and the ceiling was low. Men huddled around tables full of coins, shoe buckles, scarves, and bright-colored jackets. I'm sure I spotted a glint of gold here and there. Some held cards and dice in their hands. Suspicion and greed marked their eyes. Swords hung from their belts and cross-straps, while daggers of all shapes were fixed to their shirts and jackets. Earrings that could've looped my neck spiked their ears. There wasn't much talk. The ladies behind the bar grew their hair long, wore tight bodices, and smiled filthy smiles. Men in long hats whispered in shadows. The stench of rum almost made me sneeze.

"Stay here so, Kemosha," Tenoka said. "This place well dangerous. Let me check if Misser Caspian here."

I ignored him and walked around the walls of the tavern. Men's eyes followed me. I tried to avoid their gaze. My fingertips brushed the handle of my sword. My heartbeat bounced hard in my chest.

"How much for you, dark one?" one of the men asked.

"I will pay a piece of eight," said another.

"I will pay two!"

"Who's your owner?"

"I will pay three pieces of eight if *two* of us can entertain you until my ship sets sail in two days."

"If you clean my room and cook me a good dinner every day, I will give you a bed to sleep in."

I stayed silent, searching for Tenoka. He held his arm up, pointing at someone slumped in a corner. I had to barge my way through the crowd to reach him. He had found Edward Caspian.

But is him dead?

He lay across a bench. He wore strange garments, and no shoes covered his toes. I sniffed the ale and rum off him, and he had grown a beard since I had last seen him.

I nudged him. "Misser Caspian!"

He didn't move.

"Misser Caspian?"

"Him dead," said Tenoka.

"Him nuh dead," I said. "Him still breathing. Come mek we tek him out."

We picked up an arm each and stood him upright. He tried to open his eyes but couldn't manage it. Dribble ran over his lips. We turned toward the door, eyes watching our every move. Just before we reached the exit, a tall man stepped in front of us. He wore a high dented hat that nearly kissed the ceiling. A lime-green shirt wrapped his lean chest. Gold buckles glinted on his shoes. The five teeth he had were rotten.

"Is that your master?" the man asked. He had a strange accent.

"No," Tenoka responded. "This is Misser Edward Caspian. He's Captain Morgan's navigator."

"If he's not your master, then what are you doing with him?"

"Teking him to ah place where him cyan rest him head," I said.

"We going to fix him up good," Tenoka added. "Mek sure him eat nice and give him good water to drink."

"And why do you want to take care of Mr. . . . ."

"Misser Caspian," Tenoka finished the sentence. "Captain Morgan's navigator. Him going to help we buy ah small boat."

"A boat?" The man grinned and bared his five teeth. "You have pieces of eight to buy a boat?"

"Yes, mon—"

I punched Tenoka in his back before he could finish his words. "Mek we pass!" I shouted. "Mek we pass!"

Using our elbows and shoulders, we jostled our way through. Edward Caspian couldn't walk at all. We dragged him over the cobbled street, the strip of grass, and to the bottom of the fort steps. Hard rain smacked our faces and seemed to make Edward Caspian heavier.

"Why you tell gap-teet' stranger we buying ah boat!" I raged at Tenoka. "Your mout' too loose! If tough rain nuh fall, me woulda chop off you tongue!"

Before Tenoka could reply, Edward Caspian cut in: "Marie, Marie."

We took our rest at the base of the fort. I decided against chasing my argument with Tenoka. His eyes told me he was sorry. We allowed Edward Caspian to drop to the ground, so his head rested against the fort wall. The spray from the crashing waves mingled with the cold rain.

"Marie."

"Who is this Marie?" Tenoka asked.

I was about to answer but something caught my attention: we had been followed.

The man with the long dented hat and lime-green shirt had chased us down. Another fellow was with him. He was shorter, fatter, his white slops tight around his thighs, and his feet barely squeezed into his shoes. His hungry eyes were close together like an owl's.

"You will not buy any boat," said the taller man. "We will relieve you of your pieces of eight and any other coins you carry. How did you Negroes come to have the means to buy a boat?"

"We never t'ief it," I replied. "And we don't have anyting wid we."

"Dat's de truth," said Tenoka. "We sailed de great blue wid Captain Morgan himself. We signed our Articles of Agreement."

"Your lies will see you on the gibbet!" the tall man threatened.

A chill of dread raced along my spine.

"We will let you live if you pay swiftly," said the wide man.

"We have little time to parlay," said the tall man. "Give us your pieces of eight. Now!"

"Me nuh carry one piece of eight wid me," I lied. In truth, I had my bag of hogskin tied around my hips. *Dem would have to kill me first before me even give dem de string.*

I thought of Ravenhide, being killed by a sword in his back. In my mind I watched him being lowered into his pit. I saw white men on horses attacking Hakan, Iyana, and my people at the plantation. I imagined Lillet being choked to death by a drunken bucko. I remembered Oliver Marsh, wanting his wicked way with me before I stabbed him and escaped.

Fury erupted in my chest. My hand gripped my

sword and I rapidly unsheathed it. Blood sailed through my veins. The vengeance of my ancestors flowed with it. I swapped a quick glance with Tenoka. He nodded. He knew what I was about to do.

I sprang to my feet and in one movement, slashed the tall man's neck. I hit my mark perfectly. Blood gushed freely. He fell in an instant.

The fat man ran away—if you could call it running. He slipped over in the rain, got up, glanced back to check if I was hunting him, and hurried on again. I'm not sure how long I stood there, watching the dead man's body. It didn't move.

For a moment I thought of rifling through the tall man's pockets. *If him have any pieces of eight, him won't need it now.*

"Kemosha!" Tenoka called. "Come!"

I wiped my reddened blade on the wet grass and sheathed it. We picked up Edward Caspian and hauled him up the steep stone staircase. My leg muscles cried, but somehow we managed to pull him up to the battlements. The man in uniform peering through the spyglass had disappeared. *Thank you, Asase Ya.*

"Come, Kemosha!" Tenoka urged. "We have to get him back to Ravenhide's cabin."

"Nuh, mon," I said. "Me have to rest up."

Tenoka kept Edward Caspian upright as I sucked in all the air I could. Asase Ya stirred the skies, Epo shook the seas. Thunder echoed in the distance, lightning lit up the heavens. I tasted rainwater on my lips.

I climbed to my feet. "If Edward Caspian don't get we ah boat, me going to kill him meself!" I said.

"Even if him do buy de boat," Tenoka said, "we cyan't leave while de wind too tough."

The path was not a path anymore. We slipped and slid down to Ravenhide's cabin. By the time Isabella opened the door, we were covered in mud. Isabella locked the door behind us and I dropped to the floor in exhaustion. Marta spotted my fall.

"You find him!" she said, pointing at Edward Caspian. "This mon cyan read de stars in de sky? Him don't look like him cyan read de ground him walk on!"

Tenoka and Marta helped Edward Caspian to the bed and laid him down. I was too weary to move. Isabella insisted that I drink a mug of water before I fell asleep.

As the night wore on, I pushed opened my eyes now and then and spotted Gregory watching over me.

CHAPTER 28

The Long Wait

It was still dark when I woke. I no longer heard the rain lashing Ravenhide's roof. I was stretched out on the floor with Ravenhide's garments bunched under my head. I sensed a presence to my right: Isabella. She checked over me to see if I had any injuries. *Only tired muscles and ah weary mind.* My eyes hadn't got accustomed to her scalped head, but her lips curled into a pretty smile. She kissed me twice on the cheek and picked out grit from my hair.

I scanned the room and found Gregory, Tenoka, and Marta asleep. Edward Caspian was still in the bed.

"Te ves tan hermosa cuando tienes los ojos cerrados," Isabella said. *You look so beautiful when your eyes are closed.*

"Why you nuh sleep?" I asked.

"Tenoka say one should keep watch," she replied. "And check path."

"Me kill ah mon," I said. "Me draw me sword and

cut him neck before him could mek ah move. So we must leave this place. They will come after we and me nuh want to finish me life 'pon ah gibbet."

"Tenoka say no one follow," Isabella said. "Ketch you rest."

"No, we cyan't rest. We have to buy de boat, buy some food."

"Kemosha!" Isabella raised her voice. "Everybody tired. Wait till sun rise." She leaned toward me, held my jaws within her palms, and kissed me on the lips. "Rest, Kemosha. Save strength for morning."

I tried to capture sleep again, but it escaped me. After Isabella fell asleep, I went out to the backyard, sat on a barrel, and watched the dawn roll in. I imagined Mama was up there in the heavens, keeping watch over us.

Marta was the first to rise. She joined me in the backyard. The dark clouds had cleared, and a new sun peeped over the eastern hills. There was an amber light filling the Jamaican morning, reflecting off the sails in the harbor. It was very pretty.

"We have to buy this boat today," I said to her. "Let we leave dis wicked place."

I closed my eyes and saw Captain Tate falling at my feet. Then I watched the tall man from the Buccaneer's Elbow drop to the ground. *Kemosha Black, you kill two white mon! You will end you good life spiked to ah gibbet. Sweet Mama will nuh want to see you end dat way. And you have led de good people who you claim to love to dem death.*

"You all right, Kemosha?" Marta asked. "You don't look right."

"Me nuh feel right," I admitted. "Maybe once we riding de waters, me will feel ah liccle better."

"Speak for you one," said Marta. "Me is one foolish woman going out to de great blue where de waters never finish."

Later, Marta and I made a big breakfast of fruits, soursop, and hog meat. Edward Caspian still slept. I nudged him on the shoulder but that didn't stir him. I pinched his arm but still no response. I punched him on the jaw. His eyes opened wide. He rubbed his chin and focused on me. "Kemosha!"

"Misser Caspian," I said, "it look like you loving you sleep too much, so you have to excuse me."

"Er, that is all right, Kemosha. I . . . I was very tired."

"Me don't have too much time to talk," I said. "We must go down to de harbor road and buy ah boat."

Edward Caspian sat up, blinked, and palmed his jaw again. He glanced at Marta, Isabella, Tenoka, and Gregory. "Where's Ravenhide?"

I dropped my head. "Him dead. Him now talking to we ancestors."

"How did he die?"

I didn't want to answer. I didn't want to see the image of the pit again, nor his body being lowered into it.

"In his own way he was a holy man," Edward said after a pause. "A good matey. The best barrel maker in Port Royal and, by Captain Morgan's eye, a fine swordsman."

"Overseer kill him at Captain Tate plantation," Gregory said suddenly.

Silence.

It was still hard to accept. A moment's sorrow stopped me from speaking. I found it difficult not to allow revenge into my mind.

Edward stood up. He stretched his arms and rubbed his neck. "And Captain Tate?"

I swapped a glance with Tenoka. For a short moment, I wondered if I should share this news. "Him dead too," I said. "All de overseer dead or run off."

"If these tidings reach Antock Powell or Captain Morgan, they will come for you," Edward warned. "The English do not tolerate insurrection. Especially from a race who they feel superior to. They'll hunt you down to all the corners of Jamaica. They'll never stop."

"Why do you t'ink we come for you?" I said. "We need to buy ah boat."

"Before we buy or hire a boat, may I eat or drink something?" Edward asked. "I feel like I'm carrying a cannonball inside my head."

"We found you at the Buccaneer's Elbow," said Tenoka. "It must be drink you still carry inna your head."

"The Buccaneer's Elbow?" Edward repeated. "I . . . I don't remember."

"You don't *want* to remember," I said. "Robber mon drink and gamble there so."

"What you doing at ah dangerous place like dat?" Tenoka asked.

Edward tried to remember. He fingered the wooden cross that hung around his neck. "Sometimes . . . sometimes a man wants to forget his sins. And I have sinned."

I didn't understand what he meant.

"Me find some bush tea," said Marta. "Let me boil some water and give you ah tankard of dat. Me will give you ah liccle food too."

"That is kind of you," said Edward.

I watched him eat his breakfast and sip his tea. When he finished, he licked his fingers and smiled at me. His eyes seemed a little clearer. I guessed his head felt a little lighter. "Kemosha," he said, "how many pieces of eight do you have?"

I called Tenoka over and asked him to share his money with us.

Tenoka reached into his pockets and emptied them out onto the top of a barrel. I did the same with the coins I had. Edward counted.

"Me give you all de coins me have," Tenoka said. "But me been t'inking . . . Me nuh sure if me cyan sail wid you to ah new island."

I gave him a long stare.

"Don't forget, Kemosha," Tenoka went on, "you have you people here so. My people are still here so on this island. And de masser's lash at their plantation is just as cruel as de one you come from."

The thought that he might not sail with me bruised my heart, but I understood.

"Me will do me best to help you reach de boat and sail away," Tenoka added. "Me will never forget how you open me eyes to we people and how dem still ah suffer. Ravenhide would say de same ting."

I had forgotten about Tenoka's family and those he left behind. I embraced him: he was a brother from another mother. "T'ank you for everyting."

"Seventy-three pieces of eight," Edward finished his count. "It won't buy you a big boat but maybe I can go down to the harbor and barter for a pinnace to rent. I'm sure I can find a willing captain to trade with me."

"Ah pinnace?" I said. "What is ah pinnace?"

"Ah small boat," Tenoka answered. "They have two or three sails. Sometime captains use dem to sail around de island. Captain Morgan have three ah dem. Maybe four."

"They have oars too," said Edward. "But if the wind blesses us, we can set sail with that."

"Oars?" I said.

"Long pieces of wood to move de boat by hand and strong arm," replied Tenoka. "If breeze nuh blow, de boat nuh go nowhere."

Edward wiped his hands on his slops and belched. He glanced at the ocean before facing me again. "It might be best that I go to the harbor alone and barter for this boat."

"No," I said. "Me coming wid you! Me nuh want you

to find youself inna Buccaneer's Elbow and lose all we pieces of eight. Is dat how you lose you pretty clothes and you shoes?"

"Kemosha," Edward lowered his voice, "how is it going to look if a navigator inquires about the hiring of a boat with a Negro girl with him?"

"Me want to mek sure that you don't tek ah voyage into de nearest tavern and drink off everyting we have," I argued.

"I wouldn't do that to you," said Edward. "I give you my word. I'd swear on the Bible if I could find one."

"Me nuh know about any Bible. Me don't even know what dat is. But you cyan promise Asase Ya, Nyame, and Epo."

"Asase who?" Edward said. "Nyame?"

"You're ah white mon," Gregory cut in. He approached the navigator and pointed a finger at him. "You will tek we pieces of eight and go buy boat for youself."

Edward shook his head. "That would be another sin."

"Me coming wid you!" I pressed.

"That won't work," insisted Edward. "Any captain will be suspicious of me wanting to hire a pinnace with a Negro girl in my company. I have no papers to say that I even own you."

Frustration replaced my fury.

Isabella sat beside me. She held my hands and gazed at me for a little while before she spoke. "Debes permitirle comprar solo el bote," she said. *You must allow him to buy the boat alone.*

"No," I said. "Why you talking like this, Isabella? Me have to go wid him. Misser Caspian love him drink too much."

"No! Kemosha!" Isabella shouted at me. For a moment I was shocked. I'd never imagined she would raise her voice at me. I glared at her hard.

She shook her head. "Debes confiar," she added. *You must trust.*

Could this be de same Isabella who mek beautiful love to me? I snatched my hands away from her, stood up, and marched to the back of the yard. Everyone was silent behind me.

After a while, Isabella joined me. We looked out to the great blue. The seas were calm: the ships in the harbor barely moved. Clouds separated and drifted away. We shared an awkward glance. For a short moment, I wished we were back in her hideout in the Kingston hills. I dreamed of eating fried plantain with her, bathing in fresh waters, and listening to morning birdsong.

"Ravenhide era de un color diferente," she said. "Pero confiaba en él." *Ravenhide was a different color than me, but I trusted him.*

She went back to the others. I closed my eyes and tried to imagine a new land where I didn't have to worry about trusting anyone. I longed for Ravenhide to be with me. *Him coulda go wid Edward to buy de boat.*

I turned around. "Sí," I said. "Go and buy de boat.

And buy some food too. Fruits and vegetables. Hog meat will spoil under de sun. Tek Freedom wid you. Be gentle wid him. If you lash him, you will have me sword to answer."

Edward nodded. He selected garments and shoes from Ravenhide's chest and changed clothes. He used a dagger that he found in Ravenhide's trunk to shave his beard. He collected all the pieces of eight, put them in his pockets, and drank a tankard of water. He wiped his mouth on his sleeve before he approached me again.

"As the Lord is my witness," he said, "I shall return and sail you to a new island."

He left. I checked along the path and locked the door.

Gregory shook his head. "Kemosha, you shoulda never trust ah white mon."

"Me had no choice," I replied.

Until the sun reached the middle of the sky, we sat in the backyard, swapping childhood memories. I reminded Gregory how I taught him to walk. "You had Mama's spirit," I said. "Always wandering off!"

"You remember when we had to hide Gregory in de kitchen when Captain's wife come to check on dinner?" Marta said.

"Yes," I nodded. "Dat don't leave me memories. Me had to push him down inna de vegetable barrel."

"You hurt me head!" laughed Gregory.

"Better to hurt you head than you lose it."

"You hand too tough," Gregory joked.

"De same hand stroke you head when you sick."

"And de same hand lick me when me get too close to Captain's big house." Gregory gazed at me and smiled. He didn't have to say he loved me. But it was hard not to think of Mama.

We tried to sleep from midday but only Gregory captured any real rest.

The sun walked its way into the western sky. I couldn't help but glance at the front door or look down into the harbor.

We have no more pieces of eight to buy food. Freedom and de cart gone. Maybe Edward run away and white mon in uniform will come for we. We will end we good life spiked to ah gibbet. Mulatto girls will dig our pits. Me hope somebody will be left to chant ah song of freedom.

My anxiety caused me to walk to all corners of the backyard. I kicked a small barrel and bruised my big toe. *Arrrrgggghhhh.*

I had to do something.

"Tenoka!" I called. "If Edward nuh come back before de sun fall, me and you will have to t'ief ah boat. Dat's de only ting we cyan do."

"T'ief ah boat!" Tenoka said. "Kemosha, trying to t'ief ah boat is ah mighty quick way to get we killed."

"Me will go out to look for one if you come wid me or not!"

Tenoka shook his head. "Crazy you ah crazy, Kemosha Black!"

"Foolish chile," said Marta.

"Me might be crazy and foolish," I said, "but me nuh want to wait here so and be led by vex white mon to de gibbet."

The sun sank beyond the western hills. There was a pink sunset. The still seas looked so inviting that even Marta might have considered dipping her toe in there. No sight or sound of Edward. No swishing tail from Freedom. *Me cyan't believe it! After all de trouble to find him.*

"Tenoka," I called, "you ready to look for boat?"

A long pause. "Yes, me ready," he agreed finally.

"Cyan me come too?" asked Gregory.

"No, Gregory. Stay here so. Nuh worry youself. Me and Tenoka will find ah boat. Even if me have to kill all de buckos, mateys, and robber mon inna Port Royal."

Before we left, I checked everybody's faces. Marta wept. Gregory shook his head. "Me tell you not to trust de white mon," he said. "All me life dem give we angry lash."

Isabella sucked in a big breath. She tried to raise a smile, but it stopped at the corners of her lips. I threw her the front door key. Isabella caught it and nodded. "Pisa con cuidado," she said, locking the door behind us. *Tread carefully.*

"Kemosha," Tenoka said, "this is Port Royal. Nobody leave their boat alone here so. There are all kinda robber mon and t'ief all about."

"Then we have to *tek* one by de speed of me sword," I responded.

We started down the hill. The small creatures in the grass gave their comments. Passing a roadside tavern, we heard raised voices. We ducked under the open window and listened. There were three men talking.

"Negroes killed Captain Tate and most of his over-seers!" a growly voice said. He sounded like he dined on Ravenhide's chippings.

"Thaaaat's what happennnns when yoooou give them tooooo much meat," slurred a drunk.

A tankard was slammed on a table. A girl shrieked from farther away.

"Treat them like the animals they are, and they'll be obedient again," said the rough voice.

"Let the ones still living see their savages nailed to the cross!" said another.

"Haaaang them hiiiigh from a sturrrrdy treeeee," added the drunk.

"Or lynch them from the crow's nest!" the growly man shouted.

New cruel voices joined the conversation.

"That'll be good sport."

"They're sending word to the governor."

"He won't suffer this."

"The gibbets will be straining."

"We'll soon be called to arms."

We crouched low and hurried on.

We left the path and made our way through wild grassland and prickly bushes. The ground fell steeply as we approached the shoreline. We picked our way down over rocks, stones, and hard mud until our feet met the sand. We avoided the guards on the Port Royal Road and rejoined the path where it narrowed into a long skinny finger cutting through the sea. On both sides, the waves rolled in gently. We heard the shouts of men working on ships in the distance. Asase Ya had filled the sky with stars. It was humid, my top garment stuck to my skin.

Someone was on the road. We stood still and peered through the Jamaican night. *Asase Ya! Me hope it not ah mon in uniform.* There wasn't anything to hide behind, save the waters. We hit the ground and lay flat. I lifted my head. I didn't want to kill again but I groped for my sword's handle.

I peered closer: a man with a donkey.

"Is it just de one?" I asked Tenoka.

"Me t'ink so," said Tenoka. "Him singing ah song."

Tenoka had better ears than I, for I heard the chanting a moment after he did.

*"I want to lay down with my virgin Marie once again
And caress her smooth skin beyond her hem . . ."*

CHAPTER 29

The Boy with the Long Black Hair

Tenoka and I grinned at each other. Then we laughed.

"When him reach, me going kiss him 'pon de cheek then me going cut him up like ah hog for being so late," I said.

"Me just hope him rent de boat," said Tenoka. "Otherwise, you have to swim to this new land. And Marta nuh love de water."

As Edward Caspian approached, I prayed he hadn't been drinking. But he seemed to walk straight enough.

"Hail the potato queen of the Spanish Main," he said when he spotted me. "And what brings you out this far onto the Port Royal Road? I fear trust is lacking in you, Kemosha Black."

Freedom sniffed and snuffled when he recognized

me. I stroked his back and saw that his cart was full of fruits and vegetables.

"*What bring me out here?*" I said. "Your late hour! The night is thick. Did you hire de boat?"

Edward smiled. I was relieved when I couldn't sniff rum or ale on his breath. "Indeed I have," he said. "Fifty pieces of eight I paid Captain David Griffith. He wanted a high price for the four days of hire I requested. I told him I need it to visit Captain Morgan at his Firefly estate."

"And did this Captain David Griffith accept dat reason?" I asked.

"He took my pieces of eight quick enough. He knows how important I am to Captain Morgan. He also wants to build a big house along the coast to challenge Captain Morgan's Firefly palace."

"Did he ask why you needed to see Captain Morgan?"

"Indeed he did," Edward replied. "Captain Griffith is a suspicious man. I told him that buckos and mateys are becoming reckless and murderous in Port Royal. There have been seven killings in five days. They need order."

I thought of the tall man I killed at the feet of the fort. I couldn't rid his bent hat out of my mind. I wondered if they had discovered his dead body yet. *Of course they have, Kemosha. You shoulda pull him body out to sea and let Epo have him.*

"They need Captain Morgan and another adventure to the Spanish Main," Edward went on. "Captains prefer mateys carving Spanish necks rather than English ones. And that's not a lie in God's face."

"Where is de boat?" Tenoka asked.

"By the far side of Kingston Harbour," Edward revealed. "The very last one anchored there. I have paid a young rigger boy to keep watch on it until my return."

"How much you pay him?" I asked.

"One piece of eight. He will receive another upon my return. When he clutched the piece of eight, his grin was wider than the distance between Port Royal and Bristol."

"Should we go back to Ravenhide's cabin wid you?" I asked.

Edward considered it. "No. Go to the boat but don't board it. Stay a distance from it. There are hills overlooking that part of the bay that you can hide behind. The boat has three sails and a black-painted hull. It carries the banner of the triple sword—Captain Griffith's mark."

"Triple sword?"

"Yes," Edward said. "On a white background. No hungry pirate should dare steal it, but this is Port Royal. The rigger boy appears to be the same age as your brother Gregory. He has long black hair—if I were his English father, I'd question his mother. Don't let him see you. Young buckos have loose tongues."

"What about Marta, Isabella, and Gregory?" asked Tenoka.

"I'll pick them up," said Edward. "Three don't look

so suspicious as five on the Port Royal Road. Now begone! When the boy leaves, board the boat."

Edward pulled Freedom, but the donkey was reluctant to leave. Only when I stroked his side did he start again.

Tenoka and I kept close to the bushes and hills that overlooked the harbor road. We heard shouts and cries in the distance. Taverns and bars emptied. White men were assembling: vengeance for Captain Tate was in the air.

We crept low behind the folds and shoulders of the hills. We darted in back of trees and took cover behind thick reeds and broad leaves. The land poked out toward sea in a long arc. Smaller ships and boats were anchored there. Lanterns seemed to stretch out into the ocean: it was beautiful to see. We used the last light as our guide.

As we pushed on, the land dipped and rose in a series of low valleys. My feet were sore, and my leg muscles demanded rest.

"Kemosha, you want to stop for ah liccle while?" Tenoka said. "You look like you want to sleep till de next moon."

"Me all right," I lied. "Come, let's forward."

We crested the final rise and finally I could see the last boat. It had three white sails, a black-painted hull, and a lantern on deck. I couldn't quite make out the image on the banner that fluttered atop the main mast.

"Tenoka! See it there!"

"Me nuh see de rigger boy," Tenoka said.

I concentrated my eyes. All I could see was the light on the boat and the vast, dark seas behind it.

"We have to move ah liccle closer," I said.

"All right."

We started down the hill. Tenoka spotted a dark shape in the grass. "Hold up! Dat is him. Him sleeping! Cyan you believe it. Misser Caspian pay him a piece of eight *to sleep!*"

"Go back," I said. "Go back."

We hid in the hollow of a valley. Lying on my back, I counted the stars. I hoped Mama and Ravenhide sent us good fortune.

Tenoka chewed on a blade of grass, deep in thought. "Me will go wid you to this new island," he said after a while. "You need ah man of size on board. But me have to go back wid Misser Caspian. Me have to try and free me people from me plantation. Me want to see me mama and tek her to freedom."

It hit me hard that if we reached our new land, I might never see Tenoka again. I turned away from him so he wouldn't notice my tears. It took me a long while to reply.

"Me understand," I said finally. "Maybe you cyan go'long to de hills and join Hakan and Iyana. Maybe dem cyan help you. And your mama must ah wonder if your good foot walking . . . or not."

"Yes," Tenoka said, "dat is me plan. You have Marta, Gregory, and Isabella to keep you company and look out for you. Ravenhide dead and gone now. Who do me have?"

"If . . . if you cyan't free nobody from you plantation," I replied, "you still have all of we."

Tenoka smiled and wiped away a tear. I'd never seen so much pain in his young face. I hugged him and he cried on my shoulder. *Me should not forget him only fourteen.*

"Nuh tell Gregory about this," he laughed.

"Nuh worry," I said, "me won't."

A thin light of gold had sneaked over the eastern hills, when I heard a far-off noise. A trotting sound. Tenoka had fallen asleep. I elbowed him in the ribs. "Somebody coming. Wake up, mon! Wake up!"

We crawled to the top of the rise. Below, Gregory led Freedom. Edward, Isabella, and Marta walked behind him.

"At last!" Tenoka said. "At last dem come!"

He went to stand up, but I pulled him back down. "You nuh listen to what Edward say? We don't mek ah move till de rigger boy wid de long black hair has gone."

Sure enough, we watched the boy approach Edward. The navigator gave him payment while Gregory untied Freedom. He offered Freedom's rope to the boy.

I stood up. "Dem cyan't do dat," I said. "Ah me donkey dat and him serve me good!"

"Cool your temper," said Tenoka. "Freedom have to go to somebody else. How is him going stand up in ah small boat? Nuh worry, Kemosha. Asase Ya will look after Freedom."

The rigger boy with the long black hair led Freedom along the coastline. I couldn't push my tears back. I watched until they became a black dot in the Jamaican dawn.

CHAPTER 30

Fly Away Home

"Come, Kemosha!" Tenoka called. "Time to step 'pon de boat."

He ran down the hill but I took my time. Ravenhide entered my mind. *Him woulda loved dis moment. Ah calm sea to escape to. Ah new land. Ravenhide, why did Asase Ya tek you from me?*

"Come, Kemosha!" Marta called. She smiled a broad smile.

Gregory and Isabella waved.

I had to shake my head to rid Ravenhide's image from my thoughts. I didn't want to carry my sadness on board. I looked up and spotted the triple-sword banner flapping atop the main mast—Captain David Griffith's mark. The blades crossed each other.

"Hail Isabella!" I cried. "Hail Marta and Gregory! Hail de navigator! Kemosha ah come!"

I waded into the sea up to my thighs. The sand beneath the waters was soft and yielding. Isabella pulled me on board. The boat wasn't as steady as the *Satisfaction* and it took me a moment to find my balance. Isabella held my shoulders and gazed at me for a long while. She placed her palms around my jaws in that soothing way of hers. Her eyes sparkled under the morning sun. "Los piratas viejos nos roban pero ya estamos libres de ellos," she said. *Old pirates rob us but now we're free of them.*

"Sí," I nodded.

She hugged me tight and wouldn't let me go, until Marta, Gregory, and Tenoka joined us.

Meanwhile, Edward sat down at the bow of the boat, closed his eyes, and prayed over his tools and instruments. After a short while he gave instructions to Tenoka to adjust the sails. "The Lord has granted us some wind," he said. "Not much, but enough for a fair sail. The sun rises quick, so let us depart."

Tenoka adjusted the rigging.

"Weigh anchor!" called Edward.

Isabella and I pulled up the rope that was attached to the stone anchor.

Then Isabella paused. She shielded her eyes from the sun with her right hand and peered toward the shore. I followed her direction of sight.

"Hombres!" Isabella cried. "Hombres a caballo." *Men on horses.*

"Drop the anchor!" demanded Edward. "Drop the anchor!"

I couldn't move. It was as if my blood had stopped flowing. Coldness flushed through me instead. Many horses galloped toward us. My heart beat as fast as their forelegs covered the ground. *Boom de boom, boom de boom, boom de boom.* Their hooves kicked up sand and disturbed the crushing waves. Ripples of white crisscrossed the great blue. The gibbet erected on the Port Royal Road grew enormous in my mind.

Isabella dropped the anchor as I stood very still. *Me cyan't believe it!*

"In the sea!" Edward cried. "In the sea! But not you, Tenoka."

Gregory dived in first. Then Isabella. Marta shook her head. "Me cyan't go in," she cried. "Me cyan't go in. Waters will tek me!"

She backed away from the boat's gunwale. I managed to flex my fingers and move my feet. I grabbed Marta's wrist and pulled her overboard. We plunged into the warm seas in a big splash. Marta frantically flapped and flailed. I reached out to a ladder on the side of the boat, clutching on for my sweet life as Marta wrapped her arms around my neck. She spat out seawater. "Nuh let me go under," she said. "Epo, me calling on you!"

I snapped my head to look out for Isabella and Gregory: they were holding onto rigging two arm lengths from us.

"They going to ketch we!" Marta panicked. "They going to nail we 'pon ah gibbet!"

"If you don't quiet you mout' we will all dead," I said. "Now, hold onto you tongue!"

The hooves pounded closer. I heard the splashes on

the shore. Then a shout: "Navigator Caspian! Navigator Caspian! Do not set sail yet. I have news."

"What news do you bring, Captain Griffith?" Edward called back.

A wave rolled in and soared above Marta's mouth. She coughed and spluttered. Seawater filled her nose. "Me going to dead," she said.

"Your weight pushing me down," I whispered to her. "Hold onto de rope. You not going to dead."

Marta sneezed and did what she was told.

"Slaves have revolted at the Tate plantation," Captain Griffith announced. "They have killed the Captain and his good men. They have fled to the high hills. Make sure you carry this news to Captain Morgan."

"I will do as you command, sir."

There was a pause. I checked on Gregory. His mouth was open, and his eyes were wide. Pure fear caused him to shiver in the waters. I pushed my finger to my lips.

"Who is this Negro with you?" Captain Griffith asked.

"Tenoka," replied Edward. "A fine servant of the *Satisfaction*. He worked as a rigger when we last paid a visit to the Spanish Main. On a previous voyage, he worked as a powder monkey. He has the quickest hands I have ever seen refilling a cannon. He will assist me sailing to Firefly."

"Can he be trusted?" Captain Griffith asked. "I can give you one of my men to escort you. Maybe even two?"

"Tenoka has been a faithful servant for many years," Edward said. "Captain Morgan himself favors him. I would not like to deprive you of any of your men, as you need them all to find these wretched slaves."

"And find them we will," declared Captain Griffith. "More gibbets will be built on the Port Royal Road. We will watch their flesh rot and their bones splinter under this cursed sun."

For a moment, I loosened my grip and sank under the waters. Marta pulled me back up. My eyes stung and I tasted salt on my lips.

"When you have delivered your news to Captain Morgan," Griffith continued, "bring my boat to Old Harbour. I may need use of it."

"Of course, Captain Griffith," said Edward. "I fare you well."

"And I fare you well too," said Captain Griffith. "I trust by the next time we meet, there'll be a band of Negroes nailed from Port Royal to the harbor road to feast our eyes on."

"I will enjoy the view," Edward said.

The waters stirred. There was a long silence.

"Dem gone?" Marta asked.

"Me nuh t'ink so," I replied.

Finally, hooves kicked up the sand once again. I closed my eyes and thanked Asase Ya.

"Shall me climb up?" asked Marta. "Me nuh want to stay in de waters no more. Beast wid long tail might come for me. And Tenoka say dem always hungry."

Gregory didn't wait for my permission. He scrambled aboard as if the sea gods were hunting him.

We followed Gregory's lead and clambered over the side of the boat. Marta landed with a solid thud.

Moments later, we huddled in a circle. As we dripped on deck, Edward asked us to close our eyes. We did what we were told. The navigator spoke a few words.

"Our dear Lord," he began, "I know I have sinned, but I ask you for your eternal forgiveness. May I also plead for your divine protection on this new voyage. I hope it may lead to a new land and a new start for those I have sinned against. *Amen.*"

We opened our eyes and peered at each other. Silence and smiles.

"Hold up!" I said. "Hold up! Close your eyes once more and hold hands."

Even Edward shut his eyes. Isabella found my left hand and Gregory held my right.

"Asase Ya," I said. "Nyame and mighty Epo. Look over we and guide we to ah new land where cruel and wicked mon never trod. And in dis new land, mek sure you grow plenty plantain tree."

Isabella burst out laughing and everyone followed.

"Weigh anchor!" cried Edward.

Gregory sprinted to the rope and pulled up the heavy stone as Tenoka made minor adjustments to the rigging and sails. Edward studied his tools. Marta gazed at the waters as if they might attack her.

I found Isabella and hugged her hard.

"Nosotras tenemos una segunda vida," she said. *We have a second life.*

"Sí," I nodded, then glanced at the heavens. "Volamos a un nuevo hogar, Mamá." *We're flying away to a new home, Mama.*

This was meant to be.

The End

AUTHOR'S NOTE

After twenty-two years of not seeing each other, I was finally reunited with my father, Alfred, in the fall of 1987.

One morning, I was sitting on his veranda in Old Harbour, Jamaica, enjoying the early-morning sun. Alfred came out wearing his baseball cap. He admired his beautiful almond tree that stood proud in his front garden. He asked me what famous or historical sites I would like to visit during my stay in Jamaica.

First on my list was Nine Miles, Bob Marley's hometown, and where he was laid to rest. I simply could not leave Jamaica without paying homage to my idol. Being a poet/lyricist and a fledgling writer at the time, my second choice was the Firefly estate where Noel Coward and Sir Henry Morgan once resided. I said it would be a bonus if he could also escort me to the nearby James Bond beach where Ursula Andress emerged from a turquoise sea in the movie *Dr. No*. My final selection was the legendary pirate capital, Port Royal. In my head, I still had visions of the actor Errol Flynn doing his swashbuckling Hollywood thing.

Not being a massive fan of reggae music and possibly suspicious of me wandering off to have a drink if we journeyed to Nine Miles, Alfred decided to take me on a day trip to Port Royal.

I was immediately fascinated by the history of Port Royal and how the pirates, who had their base in 1650s Hispaniola (modern-day Haiti and the Dominican Republic), were kicked out by the island's Spanish rulers and made their way to Jamaica.

Launching attacks on the Spanish wherever they found their vessels, the pirates of Port Royal, including Sir Henry Morgan, became incredibly wealthy. The governor of Jamaica at the time, Sir Thomas Modyford, a good friend of Sir Henry Morgan, decided to grant permission to the pirates not only to attack Spanish ships but also to protect Jamaica from Spanish invasion. They were rebranded *privateers*.

In the mid-1660s, Port Royal became one of the richest colonial outposts in the British Empire. It was mostly populated by pirates, cutthroats, and prostitutes. It had a tavern for every ten residents. Goldsmiths were almost as busy as bar staff in the inns. Sir Henry Morgan was charged to boost the island's forts and defenses. He made a few pretty pieces of eight too: his raid on Porto Bello produced an almighty plunder of £75,000—an astronomical sum in 1668. He spent a fair portion of his booty on plantations.

At Port Royal I studied artifacts, historical pamphlets, and books. I was captured by the story of Mary

Read, who as a young girl dressed as a boy and had a yearning to venture out to sea. Disguised as a young man, she became a pirate working for the crew of the notorious Calico Jack Rackham.

Equally captivating is the narrative of Anne Bonny. She left her husband for Calico Jack and they became lovers, sailing the seas together with Mary Read. I suspect that Anne Bonny was bisexual and she also had a relationship with Mary Read. We writers are always imagining *what ifs*!

It didn't end well for Calico Jack nor Mary. Jack was executed for his piracy and Mary died from a fever while in prison. No historian that I can find is too sure what happened to Anne Bonny, other than she was also imprisoned, and while awaiting her fate she claimed she was pregnant. That is where her tale ends.

As I sat down to pen *Kemosha of the Caribbean*, the above history and folklore ignited my imagination. *What if*, indeed.

Weary of all the *Pirates of the Caribbean* films where no Black character plays a significant role, and outraged by the racist depiction of Friday in Daniel Defoe's *Robinson Crusoe*, I set to work creating a Black heroine for modern times: Kemosha of the Caribbean. I'm very proud of her and may she long kick ass after I cease penning such tales.

Alfred, this one is for you.

Alex Wheatle
South London

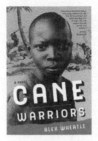